The Grottos of Barigoule

A Novel

FRANK FROST

The Grottos of
Barigoule

A Novel

FRANK FROST

ARPress
45 Dan Road Suite 5
Canton MA 02021
Hotline: 1(888) 821-0229
Fax: 1(508) 545-7580

Ordering Information:
Quantity sales. Special discounts are available on quantity purchases by corporations, associations, and others. For details, contact the publisher at the address above.

Printed in the United States of America.

ISBN-13:   Softcover   979-8-89356-543-0
               eBook   979-8-89356-544-7

Library of Congress Control Number: 2024902458

TABLE OF CONTENTS

"Veramen vous lou dise, n'i'a d'aquéli que soun eici que noun goustaran pèr la mort, d'aqui-que vegon lou Fiéu de l'ome veni dins soun reinage."

Matthew 16.28 (from the Provençal Bible)

PROLOGUE: TWO YEARS AGO

After the practice they decided to split up and play a game. The rugby field was close to the creek down there in the valley. It was hot for late September and Michael Tolliver was slapping mosquitoes on his legs.

"*Allons*," said Jeannot. "You can't just practice, you have to play some rugby, hit someone. We'll play nine a side." Young men had been leaving the village of Barigoule over the years and it was hard to get thirty players out to play any more.

Michael was the only American. He took the fullback position because their regular man wasn't there. Jeannot was playing prop on the other side. Five minutes into the game the other scrum half put a kick high in the air. A *chandelle*, they called it. Michael fielded it cleanly, ran up the field and angled his kick to bounce out of play close to their goal line. He was just standing there admiring his aim when Jeannot, running full tilt, hit him with a forearm on the side of his head.

Later, after they'd carried him into the shade under the trees, poured cold water on his head, and he finally sat up and said he was okay, Jeannot kneeled next to him, very serious, and spoke in his hesitant English.

"Michael, my friend. I am so sorry. Is how I play always, you know? *Jusqu'au bout*, you know, all the way?"

Michael was angry, holding it in. He shrugged it off. "I shouldn't have stood there that long. Just watch out next match."

Jeannot insisted that Michael ride in the back of the equipment truck up to the village, the evening sun now lighting up the buildings on the top of the hill, tan, peach, white, the tiled roofs, the gloomy eminence of the old castle rising above the town.He usually made all his players run up the hill.

Later at the bar they were all joking about it. Michael was staying with Jeannot and his wife Danielle, in one of the rooms over their restaurant. Now they were sitting around, sipping at milky glasses of pastis.

"He's just helping out, working out with the club, and Jeannot hits him and knocks him out! What a friend!" said Titou, the scrum half.

Michael knew that these big, friendly, dangerous Frenchmen knocked out their friends all the time. In rugby games, at the parties afterward, discussing politics in bars. He'd washed and was wearing jeans and a long sleeved cotton shirt against the mosquitoes. Now he just smiled and shrugged it off for the moment. He had a big welt along his right cheekbone.

They had the usual rugby club dinner at the restaurant. A big platter of *charcuterie*, salad of *gesiers*, steak-*frites*, cheeses, fresh fruit. Michael used to joke with his wife about the rugby diet: it satisfied the daily requirement for two of the essential food groups, fat and salt. Michael was facing the wall devoted to Jeannot and his storied career. There were posters, photos, old newspapers, trophies on shelves, even jerseys with the number 3 on them, some bloody, never washed after some spectacular triumph. Jeannot had played for France seven years in a row. He'd been sent off four of those times for rough play. His local team had played in the national championship match once and had lost narrowly to Toulouse. Jeannot would leap up now and then to fetch more wine and plunk down the liter carafes, slopping wine onto the table, dodging his daughter on the way. Gaby was ten. She had demanded the right to wait on tables and was bringing around more bread, platters with more steak and *frites*, smacking the rugby players on the ear when they tried to pat her bottom.

When Danielle finally had a free moment she came over and sat next to Michael, leaned over and touched the welt on his face. "Is it true?" she asked. "Did Jeannot really hit you one in the face?"

"*C'est pas grave,*" he said. No big deal. "I'll get him next practice." Dany didn't look worried. One of the locals had produced a guitar and now there were calls for Jeannot to sing "*Un jour tu verras,*" the sad old song he hummed incessantly and could almost sing well. "*Un jour tu verras, on se rencontrera...*One day you will see, we shall meet once again..."

A player was calling from the bar. "*On appèle Mike...*" Someone was on the line for Michael. He got up, muscles creaking after the workout, not in shape at all. It was Nicole, in San Francisco.

"Mike! Jerry called. They're going to auction for the paperback. He says you're going to get at least a million five." She was bubbling over. Michael tried to cut in.

"Wait. Wait a minute. *Babylon* is going to auction? But I thought—"

"Right! Ballantine liked it so much and then Jerry had shown it to Collins and now there's a bidding war. Jesus, Mikey! This is so exciting! And Jerry says Miramax called about an option."

Michael tried to calm down. *Waters of Babylon* was his third novel, something he'd written just to see if he could write a historical novel. But the hardcover sales had been surprising. And then a reviewer had claimed the book was a cleverly concealed allegory of the present Palestinian exile. An Israeli defender had angrily fired back in an op-ed column and the book had aroused a storm of political comment, resulting in four weeks on the best seller lists.

"Listen, Mike. Jerry said he'd call you tomorrow, once he has some *real* news. But this is so great! I can hardly sit still. You couldn't fly back right away, could you?"

Michael laughed and explained how the house hunting was going. "At least we'll be able to afford it right away," he said. They chatted for a few moments.

Michael looked over the room after he'd hung up. Should he tell his news to the raucous rugby crowd right away? They had virtually no idea of the money a writer could make in America, especially a writer who was a mediocre rugby player, let Jeannot hit him like that. He focused on Jeannot, the hulking host, laughing with his friends, punching one or another now and then, made up his mind.

"Jeannot! Big news!"

"Aha, Michael! I saw you talking, and I thought—"

"Yes, but this is a secret. Come outside a minute."

Jeannot followed him out the back door, where the refrigerator motor and fan from the kitchen were making a din in the night. Michael stopped in a pool of darkness, Jeannot facing him eagerly, waiting to hear. It was a moist, warm night, waiting for the first big fall rain. The *cigales* were in full voice.

"Jeannot, we're going to buy the house. We've got the money. But first, let's get something straight. Put your hands up." Jeannot narrowed his eyes, began to bring up his big fists.

Michael pivoted off his right foot, hit Jeannot with all his force, all his speed, right on his big left jawbone.

He thought for a moment that Jeannot would actually go down, crashing backward into a stack of empty wine cartons. But the big man staggered, found his footing.

"I had to do that, Jeannot, just to stay friends. That was for the late hit this afternoon. I just couldn't let that go. You want to keep on...?" Michael had his hands up, ready.

For the rest of his life Michael remembered the change in Jeannot's face, his eyes becoming slits, turning a piercing red in the reflection of the street light, his whole face darkening, his shadow lengthening as if his body were swelling with fury. For a moment Michael feared for his life. He knew that Jeannot, huge and battered, getting old, could beat him to death easily if he wanted. But he'd had to make the point.

And then Jeannot seemed to change size again, shrinking. He emerged into the full light of the street and he was grinning. He held out his hand.

"Michael. Yes. We are even. I deserved that. Come give me a kiss."

And there in Provence, where savage rugby players, remorseless gangsters, convicted killers all kiss each other daintilly on the cheeks three times in a row, many times a day, Jeannot and Michael exchanged a great hug, and scratched each other's cheeks with their whiskers.

"Now, let me tell you the news," said Michael.

PART ONE

CHAPTER ONE

The boar stood rigidly in the clearing. He had been digging summer truffles beneath the little oaks until a moment ago, but then he had heard some creature approaching. He was a magnificent specimen, over 150 kilos, with savage tusks sprouting from his jaws. He was eighteen years old—old for a boar—and had managed to evade hunters his entire life, although a long callused scar over his right hip testified to the time many years ago when a shotgun had almost put an end to his life. He knew about French hunters. And he savored the air nervously.

Until four centuries ago the wild boars of Provence had not known an enemy. There had been bears then, and wolves. But a full-grown boar was not bothered. Even the black bears, twice the size, took a look at the long yellow tusks, the little red eyes, smelled the insanity of the bad temper, and found errands elsewhere. And the wolves could always be lured down into the brush-choked gullies, where they couldn't maneuver, and be disemboweled.

Boars were virtually indestructible, with their thick, armored hide, able to run for hundreds of meters harmlessly through thorn and scrub oak that would strip the skin from any other animal.

Then came guns. Guns, and hounds that could chase down a boar, corner it, and wait for the human to come up with the gun. One big bang and the boar lay there with its brain shattered or its heart blown to bits.

Pigs are not dumb. Hundreds of years ago this boar's ancestors had learned to run from dogs because after the dogs came other creatures smelling of gunpowder, a very acrid smell, and a sudden killing or terrible wounding with a loud noise. The boar's natural instinct was to put his head down, face his enemy, race toward it, his jaw almost scraping the ground, and then get under it, set the long, sharp tusks and heave upward with the huge shoulder muscles. Even if the enemy was still alive the boar could quiet it quickly, jumping down on the beast with its small, sharp hooves, driven by all that weight of bone and muscle. The sharp hoof would go right through most animals, over and over again, as the boar stamped, and jumped, and trod its enemy beneath it. Then the boar could eat at his leisure the soft parts that had come bursting out of the enemy, eat the heart and liver and all the flesh that could be torn away. And the crows would come and sit around waiting, and maybe even in the old days, the wolves and foxes, waiting for the leftovers but staying well out of range of this huge, bloody, angry, killing machine.

Now there were no wolves. Often the foxes would hear the crashing boom of a gun and would come to wait out of sight in the brush, knowing that when the hunters had left there would be meat, bones, and guts to eat. And of course the crows were always there.

This particular boar had evaded hunters for his eighteen years. Foxes stayed out of his way. He had seen a former mate shot to death and butchered and his rage had tempted him to crash out of the brush and attack the murderers, but the dogs were there and men with guns he could smell, guns smoking with that sharp, painful reek of gunpowder, so he had gone off down the tiny trail, smoldering with his anger, saving it up for another time.

Today he had an infected tooth and pain shooting through his head. More than anything he wanted to put that tooth into something alive and kill it. And now he heard the human coming and he put his snout high in the air to smell the danger. It seemed to be a male human, no dogs along, no smell of gunpowder. The boar's little red eyes began to glisten. He dug his front hooves into the turf of the clearing and swiveled around, getting a firm footing.

Michael Tolliver was descending a narrow path in the hills above Barigoule. He had been looking for an alternate way down from the Col de Murs, the historic route between the important Provençal towns of Apt and Carpentras, and had found a finger of land with a goat trail that seemed to cut off at least a kilometer of the winding main road. The shrubbery was thick and green in May, and when he emerged into a small clearing he paused to look around, to spot any of the landmarks visible above the great bowl of Barigoule within its encircling hills. He could just make out the tallest tower of the old castle, its battlements perched above the grove of trees that crowned its hills. So he was heading the right direction. The present path should take him to the little road leading over the mountain from Barigoule to Sault.

Just then he heard the crashing of brush and was instantly on guard, moving quickly to his left, upslope. The boar came out of the undergrowth like a mad thing, squealing with rage, sticks and leaves exploding away from it.

Michael had less than a second to act. He was already moving uphill as he remembered what Jeannot had told him about the woods. *Don't wander around when the hunters are out. They will kill you. Cows, farmyard geese, sheep, themselves, anything that moves. French hunters have killed more people than cancer. Other than that, only the pig is dangerous, only the pig. They almost never attack. But if they do...? You must go uphill, on loose dirt and gravel, if possible. Only then can you get away.* Michael darted up the slope, finding it just as Jeannot would have wanted—a scree of small stones under the scrub oak and stunted pines. He scrambled twenty meters up the slope, pulling himself along on the overhanging branches, until he hit a sloping cliff with a faint trail along its base. It seemed fastest back to the left, so he ran until suddenly blocked by dense undergrowth. He wondered if the boar would actually follow.

The boar had indeed been delayed. It was heavy and had small feet and was therefore a bad climber on scree. But its rage was carrying it uphill, scrabbling away at the loose stones and dirt and now Michael found himself cornered between the cliff and the undergrowth. The beast came thrashing up the last of the slope, paused and looked around with its weak eyes to find the thing it wished to kill. Michael froze, but as the great head of the boar swiveled slowly its eyes stopped and focused on him standing there. The boar screamed in anger and accelerated toward Michael. At the last moment, thinking to climb up into the brush, he pushed some branches aside and there—a few feet in front of him—was a caver*nous* opening in the cliff. It was too large to offer any defense against an attacker—but in the back he could see a hole, an entrance to a smaller cave. Could he get in? Would the boar come after him? There was just enough room for him to throw himself onto the rock floor and scramble into the interior cave. The opening was narrow but then widened and Michael turned, pulling out his hunting knife. The boar would have to come into the hole after him headfirst and Michael figured they were even, knife against tusk, no way for the boar to get under him. He lay panting in the opening, hearing the beast approach. There was a thrashing in the brush and then he saw the boar's great head in the outer cave, lifted now, testing the air, little eyes looking directly into his, head moving up and down. He could smell the stench of its breath, the odor coming off the rotten tooth. The boar squealed again almost as if in agony, but instead of coming forward, it wheeled and trotted quickly out of the brush, back down the slope.

Michael waited for his heartbeat to slow, for his breathing to become less frantic. *God, that was close,* he thought. *Now what? Do boars pretend to go away and then circle back in ambush?* He decided to wait a few minutes. In the meantime he examined the cave behind him. Certainly no secret hiding place: in the dimness he could make out a crumpled candy wrapper lying on the sand. Beyond it, a cigarette butt. He could imagine the village kids who came up here...and why.

He worked his way as silently as possible out of the cave and the protective screen of brush, ready to dart back in again should the boar reappear. But there was no sign, not even the feeling of a hostile presence, and Michael was convinced that the big pig had gone far away. *For some reason he didn't like that cave. Did someone hide there and shoot at him?* Something like that. Michael found that the little trail along the foot of the cliff widened and led in the direction he had been going. In a few minutes he came out on the side of the hill and could see the old road to Barigoule off to the left. Now the whole basin of Barigoule was visible in the late afternoon, the crest of the great plateau of Vaucluse to the north and west, lower hills to the east, the little hill of Barigoule with its chateau to the south, surrounded by the houses of the village, and farther along, the sloping basin below the town, cloaked with wheat and hemmed by the surrounding hills that narrowed into the gorges of the Veroncle. The light was beautiful on the hills and the buildings below and as usual he didn't have his camera with him.

CHAPTER TWO

"Where in God's name have you been?" complained Nicole. She was standing in the doorway, a spoon in her hand, trying to sound angry but obviously more concerned than anything else. A slim, almost elfin woman, blond hair falling into her eyes. "And look at you! Did you fall down a hill or something?"

Michael looked down sheepishly. The front of his shirt and jeans was covered with dirt, twigs, and grass, even though he thought he'd brushed himself off before coming into town. He stroked his shirt front vainly.

"And go back out to the terrace and take those clothes and shoes off before you come in. I spent all afternoon cleaning! Did you forget the Sullivans?" Nicole blew upward at a strand of hair that was trying to get in her eyes.

"Actually, no. I was trying to find a good piece of flint. I got tired of hearing Spencer talk about his Neolithic hand ax. But wait till I tell you about my day!" He grinned.

Bathed and changed into khakis and a fresh polo shirt, Michael sat with Nicole on the kitchen terrace as the sun went down over the western edge of the Vaucluse plateau. They had opened a bottle of the local Côtes de Ventoux to sip with some warmed up *fougasse*, and he told her about the boar. She was alarmed.

"And we go walking in the forest all the time! Is that going to be a problem from now on?"

"I'm sure not. I'll ask Jeannot tomorrow. He'll probably say it almost never happens, a boar charging like that."

"Jeannot! He'll probably say that if you'd made a loud noise and charged right back it would have run away instead."

Michael had to laugh. "You've got him right. That's what he'll say. But that pig was mad! I think even Jeannot would have run like deer."

"Probably, but don't tell him that! Is that the door?"

The Sullivans wandered in and the room was full of tiny air kisses. Spencer had brought a bottle of wine, as if he were still back in California. Here in the Vaucluse you could find endless marvelous wine in the supermarket for three euros—about three dollars depending on the exchange. *Why bother?* thought Nicole. *Why not bring flowers, like the French do?* But she liked Spencer and bore the bottle off to the bar, making noises of appreciation.

Spencer was a middle-aged, medium-plump dropout from a big San Francisco brokerage. But before he'd dropped out, he'd made one smart investment after another in the boom of the 90s and now could indulge his dream of living in France and toying with his stocks on the internet. Rosalind was a superficially good-natured Englishwoman who had been a journalist, stationed in San Francisco. She had interviewed Spencer once for a magazine piece, sitting on his patio above the Napa valley, decided she liked the lifestyle, and married him before he could figure out what was going on, other than the great sex. Miraculously they were still together ten years later. Spencer was wearing a black and purple jogging suit that made him look fifty pounds heavier than he really was. Rosalind looked like a million bucks in just jeans and a light sweater, and she knew it. Rosalind had once run marathons and even now she went for a run almost every day.

"I told Spencer to bring flowers instead of boring wine," Rosalind was saying.

"And I said the whole countryside was full of flowers, you could step outside and grab a handful." Spencer was laughing.

"Cheap wine and flowers everywhere! What a terrible life we live here," said Michael. "Does anyone want a pastis?

You still have to pay over fifteen euros for a bottle of *Casa*nis."

Over the smoked salmon and goat cheese salad Michael repeated his meeting with the boar.

"And that cave! If it hadn't been there..."

"The limestone up there is riddled with caves," said Spencer, toying with his *frisée*. "But you were lucky to find one."

"And then the boar took one look at the cave and ran away. I'm sure he wasn't afraid of just a knife. It was as if there was something bad about that cave."

"The grottos! That's where you must have been!" said Rosalind. "There was some kind of massacre there. We'd heard a rumor, but the real estate lady was pooh-poohing it and Spencer was smirking at her—"

"Some kind, indeed," laughed Spencer. "In 1545. Over twenty-five women and children. Not up to the standard of the CIA's goons in Central America, but they were trying!"

"I knew this area was in the middle of the religious wars, but I didn't know that here, Barigoule, anything—"

Spencer had majored in history, with a specialty in early modern France, and he held up an imperious hand.

"Yes. The religous wars. You say it so lightly, Michael, but you should read the contemporary accounts. The slaughter, the rapine, all man's inventive nature turned to the nastiest tricks they could play on each other—"

"Spencer?" Rosalind warned.

"Yes! Yes! You can't imagine. For instance, the "Protestant communion," they called it. They'd hold down a prisoner, jam a funnel in his mouth and pour in a mixture of piss, diarrhea, and vomit..."

"Thank you, Spencer," said Nicole, coming in with a steaming platter. "Just in time for the cassoulet. *Bon appetit*, everyone!"

Outside night had fallen and gloom filled the narrow streets of the village. Two figures came up the gentle slope leading past the Tolliver house. They paused outside the cone of light cast by the lamp over the broad terrace leading to the front door. Through the lace curtains they could make out figures seated at a candle-lit table, and they heard the sound of laughter and tinkling glasses.

"They don't close the shutters, the Americans?" one man asked. He spoke with a strong Provençal accent. There was almost a sense of shock in his voice.

"They think nothing can happen to them, Americans. Come on, he's waiting."

They continued up the street for a bit, then turned into a lane that wound steeply up the hill between silent houses, some empty and dark as the night, others betraying a human presence by slits of light escaping the closed shutters, usually shifting and *flic*kering blue light of different shades from the televisions within. The village was infamous for its barking dogs, but not a sound was heard this night as the two men climbed through the village on the narrow footpath. At the top of the lane they emerged onto a small square in front of the cathedral. Here, all was dark under the surrounding trees, but they could see an even darker line where the door to the cathedral was ajar. They quickly crossed the square and slipped through the great wooden door. Inside only a few candles were burning. Both men dipped their hands into the font and genuflected. A still figure stood in front of them, blocking the feeble *flick*ering of the candles.

"Close the door. Some old woman might come by and feel like praying."

One of the men tugged at the heavy door until it clicked shut. "Where is Jean-Claude?" he asked.

"The priest is in his house, eating, I suppose. He knows better than to bother us here. Anyway, tell me what you heard."

"The American was in the grotto today. A pig chased him and he was lucky, he found the big hole."

The big man was angry. "The 'American,' the 'American.' Don't be such a peasant. They have names, you know. He is Tolliver, the other fat man is Sullivan. And the Sullivan woman is not American, she is English. The Tolliver woman is Canadian, speaks perfect French. We are in trouble here, maybe danger. They could be threats. Think of them by their names, so they are real, not just outsiders."

"But they are outsiders. Like the German—"

"Like 'the German,' he says. You see your ignorance? Monsieur Hauer is Dutch, a former judge, an important man. If he should start looking into our affairs... And he speaks French perfectly too. Do you speak Dutch? or German or English, for that matter?"

"No, but—"

"Enough. Let's get to business. The fat Sullivan man knows French history. Now we have to watch out, that they don't get curious about...about the grottos."

"What could they learn? Where would they go?"

"Where? In the archives. Some in Gordes, but many documents in Avignon, in Aix at the university, in the Palais des Papes. It is there, for those who know how to look."

The first two men looked at each other, turned back to the big man, questions on their faces.

"What do you suggest?"

"First, I think, we should have someone in town tell about the grotto. Just a bit of local color. Insignificant, compared to what happened over there at Lacoste, Merindol, other towns. You give these people a story, it satisfies their curiosity, eh? Then go on to explain our famous asparagus festival here, make the stories all seem just as important, *colorful*, we quaint Provençal natives."

One of the men was nodding his head, agreeing. The other wasn't so sure. "And if they go on looking?"

The big man was still, completely silent, and the cathedral suddenly seemed darker and colder.

CHAPTER THREE

Michael had been sitting at the computer for an hour or more. Now and then Nicole passed him, carrying out the laundry, doing other tasks.

Once she stopped, looked at his motionless fingers and a blank screen.

"Did we get any mail?"

"E-mail? Yes, of course. I can enlarge my penis, I can watch young men taking it in the ass, I can invest in sure-thing dot.com stocks, I can download pics of hot and wet teens—"

"Michael! How did your name get on—"

"No, that was just *your* mail. Mine was pretty boring. No. I have no idea what lists we're on. And they have no idea that they are reaching us in France. We're just lucky the French spam hasn't reached us yet."

"So. How is your writing going?"

Michael turned to her, grimaced. "I was just trying out the beginning of a story, but my fingers kept on wanting to write something about Barigoule. You know, sort of a historical novel, set in the religious wars?"

"Are you going to have prisoners with funnels jammed down their throats and—"

"No, no!" He laughed. "Maybe sort of a 'West Side Story,' theme. A Catholic boy, a Protestant girl, falling in love, but trapped in a centuries-old legacy of hatred and intolerance, that sort of thing."

Nicole considered, a finger poised on her cheek. "Alright. So what about the big Michael Tolliver commandment: write what you know about?"

"I was worrying about that. Of course I didn't know anything about the *Babylon*ian captivity either."

"But you didn't have to, did you? It's all in the Bible. And look how well *Waters of Babylon* is doing."

"Was doing. And that's another thing. Jerry's been reminding me that two years is a long time between books. He said—"

"I hate that. You have to write a book a year or something?"

"Some authors do...just look at the best seller lists. Just like clockwork, Cornwell, Grisham...and after all, I wrote *Babylon* in what?...eight months?"

"But¬—"

"And you know, that's another thing. What we were saying about wine and flowers the other night. Life *is* too good here. We go to the street markets, we buy food, we cook it, we eat it, or eat with the Sullivans, or the Bérards. Drive around, take walks, explore—"

"Explore. Yes. That's what you have to do, but focus it on the wars of religion. You know, what happened here, locally."

"Well, maybe I can find out what I need to know. And after all, we're here, we know Barigoule fairly well. I can at least do the local color."

"We get enough of that from Madame next door." Their neighbor, Madame Bertrand, knew every secret in the village, and what she didn't know she made up.

"No, I don't mean who is screwing the grocer's wife and how much the garageman cheats his customers. You know what I mean. The real history of Barigoule. Did anyone ever write one? The other day, over at St. Saturnin? At the pottery market? There was an old man selling his book about, what? Was it Lacoste? It must have been privately printed. Maybe there's something like that about Barigoule."

"Well, Jeannot would know."

Jeannot laughed, shrugged his shoulders. "Barigoule? Well, yes, there's the book by what's-his-name...Fauré, used to be a neighbor of yours. An old man, lives in Paris now. He had property here, his family before him, I don't know, two hundred years maybe they were here. Anyway, he wrote a book forty years ago... look...I'll find a copy, somone's copy here, and you can borrow it. Okay?"

They were sitting outside the Café de la Platane, Jeannot's bar, in the dappled sun under the plane trees. Michael was drinking a pastis, golden and milky. Jeannot took tiny sips from a *ballon* of local red wine. They were watching a stream of German, Belgian, Dutch cars wind through the village in both directions, headed for Roussillon, or Gordes, famous tourist destinations. Jeannot's eyebrows shot up as he spied a young woman strutting by in dramatically short shorts, the lower curve of her buns jiggling beneath the hem. Michael ogled too, met Jeannot's glance. Both men whistled softly. Jeannot groaned. But then Michael brought them back to earth, reminded his friend.

"You, Jeannot! The book would be fine. But you...you know everyone in town. You must know something...?"

Jeannot was waving his hand, chuckling. "Me? No, my friend. I moved here from Gordes twenty years ago. And here they still call me *le Gordais*. The guy from Gordes, what is it, eight kilometers away? As if I were a stranger, a newcomer? That's their way here. Now the deputy mayor, Marius, you know the big old man? He runs the library, everything really, sends out the village truck and the imbecile boy to repair things, has a key to everything in town. That's the man who lived here forever. We'll have a talk with him sometime. I'll translate."

Michael was about to say that he spoke French fairly well, then remembered to shut up, let Jeannot do the talking. Sometimes the thick Provençal accent was nearly incomprehensible. There were two old men across the street now, sitting on a low wall, talking, punctuating their remarks every three words or so with a "pah!" or "oof!" slapping their wrists, stroking their cheeks, raising their chins to emphasize some point. Michael could make out words in a sentence now and then but had no idea what they were talking about. He'd let Jeannot question the man.

"Have another *Casa*," Jeannot was saying. "You can't just drink one, a fine morning like this with young ladies walking by showing us their *fesses*."

Michael was about to beg off but just then he saw the man they'd been talking about, big Marius, coming their way.

"Okay, and stop Marius, let me buy him a drink."

Marius Pellenc was not so much big as hulking, his huge hands hanging way below the sleeves of his ancient, patched leather jacket. He had the usual cloth cap on his head and was wearing a white shirt buttoned at the throat and a shapeless pair of black trousers, too short, above his large, scuffed brown shoes. His face was long and craggy, devoid of expression. His grey eyes looked everywhere except at Jeannot and Michael, but he accepted the drink.

"I'll take a quick *ballon*, thank you, monsieur," he said to Michael in French, sagging down on a café chair that splayed beneath his weight. "But then I have to see to the fountain. Something's plugged up the drain again."

Jeannot asked a few questions about town affairs, offered an opinion about several of the locals passing by, then asked his prepared question.

"What was the name of old Fauré's book? The one about Barigoule? I was trying to answer a question for Monsieur here."

Marius gave him a keen look, then his eyes darted away again and he rubbed one side of his long nose with a calloused index finger, obviously thinking.

"Aha, Fauré! Yes. A good book. We had a copy in the library here, but it's disappeared." He thought, scratching his head. "You can find the book in the library in Apt, I'm sure. Cavaillon certainly. Why would you read that old book, monsieur? We have a touristic book at the *mairie*, colored photographs, excursions, all the festivals—"

"And a marvelous description of our one restaurant, the world famous Tapounado." Jeannot was laughing. "Where you can get poisoned any day of the week except Wednesday, when they are closed."

Marius was making shushing noises. "*Incivisme*! You're being uncivilized! Don't say those things, Jeannot! It was only two Germans last year." He looked for a moment as if he were going to say good riddance, but he didn't, a skilled civil servant. He turned to Michael, trying unsuccessfully to frame a friendly smile with his broad mouth and crooked teeth. "Now you should read about our asparagus festival, monsieur. And next weekend, the famous exposition of pottery. They come from Paris, even!" He consulted his watch and gulped the last of his wine glass. "And now, the drains. Thank you for your kindness. Till the next time." He lurched to his feet and plodded down the street

"That one is a type," said Jeannot in French, then looked around and switched to English for greater security. "But our Madame the mayor could not do without him. She is a dodo, understands nothing on a map although she has to make dozens of permits for building. The fucking developers pray that Marius will not be there when they come in for her signature. He knows every inch of Barigoule."

"How complicated is that?" asked Michaal. "So few hectares of land..."

"Aha!" burst out Jeannot, triumphantly. He put his face close, conspiratorially, then quickly turned and yelled into the bar. "Gaby! Bring monsieur his *Casa*! He's dying of thirst, child!

"No, no." He turned back to Michael. "You see that derelict house across the street with the '*a vendre*' sign? Typical! Old Vernis has been trying to sell his place for seven years. You go down his drive—there is the little road to the garden belonging to the house and the garage. But old Pichaud across the way owns a strip of land across the road. He's just waiting for the land to sell so he can build a fence across it. Then the unlucky fool who bought the land would have to pay God knows what price just to get into his own garage. Last year a Dutch almost bought the place. He was at the *mairie* asking—the Dutch are not stupid about money, you know—and Madame the mayor says, "Oh yes, a beautiful property, monsieur!" And then big Marius, standing there like a ghost, says, 'But there is this little bit of land...' and there went the sale." Jeannot roared with laughter. "So why do you want to know ancient crimes, Mike? Everyday here there are such stories. You could write a book like the Englishman, what is his name? Mayle? and make millions of dollars like he did! Now he lives over there by Lourmarin, eats six-hundred-franc luncheons at that fancy restaurant. You're a good writer, you just listen to the stories I'll tell you about Barigoule. We'll call it, 'A year in Barigoule.' It will sell millions, they'll make a movie, they'll come here to Barigoule to shoot it, all those beautiful actresses." Jeannot leaned across the table again. "Those Hollywood girls, we'll take them up to the grottos, tell them scary stories, make love to them there in the caves, like the kids here in town do with their little friends."

He leaned back, slapped the table and made their drinks jump, laughing.

Later, back home, Michael told Nicole. "We've got to go look at those caves again. Us and Spencer and Rosalind. Let's go tomorrow, take up a picnic lunch?"

That night Nicole was rave*nous* in bed, insistent, touching all Michael's secret places, finally rolling over on top and ravishing him, crying out over and over again.

"I had this feeling that you were in danger," she said afterward. It was so intense. And I must have you with me always, Mikey. I can't lose you...I would die!" As they relaxed, sweating on top of the sheets, the full moon came into view through their western window, so bright and intense that they both felt as if they were being watched, and they pulled the covers up.

CHAPTER FOUR

The village of Barigoule lies in a shallow basin on top of the plateau of Vaucluse, for which the whole department is named. The big city of Avignon, at the confluence of the Durance and Rhone rivers, where the popes once lived in times of lively religious dispute, is the capital of the department. If you take any road east from Avignon you will soon run into the plateau of Vaucluse, running east toward the Alps, of which it is a minor outlier. From the south, on the RN 100, you will take a small road northward and up the slope of the plateau, passing through the picturesque, touristic village of Gordes, with its castle and overpriced shops. Five minutes later, after driving past a gorge and through forest and orchards, you see, across the basin, the village of Barigoule, a cluster of buildings in various shades of cream and tan with their tile roofs, huddling around the low hill crowned by the chateau. The original castle was just a rough fort, built in the ninth century against Saracen raids. Beginning in the thirteenth century a noble family began to improve it and added a fine church to its western courtyard. It now makes a fine photograph from the hill to the east, with its crenellated battlements and high walls. The last member of the family had his head removed in the Revolution. In the years between the great wars an obscure family of great wealth inherited the chateau and all the fields around Barigoule. The chatelain is a recluse and no one in living memory has been invited to a social visit. The townspeople approve of him because he refuses to sell any of his land for development—the curse of Provence.

The main road goes directly through the town and out the other side, winding down the hill gradually to Apt in the valley of the Calavon. A smaller road leads northward out of town across the highest part of the plateau and eventually descends to the valley of Sault, where Nazi troops were stationed and vainly tried to control the French partisans during the big war.

As you drive slowly past the housefronts of Barigoule along a lane of plane trees, you will count the few shops: a *salon de beauté*, a bakery, a butcher shop, Jeannot's café and bar right on the corner of the Place de la Paix, under the plane trees, with a few old men sitting either inside or outdoors, depending on the weather. Out the road to Apt is a little park, a service station, and a small grocery store. On the east side of the Place, next to the restaurant, is the *mairie*, a three-story building that also houses the village grammar school. When Michael and Nicole had completed the financial negotiations for purchase of their house, they still had to go with Jeannot to meet Madame the mayor. Jeannot had explained that it was only a formality but that mayors in France had the right to deny a sale to someone they thought might be undesirable. Madame the mayor had been delighted to welcome wealthy Americans to her town; she had greeted them warmly, gazing from one to the other through her thick glasses, then casting a glance over at the silent figure of Marius, who might have been part of the furniture.

From the Place a narrow street, almost too narrow for a car, leads vaguely northwestward with turnings up to church and chateau, making a dogleg to avoid an inconvenient spur of rock thrusting out from the hill. The limestone formation here makes a natural terrace about three feet above the street, a terrace leading to a deep vaulted hollow in the cliff face. Perhaps as long ago as Roman times an enterprising miller had realized there was room for him to set up a flour mill, in the shelter of the overhang, protected from wind and rain, with a donkey pulling the shaft of the upper millstone around and around. Romans came and went, Gauls gradually became French. Humans change, but bread is forever, and miller succeeded miller for over a thousand years during which the donkeys wore a circular track inches deep in the limestone floor. During the Middle Ages a skillful architect extended the roof of the cave with a clever vault of cut stone. When larger mills in the valley put the little mill out of business hundreds of years later, someone continued to use the cave as a stable and built a small living area to one side. Over the course of following centuries, succeeding owners expanded the site, quarrying away the cliff and erecting walls around the mill. It was discovered that the cliff was composed of a particularly fine creamy white limestone, of structural quality, not too hard, and much of the rest of the cliff was quarried away bit by bit. When the good stone gave out, a later owner kept building rooms, one here, one there, on various levels of the quarried rock, wherever they would fit. A staircase cut through the rock wound in random fashion up to the rooms, and haphazard landings and entryways connected the whole rabbit warren. For a while after the revolution the edifice was occupied by homeless squatters until a sensible mayor declared it a public building, needed for administrative purposes. He then appropriated funds to build what is now the present *mairie* and subsequently sold the building to his cousin's son-in-law.

By the end of the last world war the building was in terrible shape. An unscrupulous landlord had managed to make five tiny apartments out of it, using the great vault for himself as a small, overpriced village store. But in the last decade of the twentieth century Jean Bérard, our Jeannot, through a series of clever real estate transactions, gained complete ownership of the hulking labyrinth for almost nothing. It was said that new French laws made it impossible to rent out apartments without bathrooms and kitchens and no one could imagine how else it would be used. Jeannot, however, had seen the beginnings of the real estate boom in the Luberon and he thought some rich English or Germans would buy the whole building—if it could be made presentable. He hired the local louts, many of them his rugby players, to rip out all the substandard rooms and build new ones, airier, lighter. He floored the ancient vault with local stone and then quarried through the cliff to make a large window to the east so the first sunlight would pour into the room. He tore off all the old decrepit roofs and rebuilt them with timbered ceilings, then covered them using the old tiles, but weatherproofed this time. The old exterior walls had been built of stone blocks, as the locals had been doing for two thousand years. In the last century the walls had been plastered over, as petit bourgeois owners all over Provence believed that rough stone walls were the mark of peasants. Jeannot had scraped all the plaster off and restored the original stone facing. Then he plastered the inside of the house, painted everything white, and waited for customers.

When Michael and Nicole first went househunting in this part of Provence, they ran across Jeannot and saw the house he was offering for sale. Nicole stood in the great vault and looked around in wonder. It might have been a palace in fairyland, if you read the look in her eyes. They walked from room to room, up stairs carved in the rock.

"My God, Mikey! This is incredible! There's no rhyme or reason to the architecture. Nothing whatsoever! We must buy it."

"There's also no heating, electricity, or plumbing," Michael pointed out.

Jeannot cleared his throat. "I left it unfinished so you could make your own changes," he said. "If you want to put walls in the big room below—"

"Walls?" they both said at once, turning, looking at each other. "Who wants walls?" And they laughed.

Jeannot then showed them a list he had made¬¬, estimates for putting in the electricity, plumbing, two different figures for electric or central oil heating. They totted up the sums, added them to the price of the house, gazed into each other's eyes again, heartbroken. It was much too much.

Jeannot was impressed when he learned that Michael had played rugby at Berkeley. But that didn't bring the price down very much. "I have some other properties—two here in town, several around Gordes and Les Imberts," he said. "Come back in the spring and look around."

But that was before Michael's book turned into gold and the movie option opened up unimaginable vistas. In six months workmen had run all the various utilities through the house and had installed an oil heater next to the old wine cellar carved out below the vault. Nicole came over to France, sent Michael home to work on his next book so she could avoid his advice, inspirations, or other interference, and spent several months driving back and forth from the great shopping malls of Avignon, bringing back furniture, lighting, appliances, rugs, curtains—everything to make the house livable. They moved in on a November day when the mistral was blowing sixty to seventy miles an hour with a temperature just a few degrees above freezing. Jeannot had come with his van to help them move from their rental in Gordes.

"This is perfect," he said, looking up, catching his cap as the wind blew it off. "You have to love the mistral to live in Provence. It shows you if you have a good house or not."

And indeed the mistral proved the worth of their house. The structure was built into the cliff with its back to the fierce north wind. The stone walls were almost three feet thick, except in the cave proper, where they were up to twelve feet of solid cliff. The great fireplace they'd built in the vault threw out heat that traveled all the way up the labyrinth. The state-of-the-art central heating ran boiling water into the radiators and made the house toasty with very little effort. Nicole insisted on making their first meal in their new house, a simple oven-broiled chicken with potatoes in the same pan, and a salad of *frisée* with lardons. Jeannot had brought two bottles of Gigondas and gladly stayed for dinner.

"Here in Barigoule," he said, "you will find some people friendly, some are Communists and think all Americans are from the devil. But they will all like you. I have said you are a rugby old-boy, and this is a rugby town. Just don't believe anything you hear about our ancient history, *hein*? Hundreds of years ago? Who cares?"

CHAPTER FIVE

Spencer was grumbling, moving up the rough path among the little pine trees.

"You sure we couldn't have parked closer, for Chrissakes?" The big man was sweating, red in the face.

"Don't be a sissy!" said his wife. Rosalind was just behind him, carrying the heavier pack with the *jambon du pays*, the bread, the *paté de campagne*, two bottles of wine: a cheap Côtes de Ventoux red and a much better Viognier from the Luberon, a recent discovery, wrapped in bubble wrap to stay cold. Spencer was carrying only a camera. Michael and Nicole were forging on ahead, carrying a picnic basket with knives and forks, a roast chicken, and a corkscrew, which they always swore they would never forget again after the last picnic, when they had to push the cork *down* into the bottle and then let it gurgle out slowly into their plastic cups.

They had parked two kilometers north of Barigoule on the little road up the mountain and were now walking down a path that branched through the pine forest to the west of the main road. The land was beginning to rise to their right and fall away to their left into a valley filled with pines and brush. On the other side of the valley they could see the cherry orchards that covered the hillsides and the two houses of the local farmers who shared them, the homes perching on the last level land before the slopes became too steep. But the side of the valley they were walking along now had always been too rugged to cultivate, the land rising in a series of abrupt steps in the limestone massif. The cliffs to their right rose higher and higher and Michael was looking at the trees beside their path.

"There!" he said. "See the red paint?" There was a little spot of red on a tree stump. "That marks the path up to the foot of the cliff. Now it really gets hard, Spencer!" He turned right onto the barely visible track up through the scrub oaks. "Follow me! And keep your heads down under the low branches," he added, as his cap was knocked off.

It was only a short climb to the foot of the limestone cliffs, but irritating, the branches too low, the scree slipping away under their feet, flies buzzing their sweaty faces. But they found themselves facing a deep cave in the cliff face and even Spencer stopped complaining.

"This isn't the one I ducked into," said Michael. "I think it's more to the north." There was a generous ledge of rock at the foot of the cliffs and they walked easily along it, only now and then having to duck beneath oaks and other young trees whose tops brushed the rock face. Several times they stopped to investigate openings in the rock. One archway led them into a great chamber, a cavern in the rock whose top had fallen in and they found themselves looking up at the sky through a large hole above them. It was Rosalind who first looked down and saw the dead rabbit in front of them. She screamed softly and everyone flinched. Michael looked at the rabbit, up at the hole above them.

"Whoa! That's a nasty trap!" He looked up at the brush surrounding the cliff top. "The edge up there is so well hidden even rabbits don't see it. That's amazing!"

"I don't see any bigger bones, sheep, or whatever," said Spencer. "I wonder if there is a little fence around the hole? Probably not. I keep thinking about American insurance companies and billion dollar damage suits. But Mr. Rabbit here, uninsured, running from a fox, probably, comes dashing along and, hasta la vista, bunny rabbit."

"I don't think it's funny," said Rosalind. "And what about kids wandering around up there?" They were all relieved to get back on the path along the cliff. There was another narrow opening that seemed to open out into a larger cave. Spencer stuck his head in and pulled it out quickly. They could all hear a nasty, high whining.

"Hornets!" Spencer said. "I hope that's not the grotto."

"No, there's a lot of underbrush in front of my grotto. Keep going a bit."

Finally Michael stopped.

"This has got to be it," he said. "Everything looks the same up here, but there's only one place where you can come scooting up the slope and then get cornered against the underbrush. Let's clear this stuff away a bit." He'd brought a pair of heavy loppers along and quickly cut away the thickest branches to enlarge the entrance he had thrust himself through a few days ago. Now there was room for all of them to stand in a half circle, inspecting the cave in the cliff.

"If I'm not mistaken, this is the famous grotto of Barigoule."

"In that case," said Nicole, "Let's have our picnic out here in the open and Spencer can give us the background."

They sat around on rocks and distributed the food and wine and for a moment there was contented eating and drinking. Finally Spencer drained a cup of wine and cleared his throat..

"I was just reviewing last night, the few books I have here, so there might be a few gaps. I believe it all started with the Vaudois," he said. "Pierre Vaudo, or maybe Valdès—the texts differ—was a rich merchant in Lyon. In 1172, hearing a priest read the bit from the Gospel of Matthew about it being easier for a camel to pass through the eye of a needle than a rich man to enter heaven—you all know that?—he was inspired to sell all his possessions and give the money to the poor. Then he went around persuading others to do the same and follow him, preaching the Gospels and the life of apostolic poverty."

"I bet the other rich people in Lyon loved that," said Nicole. "And give me another piece of chicken. Did they burn him alive?"

"No, no!" insisted Spencer. "You have to realize, this was an age of faith. People didn't read the Bible all the time—it wasn't really available, like in your hotel night table, whatever. But if you took the trouble to look it up, *Matthew* 19, 21 to 24, there it was: all about giving your wealth away and following Jesus. Valdès soon had a large following—they called themselves the *pauvres de Lyon*, the paupers of Lyon—and in ten years they had attracted believers all over Provence. Even over the Alps in Piedmont."

"But didn't the church...wasn't the Inquisition...?" Michael started to ask. He reached over and poured Spencer another cup of wine.

"Ah yes! The Inquisition! Certainly. But they, the church, was busy fighting the Albigensian heresy out west in France. That was a real heresy, the Cathars, they called themselves, the pure ones. They'd made up their own theology—virtually a whole new religion, rewriting Christianity—but the Vaudois were simple people, insisting only on the sacred word of the Gospels, no theology at all. *And...!*" Spencer raised a hand for emphasis, "The Vaudois offered to go west and preach against the Albigensians! How could the church resist?"

"Okay, Vaudois, poor people...but the massacre here was in 1545, almost four hundred years later. What happened in the meantime?" Nicole was sounding irritated, ripping the end off a baguette.

"Just background," said Spencer. "As far as I've been able to figure out, many of the people around here were dedicated Vaudois.

They were all poor as hell anyway, and except for a persecution here or there nobody really bothered them systematically until the Protestant Reformation. Maybe a few of them burned here or in Italy. But when Martin Luther nailed his theses to the cathedral door in 1517, the word spread like wildfire all throughout Europe. The folk around here who were still Vaudois heard about it and thought, 'Hey! That's what Valdès said.' It wasn't at all, of course, but simple people like their theology simple, and it certainly looked that way. The Vaudois preached the word of the Gospels. But they went further and denied *everything* that wasn't in the Gospels. Just think about it. No sacraments except baptism and the Eucharist. No cult of the Virgin Mary. No saints. No purgatory—and of course that meant no paying indulgences to the church to get out of purgatory quicker. And that's what had provoked Luther too, the fraud involved with the indulgences. So the Vaudois began to seek out other Protestants. Of course, the word 'Protestant' didn't exist then; they were thought of simply as heretics, or *Luthériens*. But the Vaudois had been accustomed to being overlooked by the church and they thought they were on safe ground."

"You mean, there were Vaudois around for four hundred years and nobody really bothered them until Luther?" asked Michael.

"I think so," said Spencer. "I'm not really clear on it. I haven't worked on this for a long time, but from what I remember, the religious wars started in the German-speaking world and they were fierce. They were supposed to be about religion, but pretty soon it was obvious they were about real estate, and sovereignty, and rich nobles resisting the Catholic central authority. So Francis the first of France took a look at what was going on in Germany and said, 'I'm not having that bullshit here,' and started clamping down on heretics."

"God! Isn't that typical," said Rosalind, who had supported every radical movement that had emerged since high school. "You could just figure, a bunch of people who wanted to follow the Bible, they'd be the first to be eliminated. Simple, peaceful people..."

Spencer held up a hand to his wife. "Ah! Not quite, my dear. Simple? Yes. Peaceful? Not really! When the local authorities and the Inquisition started clamping down on the Vaudois, the simple peaceful people began to fight back. They armed themselves. They fortified places in the hills. They chased one group of soldiers all the way to the Durance and besieged them in a abbey for two days. And then at one point they went over the hill to the monastery of Sénanque, beating the poor monks and pillaging the monastery."

"That sounds like the Spanish civil war," said Michael. "How did following the Gospels turn into pillaging monasteries?"

Spencer grinned. "Historical forces. Historical forces, my boy. That's what we say when we don't know the answer. At any rate, the local Vaudois might have escaped notice if they hadn't started fighting back. But what happened was that local landowners, bishops, everyone who felt threatened, made their voices heard up in Paris. Some prominent Vaudois around here had been arrested by the Inquisition and interrogated. There are records somewhere. They identified all the households that were 'heretical.' Including sixteen households here in Barigoule. So early in 1545 King Francis issued an order to 'execute' fourteen villages here, on Vaucluse and in the Luberon."

"Execute? How can you execute a village?" asked Michael, helping himself to the last bit of *paté*.

"You kill everyone and then burn down the village," said Spencer, almost smacking his lips as if he'd just been waiting for the question.

"Burn stone houses?" asked Nicole, incredulously.

"Ah yes. You pile all the wooden furniture and everything else burnable in the main room, pour cooking oil over it and light it. The roof timbers burn and usually the house just collapses when the roof tiles fall in. It's all in the barbarian handbook."

They all laughed politely, giving Spencer his due.

"And now...," he said, scrambling with difficulty to his feet. "Let's have a look at the famous grotto."

Michael showed them how he'd slid into the hole in the back of the cave and then turned around to face the boar.

"It's not as hard as it looks," he said. "The cave widens out in here. Pass me in one of the flashlights and then follow me in."

Rosalind entered without difficulty, sliding on her stomach, but it took Spencer far more time and some horrible curses before he finally got to his knees and shone the other flashlight around. They were in a large chamber high enough to stand erect. To the rear of the cave there seemed to be another narrow tunnel, a hole of stygian darkness.

"Might as well check everything out," said Michael, looking around for Nicole and not finding her. "Nikki?" he called out. Her voice came from outside.

"You guys go ahead. I just don't do grottos, if you don't mind. I'll just stay here within earshot, in case I have to go for aid and succor."

"Why didn't I think of that?" asked Rosalind, but she crouched down and looked at the dark cranny. Spencer obligingly shone the torch over her head.

"It's a...I don't know," she said. "Here, Spence give me the torch, there's a dear, and I'll lead on. Yuck...!" Her voice floated back out of the hole.

"What's wrong" Spencer's voice wavered a bit.

"A stupid *preservatif*—a condom, used, naturally. And I almost put my hand right down on it."

It's nice to know the kids around here don't get spooked very easily," said Michael.

"Kids?" put in Spencer, laughing now. "It could have been any of the local husbands up here with someone else's wife." The second hole was small, jagged and not inviting, so they turned back to the larger chamber, looking more closely. It was higher than they had thought at first, the roof swooping up to twelve feet or so. In the back of the chamber a shelf of rock stood four feet above floor level. Michael jumped up on it and thrust the torch into the dim recess at the top of the chamber.

"It looks almost like a little loft up here," he said. "Room for maybe five or six people, not more."

"I think I remember...," said Spencer. "The soldiers fired their muskets into the tunnel before they got mad and lit the fire."

"The fire?" three voices inquired.

"Oh. Actually, I left out the details about the massacre. I thought you might not come in here if you knew—"

"Knew what? That there were two dozen or more dead souls floating around in here? Thanks a lot, Spencer!" said Rosalind. "I thought you meant they'd just shot them all or something."

"Nastier than that," said Spencer, grimacing. "They told the fugitives that they wouldn't hurt them, but of course no one believed them. So they built a huge fire out of brushwood—"

"Do we want to hear this?" Rosalind said.

"Well, it didn't burn them alive. But it sucked all the air out of the cave and they suffocated. The captain in charge thought it might frighten them enough to come out, but after a night and a day of silence some soldiers crawled in and said they were all dead. Something like that. I read about it in a very general history book."

"It's getting a bit close in here, I find," put in Michael.

"Can we leave now?" asked Rosalind.

They emerged into the entry cavern, blinking in the brighter light. A shaft of afternoon sun was shining through the trees outside, striking the entrance to the cave. Nicole was waiting for them. Rosalind started to speak, but Nicole interrupted.

"I heard, I heard," she said, wrinkling her nose. "It was horrible."

"And I suppose everybody just forgot about it?" asked Michael. "No investigative reporters in those days."

"Well, not exactly." Spencer was brushing the dust and leaves off his safari jacket. "You see, the reason we know as much as we do is that there actually *was* an inquiry. The royal troops were a bit thin on the ground down here and they'd been beefed up by mercenaries and papal troops from Venasque. The local troops were only interested in heretics and they tended to respect the big landowners and churchmen. But the mercenaries were always accustomed to amplifying their pay with rapine and plunder. Rapine and plunder," he repeated, with relish. "They burned barns, shot cattle and other farm animals for their feasts, raped any woman who wasn't hidden in the root cellar, and strung up any local knights who tried to stop them. The aristocracy of this whole region, bishops and nobles, made such a fuss that King Francis actually appointed a distinguished cleric to conduct an inquiry."

"I don't believe it," said Nicole. "Like My Lai, or something?"

They were making their way carefully down the slope through the brush, trying not to slip on the loose dirt and gravel.

"You can read it word for word in the records of the investigation."

"But that must be hidden deep in the archives somewhere," said Michael, disappointment in his voice.

"That could be. But you'd have to go to private libraries and archives, probably in Aix and Avignon, and root around."

Spencer was beaming triumphantly. "That's what we historians *DOOOO——*"

His last word came out in a shout as he slipped and slid on his bottom for a few feet until he could fetch up against a young oak tree.

"I'm still glad you went into stockbroking instead of history," laughed Rosalind. "You...who the hell is that!"

They were all looking down at the main path below. There was a large young man standing there looking up at them, his mouth wide open. His head was completely bald except for a topknot sprouting from the very center of his head. His hands were twitching.

"Oh my God! It's Lomu," said Spencer. "Lomu!" he called down the slope, in French. "What are you doing here? Where is you aunt?...The village idiot," he confided in a low voice. "Don't worry. But Ros? And Nicole? Get behind Michael and me."

"That doesn't quite sound like not worrying," said Nicole. "Anyway, I've seen Lomu around town. He's harmless, isn't he?"

As they paused on the slope, standing there looking down at Lomu, he suddenly shouted, "*Boop, boop, boop!*" waved his arms, and ran back along the path toward town.

Michael jumped down onto the path, held his hand up to help Nicole down. "I've seen Lomu around a few times. Isn't he just the local retard? I thought his aunt was usually with him."

"His aunt? Sure!" said Rosalind. "I've heard the stories too. Her sister got pregnant and left town to have the baby. And so did her brother. Neither of them have been back in twenty years, and Henri, at the grocery, says the brother did the dirty deed. That's why he, Lomu...he's so weird. Inbreeding."

"And around here they all intermarry too much anyway," said Michael. "Jeannot was telling me."

They started walking up the path to the car, looking nervously around now and then, not completely convinced that Lomu had run all the way back to town.

"Where does the name 'Lomu' come from?" asked Nicole.

Spencer laughed. "It's from that rugby player. The back from New Zealand? Two hundred sixty pounds and runs like the wind? The kid saw him on TV ten years ago kicking the shit out of the French team. And in his limited means of communication he told his aunt that he was to be called Lomu from now on. And he keeps his skull shaved like the real Lomu, who evidently does it for Polynesian religious reasons."

"Lomu plays rugby?" Michael asked incredulously.

"This Lomu? Absolutely not! He's completely uncoordinated. But he weighs at least two-fifty and he's incredibly strong."

"And he has this little bad habit," said Rosalind. "Which is why he's not supposed to go out without his aunt."

Spencer guffawed. "Right! He has a bad habit of whipping out his shlong and masturbating in public if he's suddenly stimulated by the sight of a good-looking woman."

"Eeuwww, gross!" said Nicole. "Does he do it often?"

"Well, I understand the mayor told his aunt that if he does it again he's going to a home."

"Or to have 'shots,'" added Rosalind. As they walked down the path back to the road, Michael realized that he'd forgotten all about the massacre of the grottos. Then he wondered what had brought Lomu up to the grottos at just that moment.

CHAPTER SIX

It was almost noon the next day in the Place de la Paix, the main square of Barigoule. Women were returning from bakery, butcher, greengrocer, their shopping baskets full of the day's lunch-to-be. It was Wednesday, an early closing day, and lunch was traditionally of greater volume and more drawn out, because most villagers would not have to return to work. Four locals, elderly men, sat at a table outside Jeannot's café. Three were dressed in the usual village garb: old trousers, old plaid shirts, cloth caps; the oldest was wearing the old fashioned *bleu de travail* of the French manual laborer: work pants and jacket that had once been a bright, royal blue, now faded and stained. They were all smoking and drinking—coffee or pastis. Now they were watching Jeannot and Michael emerge from the café and start walking down the hill road.

"They went up to the...the place yesterday," said the old man, whose name was Anselme. He shook his head. "Lomu saw them there."

"Jeannot went with them?" There was disbelief in the tone of the questioner.

"No. I don't think he tells them anything. But the fat man, the Sullivan man knows about the place, what happened. Just from history books, of course."

Another man laughed harshly. "History books! Everyone knows the history books. That old man in Bonnieux sells his book in all the street markets, whatever he calls it."

"*Blood and Steel on the Land*," supplied Anselme. "Everyone knows, as you say. The story is in old Fauré's book about Barigoule. Everyone knows," he repeated. "Just so much and no more. It worries me that they might look for more."

"Marius says that Fauré's book is now lost."

"Yes. And it was stupid to 'lose' the book. It only makes them curious." One of the other men started to protest, but Anselme shushed him abruptly.

"Don't tell me how to keep secrets," he said angrily. "I was here, a young man, when the Nazis were here, hunting the partisans in the hills up there beyond Sault. The Nazis were curious all right! You wanted them not to be curious at all. Anyone who tried to hide something, some information—even looked like they were hiding something—they would wind up in the cellar of the Hotel de Ville there," he said, pointing at the Mairie. "Believe me, that captain knew how to run a quiz show." He chuckled grimly. "You know, they'd already had ten years experience asking questions, with the pliers, the fire, the electricity. I saw a good, brave young man betray his father and brother..." He broke off suddenly. "No. You must never let them think there is something to hide."

"How can you stop them?" asked the youngest man there.

"We stopped that captain all right." Anselme lit a Gauloise and took a sip of his coffee. "But that was at the end, of course, when they were leaving. He got careless and the boys took him out of the Mairie the last night and up into the hills, up there around Lagarde. We tied his feet to a tree and his arms to a truck and pulled him apart. Very slowly. He screamed...I can't tell you how long, maybe an hour or two. It would have been longer but old Jacques, his foot slipped off the clutch."

They all laughed, the younger man uneasily.

"If you want to write a story," said Jeannot, as they were walking down the hill, "write about the mills of Veroncle."

Michael had come to the café that morning with fresh questions about the grotto. Jeannot had told him instead about a great miracle, four hundred and fifty years ago, and led him down the winding lower road out of town. They were now on the flat field bordering the stream where Michael had played rugby two years before. Jeannot stopped, gestured all around.

"You see? The rugby pitch? Probably no more now. Not enough young ones in town, and those, they want to play 'thirteens,' the professional game, make some money. My best scrum half, Titou? You remember? He's playing for Chateaurenard now. What is it? A forty-minute drive? And he might even move there, drive a truck."

Michael looked around. "It's sad, I know. But the game went professional ten years ago. No more small town rugby, that's what I thought then." He brightened. "Do you think we can get an old-boys game somewhere? I'd still like to hit someone now and then."

"Old boys!" Jeannot laughed. "Maybe a tournament next fall. Drive down to Beziers and choose pick-up teams. It's a game—but not like having your own lads, your own town team, practicing set plays, tricks, scissors...you know the system." Michael started to speak but Jeannot interrupted him.

"That's not what I wanted to show you. You see this little plain here, along the stream? Back up there is the town, the hills close around like arms..." He was pointing downhill, then east and west. "And here is the old basin. Down the gorge there, only one way out."

"That's obvious," said Michael. "That's where the stream is going."

"The stream. *Le ruisseau.* Come let's speak French, I can talk better, explain.

"You see, the stream is only in winter and spring. When it is dry there is no water, or it goes underground. So listen, almost four hundred and fifty years ago the lords here were complaining about taking their grain to Joucas to the mill. A long trip down the hill in wagons. And then wait, pay the miller, and come back up again. There was one little mill right down the stream there. And during the winter they could grind while the stream was running. But not too much...and of course one had to save the grain for months until the rains came in the fall."

"So they built a dam," said Michael.

Jeannot roared with laughter, clapped him on the shoulder, making him trip and almost fall. "Michael, I love you! You figure everything out before I can tell you." Then his voice lowered, becoming almost conspiratorial.

"The lords up there with their great wheat fields, they couldn't think what to do until...But come, let me show you what happened."

They walked along a footpath by the bed of the stream, which gradually disappeared in undergrowth, scrub oaks and brambles. The valley began to close in on them and Jeannot pointed to the east.

"Only there, you can still see the remains of the dam, that ridge of earth. Now we start downhill. Watch your feet! It is slippery from the last rain."

Michael was wondering what they could possibly see. In late May the trees were in full leaf and the trail was now hemmed in on both sides by underbrush. But after a bit the greenery thinned out and he could hear the stream again, not just trickling along as before, but rushing now, splashing ...and then he saw the waterfall. It wasn't much of a fall, but it was coursing over a ruined masonry wall. In the darkness under the trees he could make out a large square stone building, its outlines concealed by the woods around it and the vines that almost smothered it. Jeannot had been whistling his little tune, Un Jour Tu Verras..."one day you will see..." but now he pointed.

"The first mill," he said triumphantly. "Built almost four hundred and fifty years ago. You see, first they built the dam up there and made a lake in the winter and spring. Then they built the mill house here. You can't see, all the bushes now, but they cut channels in the rock to make the water come under the house and run the wheel. Every July, when the grain was all dry, they let the water out through a lock in the dam and it ran the mill."

"That's incredible," said Michael. "That technology, so long ago—"

"Bah! All over Europe they built mills. Since the Romans. But it took brains." Jeannot tapped his forehead. "You couldn't go to the yellow pages then and find 'dam builder.' And the big landowners here didn't see how it could be done. It was one young man—Jean was his name. Just a peasant. But they say his father took him to L'Isle-sur-la-Sorgue, you know? Where the river runs all around the town, and through it too? And young Jean—he was just a boy then— he saw the water wheels, all over town they had them then, and understood immediately how they worked."

"And he designed the system, still a boy?" Michael was amazed.

"No, not for a few years. His father had no wheat fields. He had a small mill for olives. And he raised pigs in the wood over there. Why should his son tell the great lords how to mill their wheat? This was not America, you know, with everybody giving everybody else advice, sharing ideas, maybe getting patents for inventions. You couldn't even speak to a noble unless he asked you something first. No. But they say Jean and the other boys, some of them noble, were playing down in the meadow and they decided to dam the stream to make a pond for swimming, just a little pond. But Jean saw the principle right away and told the others how a bigger dam could hold enough water to run a mill all summer. Most of them just laughed, because Jean was quiet and they thought he was simple, but one of the lord's sons supposedly told his father. The lord called Jean before him and demanded an explanation, and when he understood how it would work, he ordered—*ordered*, mind you—Jean to use all his farm laborers to build the dam, and then came the first mill. The story is in our history of Barigoule, if you can find it in the library."

"I really want to find that book," said Michael. "It must have a lot more about the Vaudois in Barigoule."

"Still you are worrying about the Vaudois?" Jeannot laughed. "They were of no historical interest. Simple people who were at the wrong place at the wrong time, like...like over there in the Balkans, Bosnia, Kosovo, like that."

"But they must have had names...some of them, anyway."

"Like Jean, of course, the olive mill boy. The priest was Vaudois too, but more people listened to Jeanne Serre, an old lady...I remember from the Fauré book," said Jeannot quickly. He was looking out over the valley now, talking almost to himself, as if telling an old story.

Madame Serre...some called her a witch, but she just did spells, and prayed for people. They said she knew all the Gospels by heart. She could—" Jeannot suddenly seemed to remember that Michael was there. "We know her name because she was reported by someone to the Inquisition down there in Apt. It's in Fauré's book. And the Inquisition records...they are in Aix, and probably some in the library of the Palais des Papes in Avignon. Now we have to go back...the lunch crowd is coming in and I'll be in the shit with Dani if I don't get there to help."

"You can't believe what's down in that gorge," Michael was explaining to Nicole and the Sullivans that evening. They sitting on the terrace behind the Sullivan's house by the pool. Spencer's famous shoulder of lamb studded with garlic and rosemary was roasting in the oven and the aroma was beginning to waft over the lawn.

"But here's the thing! There are supposed to be *nine*...nine mills all the way down the gorge, what's left of them, anyway. Jeannot said that after the first mill, the big one, they realized there was lots of water power left, so they cut canals and ran water through eight more mills. It got steeper and steeper so the water was more powerful and...and, the last mill, the water supposedly plunges down an almost perpendicular hole they carved in the rock and it hit—back then, anyway—it hit what must have been something like a turbine blade with terrific power. Jeannot says there's a book in the library here all about the mills of the Veroncle. Just a few years ago they wrote it. I've got to go explore that gorge. I was thinking how I could get that into my novel... young peasant boy, but like Thomas Edison, figuring out how to run water mills. Jeannot didn't have time today...said there was a book in the library about the mills, but we could all—"

"Just a moment my boy." Spencer was in total relaxation mode, except for the glass he was extending for a refill. "Maybe in a week or so. But the grottos wore me out. Take Nicole and Rosalind. They're always game."

"It sounds like a nice walk," said Nicole. "We've been all over the trails here, but never south. I'd like to see the mills."

She poured Michael another glass of the ice cold Viognier Spencer had discovered at a local winery. The others were nibbling at duck *rillettes* on toast while they waited for the lamb.

Rosalind was skeptical. "The mills sound nice. But shouldn't you have some sex or violence to start a novel? Just to get people interested?" Spencer roared with laughter.

"If this is during the wars of religion you'll have enough violence, soon enough. Is that all they have in the library here? Books about the mills"

"Anything about the massacre in the library books?" asked Rosalind, not giving up on sex and violence.

"Madame Morot—you've seen her? the librarian? Looks like a kindly witch. Last time I asked she said the book about Barigoule was borrowed but she can't remember by whom."

"That probably means you'll have to find another copy," said Nicole.

"Shouldn't be hard," put in Spencer. "There are acres of old books at every street market. Let's ask around at the *vide grenier* at Bonnieux tomorrow afternoon. With all four of us asking in different directions we'll have to find something."

CHAPTER SEVEN

After lunch the next day they piled into Spencer's big Peugeot and drove across the valley to Bonnieux, perched halfway up the slopes of the Luberon. The *vide grenier*—or "empty the attic"— is the French equivalent of a garage sale, but it involves the whole village. Here at Bonnieux it was giving the inhabitants an opportunity to sell all the junk that had accumulated over the past months or years and as usual there were stands all the way up the streets that curved through town. Brass bedsteads loitered beside tables nm covered with old crockery and mismatched silverware. There were andirons, cloisonné chamberpots, rugs, helmets from the First World War, copper pots and pans with the tin all gone inside, dolls and stuffed animals, chairs and chests of drawers, glass figurines, hubcaps, garden gnomes, clocks that didn't run, bells that had no clapper, a collection of steelyards. And of course the bookstalls. In the *place* alone there were five tables of used books and they could see more on the street leading up the hill.

"Why don't we split up?" suggested Michael. "Just ask the seller if they have anything on the Vaudois and the massacres of 1545."

"If they know what they have at all," said Spencer. "But we might get lucky. He headed for one of the booksellers in the square, a tiny little old man in a black suit who was chatting with his neighbor, a gaunt woman trying to sell ugly pottery.

Spencer let his eyes rove quickly over the books, mostly old and tattered paperback fiction. But there were also a few older leather-bound volumes: a set of Dumas, a lexicon of Provençal-Français, which he picked up, deciding to buy it for himself.

"I have many more books in my store," said the bookseller, noticing a potential sale. "Is there something you are interested in?"

"In fact, yes," said Spencer, mustering his far from perfect French. "I interest myself in history, especially the wars of religion. Do you have anything on the Vaudois and the—"

"The execution. Of course!" The old man was excited. "I have written something myself. It is just what you want..." and he reached into the pile of books and brought out a paperback with a garish cover, portraying an evil soldier slavering with passion about to violate a beautiful and chesty maiden who was embracing the bloody corpse of a young man.

"It is a *romance...Blood and Steel on the Land.* The story of the rape of Lacoste. You know the history?"

"Yes, of course," said Spencer, trying to hide his disappointment. "You say this is about Lacoste?"

"Yes, yes, the village...right down the hill there," said the man, pointing. "It is about two lovers, Vaudois, children of God, and how they were torn from each other and murdered by that vile devil, the Baron of Oppède. You must read it! Only ah...ah, four euros."

"It says three euros, here inside the cover," said Spencer. "Does your book have anything about Barigoule in it?"

"Bah! Barigoule! A few women and children! Here at Lacoste hundreds were murdered. Young men were tortured to death before their lovers' eyes, then the maidens were stripped and raped by thousands of filthy mercenaries, and finally thrown off the walls to be eaten by dogs, some of the girls still alive!" The old man was so excited that he was spraying Spencer with spittle at every fricative.

"Does one find these things in documents, or is it in your *romance*?" asked Spencer calmly, refusing to rise to the bait.

"Documents!" the old man almost shouted. "Who reads documents anymore? That which is in my book...it all happened, you can trust me." He leaned forward, looking in all directions as if to detect hostile listeners. "There are still Vaudois, you know," he said in a low voice. "We...they still follow the Gospels, only the Gospels, and the vow of poverty! They preserve the old stories!" He stood triumphantly, watching Spencer count out the coins for *Blood and Steel on the Land*, by Henri Rousset, as well as the Provençal lexicon.

Spencer found Michael at another *bouquiniste* on the village square.

"Rape and torture, Mike. Better put it in your book. I heard it from the mouth of a true Vaudois. You'll have to read his novel."

"He said he was a Vaudois?" Michael was incredulous.

"Well. I don't know about the vow of poverty after he tried to overcharge me by a third. But look, let's find 'Barigoule' in this lexicon. I've always wondered what it meant."

"I've seen it on menus and it's usually something cooked with little artichoke hearts."

"Well, there you are. So what does it really mean?"

Nicole had wandered up the winding street toward the center of Bonnieux village. The book stalls she'd seen were all junk but now she was looking at an antique bookcase that was at least a year old, and some old volumes had been put on the shelves as props. They were old paper-covered books, yellow, and dated from the advent of acid paper in the early twentieth century, which meant that they would soon fall apart if handled. The titles were tantalizing: *Provence and the Wars of Religion, Luberon under the*

Sword, and a modern book with a garish cover, *Blood and Steel on the Land.* She looked in the back of the last book for the table of contents, where it would usually be found in French books, and instead found the last page of the novel, which instantly drew her eye.

Marie Claire pulled down her bodice, exposing her creamy breasts with their pink nipples like primroses, trying valiantly to forget her last sight of her lover, Pierre, torn and mutilated with the red hot iron pincers. The evil fat Baron, sweating and stinking, licked his lascivious purple lips and loosened his codpiece. Perhaps this little morsel could provide a bit of pleasure to cap off the evening of monstrous cruelty. He beckoned with a greasy hand.

Marie Claire tried to smile seductively and to conceal the razor sharp dagger hidden in the folds of her apron. She approached the toadlike hulk of the Baron, offering her sweet flesh to his prurient eyes. Then, as he reached for her with a twisted smile, she snatched out the dagger and screamed, "This...for Pierre!" smiting the front of his stained tunic with all her might!

Alas! She felt the dagger stopped by a hidden coat of mail and the Baron roared with laughter, spraying her face with noisome breath and filthy bits of food still lodged in his decaying teeth.

"Guards!" he cried. "Take your pleasure with this bitch. Then throw her off the walls onto the iron hooks. There she can hang till she dies, remembering how her whole village suffered from the vilest tortures we could devise.

THE END.

Nicole's lip curled with disgust.

"Yes, it is very awful, is it not?" The woman selling the bookcase was smiling at her. "I had to put something in, you know, to make the bookcase look right."

"It's the worst garbage I've ever read," said Nicole. "How can trash like that be published?"

"He paid for it himself, the author. Henri

Rousset is his name. In fact, he's right down there in the square selling books. He's crazy, you probably know, if you read two words." The woman had been smiling but now she frowned. "You are not French. You speak perfectly, but...where are you from?"

"Canada," said Nicole. "I...I grew up speaking both French and English. You can tell?"

"Ah! Canadian French. Now I remember. Montreal, *hein*?"

"Well, close anyway. *Québecoise*. But I've lived in France for several years now."

"Here in Provence we can tell. First when we listen we say, 'not *Provençaux*.' Then we listen more and say, 'Gascon, or the north.' Mostly Paris, of course. That's who comes here. They are very rude and we are rude to them too. But then...I am boring you, no?"

"No, no!" Nicole protested. "I love to learn these things. We live in Barigoule...over there," she pointed across the valley. "We've been there almost two years and I still know nothing about this area...you here in the Luberon, and us over there on the Vaucluse."

The woman laughed. "Welcome. We are a welcoming people here in Provence, and I have lived here...oh, my family lived here forever. My grandfather swore that our land was given by the Romans."

They chatted comfortably for a few minutes. Nicole learned that the woman's name was Annie Serre. She was a widow and owned a small vineyard up above Bonnieux, selling her grapes to the cooperative every year. Nicole sensed that Annie was just scraping by. She finally came back to her original quest.

"But I am keeping your customers away. Actually, what I am looking for is information, old books, about the execution. You know? in 1545?"

A cloud came over Annie's face. "You mean, like that stupid book you were looking at?"

"No, no! Not that nonsense! But my husband is a writer, and he is trying to find the original sources for the history of that time."

Annie just shook her head. "We should try to forget those times. Can you believe! Looking around the Luberon today? So peaceful? That actually whole villages were slaughtered? It was as stupid as...as those countries in Africa where they kill each other."

"Oh, I agree completely. But my husband heard about the massacre in our village, in Barigoule, and he thought he'd write a novel about it."

"I don't know." Annie looked dubious. "Poking into those old things. But there are books, you know. Maybe even crazy old Rousset down there, with his blood and steel, maybe he knows the old books. There might be something in it..."

"I should probably buy this book," said Nicole. "Michael might get some ideas from it."

"It's only three euros," said Annie.

"Oh. Inside the cover it says two and a half."

"Ha ha, what an idiot I am! I was thinking of one of the other books. I am desolated. Two and a half, of course. Thank you so much, Madame. *Bonne journée.*"

Nicole took her book and walked back down the hill, trying to conceal the cover of *Blood and Steel* from the growing crowd of tourists and other shoppers. Going by the *place* she heard a whistle and saw Michael and Spencer waving from a table under the plane trees outside the Café de la République. Michael was waving a large green book, actually more like a bound album. He was about to say something but Spencer broke in first.

"Oh my God! She's bought *Blood and Steel* too! We now have two copies of the worst book ever written!" Spencer and Michael were laughing, Spencer thumbing through his copy to find some precious morsel.

"Oh, go to hell, both of you." Nicole sat down, snagged the boy waiter on his way by and ordered a glass of rosé. "What treasures did you find?"

"I bought a treasured scrap book from an old lady," said Michael. "It's actually got old photos of Apt and Gordes a hundred years ago. You won't believe Gordes—it was a ruin!"

"How about grottos?"

"Well...I asked about the massacre and someone said there was a book about Barigoule. I think it's the same one that's missing from the library. By Fauré. *Old* Fauré, everyone says. But I think we've come on a fool's errand. I'm beginning to think nobody's ever written a decent word about...here comes Rosalind. Maybe she—"

Rosalind came empty-handed. "I went to six *bouquinistes*," she said. "Finally the last one just said, 'Why don't you buy Audisio's book?' 'Who?' I said. So he says—he's a youngish man, the first one I've seen who actually seems to know books—he said, 'Audisio. A professor at Aix. He wrote *Histoire des Vaudois*. It's quite recent. But then he said Audisio also published the original investigation of the massacre by Jacques Aubery. From 1555. So I asked if he had a copy and he said yes, but he wanted to keep it, why not just order it online...like at fnac.com?"

"Fnac.com?" Michael remembered shopping at a giant FNAC store in Paris, all manner of books, records, videos.

"You mean we've been looking for ancient documents and all the time we could just buy the whole thing on the internet?" Spencer looked shocked.

Five days later the package plunked into the Tolliver mailbox and Michael and Nicole raced each other to retrieve it. *Documents*

inédits sur l'histoire de l'exécution de Cabrières et de Merindol.
Michael leaved through it hastily.

"This is just what I wanted! A chronology of the massacre with the testimony of all the witnesses! Not just Barigoule, but the whole area, all the 'executed' villages." They were sitting in the living room, Michael reading passages out loud when the big bell outside their door rang and Spencer walked in.

"I found this title on the internet last week and ordered it from fnac.com. Do you think it will help?" Spencer was grinning ear to ear. He was holding the slim volume of *Documents inédits* like a tray of sliced air-dried duck breast. In his smile one could read the message: *I am the French historian here!*

"All right, Spencer. You found it too. What have you read so far?"

"Well, there's a manuscript source, transcripts of testimony from witnesses to the massacre. And the Inquisition had been questioning people about the Vaudois so-called heresy for years before the execution started."

"Jesus! You mean they were torturing people around here for years?"

"No, no! They gave willing testimony!" Spencer was laughing. "You have to know, the Inquisition just gathered information. Most of it from loyal Christians. Now and then, if someone was reluctant, they'd show him the instruments for questioning. Usually that was enough. Remember Galileo? They showed him the thumbscrews and the ankle crushers and he said,'Okay, I give up, the sun goes around the earth...,' words to that effect. *Anyway,* You'll be reading the book...you'll see. But you know, before we read all this raw data I thought we should all talk to Professeur Lebarbe. I met him at the university in Aix, oh...three years ago? He's a historian, but professionally a *géologue*, a geologist. His specialty is the limestones of this area, Luberon, Vaucluse—the whole area. I phoned him last night and he's eager to talk to us. Said he'd meet us at the Fontaine tomorrow for lunch, okay?"

The old man in *bleu de travail* was walking through town when he saw Marius sitting with two contractors at the café. He looked hard at the lanky man and went inside, where he ordered a pastis at the bar. In a moment Marius came in, bought a pack of Gauloises, pretended to recognize the old man for the first time, came over and shook his hand.

"They are going to talk to Lebarbe," the old man said softly, but waving his hand as if mentioning the weather outide.

"Lebarbe? But...but he knows nothing! Rocks! That's what he talks about."

"Don't be an idiot!" the old man hissed. "His name, 'Lebarbe?' He is old Vaudois, no doubt! Who knows what he will tell them? But now, the problem...everything they learn, they become more interested, involved. They will dig, dig, looking. They were in Bonnieux buying old books the other day. They bought *two* copies of old Rousset's book—that nonsense about Lacoste."

"*Two* copies! What can they learn from that?" laughed Marius. "That old man is obsessed with rape and torture! They will throw it aside after reading any page—"

"Well, don't forget that there *was* plenty of rape and torture there at Lacoste. And in the other villages too. Rousset didn't just make it up. He knows the sources. It is a question of these Americans putting too many things together and maybe—"

"Ah! Marius!" It was one of the contractors looking in the door of the bar. "I thought you'd fallen in. Come look at these plans, eh? We have to get back to Cavaillon."

Marius shrugged helplessly, patted the old man on the shoulder and went back out into the sun-filled court.

The sun streaming through the window of his narrow apartment in Avignon woke David Dreyfus from a disturbing dream. He sat on the edge of his bed for a moment, the sounds of market day in the square outside reminding him of time and place. He had had troubled nights before, his sleeping mind chewing at the remains of a relationship that had foundered. But this dream had nothing to do with his lost love, his Chantal, who could not tolerate the demands of his other relationship. David Dreyfus was an inspector for the *Police judiciare* of the departmental prefecture. He was sent to investigate crime, wherever and whenever it happened. After army service he had drifted into police work because in French law there was an automatic opening. He was natural at investigation and he had risen quickly, as quickly as a Jew could in French law enforcement. But Chantal had her own priorities. There was this fabulous party, a promotion for the new CD of a singer, so fantastic...David, we must go! And there was a rash of professional car thefts that required his attention for a while, fifteen hours a day it seemed sometimes...and Chantal pouting.

Dreyfus reached for his clothes. This dream had not been about Chantal, not about the bastards high up in Avignon police administration. This dream had led him into shadowy places, menaced by a pale phantom all in black, onto a snowy plain, voices clamoring behind him in a chase...and then he had woken in a sweat. He wondered if there was some terrible threat ahead in this career.

But it turned out to be quite different when he arrived at the ancient stone building on Blvd. St. Roch where his day usually began.

"Inspector Dreyfus," intoned his superior, the commissaire Barbu. "You have long needed some backup. I've decided to assign a young woman to you. Now don't start complaining!"

Dreyfus had his hands in the air and his eyes wide open.

"Wait, David...Just pay attention. She is the daughter of a Marseille career policeman, a legend. She has the highest marks in every aspect of her *formation*, her training."

"But...Barbu! Listen...I've been doing very well without—"

Barbu stared him down, a good friend, but relentless in the organisation of the *police judiciare*.

"David. It is required by..." he pointed up in the air Those people up there. "It has been ordered. All inspectors must have backup, if only to write the reports." He smiled, shrugged his shoulders.

"Come on David! It won't hurt. And they say she's a looker too. Tomorrow come in early, meet her then."

"Great! A looker! One of these girls who only wants to hang out in clubs and chase after the singers and musicians. Tell me? She drinks, smokes...sleeps around?"

Barbu looked up calmly. "No, David. None of those things. Your corporal is a moral young woman. *Leyla Abdelaziz*. She is a good Muslim."

CHAPTER EIGHT

The asteroid hurtled into Barnswallow, Kansas, and turned it into a crater thirty feet deep and a mile wide. The crater was filled with a shallow layer of smoking debris, the remains of Barnswallow and everything around it.

After remote instruments indicated a perimeter temperature 67°C or less and the level of radiation hovering under 5,000 millirems, the first responders wandered in through the rubble wearing their hazmat suits and helmets, not expecting to find anything. With the world's television cameras focused on them, they found a child. The child was reported to be female, approximately eight or nine years old, dressed in underwear appropriate for a child, dusty, dirty, scraped and scratched, but otherwise healthy. Except she could not speak.

The asteroid was not unexpected. It had been picked up by observatories all over the world weeks ago and was expected to land harmlessly in the Pacific Ocean, until a sudden weird deviation aimed it at the center of the North American continent. A hole in northwestern Kansas was judged by all but Kansans to be a not much greater loss than a bunch of Pacific water. The public dutifully regretted the 329 inhabitants of Barnswallow. And now, here was one.

The news cycle during the approach of the asteroid had been dominated, to the exasperation of televangelists trying to get their oar in, by the Center for Extraterrestial Events, whose website had alerted the world to various possible scenarios that might affect the planet. The Center was piloted by two aerospace billionaires, one American, one British. Rick Doulton, the American, whose famously tousled hair and youthful energy belied his sixty-one years, had enlightened the public for weeks about the approaching asteroid, and now took it for granted that the Center owned the Barnswallow space child franchise. The girl had been moved to a Kansas hospital with armed guards keeping the curious crowds at a distance. She had been cleaned up and her scratches and bruises repaired by fascinated doctors and nurses. Kansas had recently declared bankruptcy and couldn't afford an extra bandaid, let alone sophisticated medical care, so no one objected when the Center descended in a sleek, shining private jet and spirited the child away to its campus and research estate along Rte. One north of Princeton.

A spacious dormer with every facility had been prepared for the girl with bewildering speed. she was met by warm and friendly nurses and psychologists, all female and dressed in casual civilian clothes. The room was filled with dolls and toys and nine-year-old-girl clothes. The little girl smiled for the first time and went to sleep almost imediately, hugging a furry green dinosaur.

No one else was tempted to sleep across America and the world. All media claimed that survival from an asteroid landing was utterly impossible. Speculation was feverish about the origin of the space child, as she was being styled. But the FBI had not been idle. Someone had slipped a swab into her mouth at some time and within a few days the FBI's DNA lab identified a cluster of possible relatives, distant perhaps but still within parameters, in northwestern Kansas. Space child was from Barnswallow.

Rick Doulton was also president and founder of Spastek, a space shuttle and satellite company in the neighboring New Jersey pine barrens. He now took up almost permanent residence at the Center and began inviting the world's foremost astronomers, astrophysicists, and pediatricians to come and consult. He was accompanied as usual by his gorgeous companion and publicist, Katie Masters. As a young girl, Katie had accurately targeted every advantage in the free market open to brains and beauty. Now with her face and figure on every screen, she enjoyed weapons-grade celebrity. Katie inspected the Barnswallow space child tenderly and kissed her sleeping head.

"Rick, this adorable girl needs a name. How about Dorothy?" Laughter rang through the lounge and space child became Dorothy. The girl woke to find a 60" television playing cartoons and, at an inviting child's desk, a computer, on the off chance that she was cyber competent. A motherly nurse, flown in from a children's home in Dodge City, bustled around bringing her pancakes and sausage, fried eggs and hash brown potatoes. Everyone was happy to see that Dorothy had a heathy appetite.

"That's an interesting earring you have, sweetheart," ventured the nurse. "Can I take a closer look?' Dorothy clapped a hand over her left ear. But then she relented and removed her hand a bit and smiled, letting the nurse — and all the surveillance cameras — see a round black stone, about the size of a pea. A Kansas physician, who had examined Dorothy under sedation when she was first discovered, had written a note: "Plain black non-gem stone, evidently inserted all the way through lobe."

"Examine earring" was added to the list of queries prepared for the coming group of scientists and select donors. Once again the televangelist community fumed at being ignored, but the Center had always rejected and proscribed any mention of divinity in their research; it was in their charter.

Another sleek, silvery jet discharged the noted British astronomer and billionaire Sir Alistair Spilhouse. The old gentleman served as Chair of the Board of Directors of the Center. "Come see our little girl," said Rick. "She's a darling. Katie and I might just adopt her."

The research group was now assembled, boasting three Nobels and a host of other distinctions. But the subject was still not talking. She did, however, seem to understand and could be seen laughing at cartoons. Rick and Katie sometimes ate meals with her and tried to attract her with family chat. Dorothy listened and sometimes smiled but didn't speak.

To a room of frustrated scientists spoke a young physicist, hemming and hawing before the illustrious company. "I feel I should suggest something... I have three young teenagers, girls, and they would all give an arm and a leg just to be on TV. You want to open her up, get her on some talk show. That just might do it." Heads nodded and the experiment was set up. Katie Masters entered Dorothy's room and after a bit of fussing about asked her, "Dorothy, how would you like to be on TV?" Immediate nod. "OK, then, let's look at some shows." It was assumed that any of the top celebrity shows would take Dorothy in a hot minute.

Using clips from YouTube, they went through Fox (hard headshake), Kimmel, Fallon and others (a yawn) until they finally hit Stephen Colbert (big smile and nod). The Colbert show was immediately offered Dorothy the Space Child. The producer was helpful. "Stephen is featuring another eight-year-old prodigy, a tap dancer. Could we get them on together?" The deal was signed.

Seven men were huddled in the lounge of a radio station deep in Tennessee. They were intent on the words of their leader, an obese man in a white suit. His face appeared young, but in the weary late hours it had come undone. He was talking relentlessly. "That earring... the stone practically burned a hole in my eye.. It must the temple stone sent to us from the heavens... From *Revelation* 21:19. I ransacked the Holy Book for stones, even thought about the stone that David killed Goliath with. Too big. Anyway, that one is locked up in some rubbishy church in Poland. But *Revelation*!

The first stone was Jasper...,' said the Saint. That's it. All the other twelve stones are light colored."

"Jasper is red," said one of the men.

"Red, yes. But black jasper is famous. I Googled it. It has fabulous health properties. It must be the Message and we must have that stone. The Lord has sent the first jewel of the temple to us back from space!"

"I've read about the security at that joint; it's air tight, they say."

"Nonsense, and we have the Lord with us to help recover his Message. We have a network of brave workers, some even in New Jersey. It is nothing to incapacitate a caregiver or attendant, assume his identity and infiltrate the area." The leader was named Homer Spode and he was calling on years of experience during his youth as a bank robber in the South before he found Jesus and a more profitable line of work. "I was thinking of sending our Deacon." They all looked over at the Deacon and back quickly. The Deacon was a spooky looking medium sized man whom people tended to turn away from. Spode went on. "But we've got somebody on the spot, can get in, try to get the stone out quick an' skedaddle."

The Center entourage could scarcely wait for the show, three days away. Dorothy remained silent but spent hours at the computer, showing experience with typing and browsing on the powerful Mac. Although the computer had been skillfully programed to transfer all her content to another pruvate monitor, there must have been a glitch. Nothing she did or listened to on the Mac produced anything more than a pixilated screen and a farting sound. So feelings were high on the given evening, as she rode with Rick and Katie in a limo, escorted by four New Jersey Highway Patrol vehicles and trailed by the scientific cordon. At the Ed Sullivan theater on Broadway an enormous crowd was waiting. Security forces lined a passage to permit the space girl and her company to pass. Crowd excitement came to a peak, not over the small figure of Dorothy, in $289 *GrlFrnd* pre-torn jeans and a George Floyd T-shirt, but over their close contact to the almost nuclear celebrity glow of the semi-clad Katie Masters and tousle-haired Rick Doulton. Then they were up in the Green Room. The tap dancer, eight-year-old African American Tiffany Gardner, was already there, with parents and agent ready to do battle over precedence. Tiffany immediately ran across the room and embraced Dorothy, who responded gracefully but still did not speak. Colbert stepped into the room, joked at bit with the rather large crowd and left to prepare.

Tiffany's agent had insisted that she go on first and so the giant nationwide audience was treated to an extraordinary selection of Fred Astaire choreography, from "I'm Old Fashioned" in which Tiffany did parts of both dancers, and a solo from "Puttin' on the Ritz." The audience forgot all about space girl and went wild. When the applause died down, Colbert called both girls before him and asked, "You two girls are unique. Eight years old! Tell me, where are you going from here?" The Dorothy entourage held their breath. Would she speak?

Tiffany: "I'm going to be a star!"

Dorothy, after a hesitant moment: "I *am* a star."

Colbert, flustered: "Well, of course you're a star, but darling, you haven't performed anything. What can you impress us with, other than remarkable survival qualities." (laughter)

Dorothy: "No. I *am* a star. This part of me you see is just for appearing and speaking. The star is this black stone in my ear. It is now actually a black hole but otherwise is a giant star with a mass of 6.5 times 10 followed by seventy-two zeros. That's kilos."

Colbert, never at a loss: "And Kirstie Alley was complaining!" (troubled laughter)

Colbert goes on. "I'm thinking I should be discussing the work of Stephen Hawking with you, Dorothy."

Dorothy: "I've been reading his work lately. It's amazing how much he gets right."

Tiffany, not to be ignored: *Tippity tappity tap*

The producer, seeing audience members checking their watches, is flailing his arms at the band to start cueing a break. The Dorothy entourage is exchanging glances that all mean: Let's get back to the Center! Rethink! Holy shit! But on the way back Dorothy fell asleep in the limo on Katie's lap so they put her to bed right away. Questions in the morning.

Benny Persons figured about 4 a.m. or a little earlier. Some burglars were impatient, went too soon after midnight and ran into insomnia, nagging money worries, or just plain ill-timed sex. He managed to follow an off-duty Center guard to a bar, bought him a drink with something in it, took his uniform and credentials and left him in a dark corner of the parking lot in his underwear. They were both African American, making confusion easy. As it was, no one even checked the cheerful, whistling security man with the easy smile. Benny figured he'd see if he could pop the earing out without waking the kid and disappear into the night. From down a long hall he could spot the target door. So he waited, and waited until a nurse emerged and went down the other way. In a second he was in the room, found the big bed and... the wrong side of her face was up. *She's dead asleep*, he thought, and he spoke softly: "Turn over sweetheart, y'hear? Gonna pull your blanket up." and he tugged it gently. Dorothy turned over obediently. The ear was there. The stone was there. How hard could this be? Benny's skillful fingers gently encircled the stone and began to push it through its hole. Except there was no hole. Dorothy suddenly said "What!" And Benny disappeared. One second he was there, the next...nothing. Dorothy put her head down and went back to sleep.

Katie seemed to have the best rapport with Dorothy so far, so she brought in Dorothy's breakfast and ate a pancake with her (cringing at the thought of the hours on the stair-master to get it off her creamy thighs). Katie had also been selected as the best person to ask the girl a question on everyone's mind. In between bites and as casually as she could contrive, she brought up the former town of Barnswallow and its residents.

"We're all wondering what you can remember about, uh, your folks and your town and like that." She was prepared for tears or worse, and was surprised when Dorothy simply cocked her head to one side and concentrated, as if contemplating a classroom problem. Finally she shook her head and answered haltingly at first.

"I wonder, myself. You know...everyone asked. You know, the...the doctors back in Kansas...people on the plane. That was before I could talk, and that was funny too. It wasn't like I forgot to talk, it was like all a blank, like I never talked before. Then when Mr. Colbert asked me who...uh, what I was, it wasn't me who answered. It was my star and I could feel it moving my lips and talking, and then I could talk myself."

Katie: "But Barnswallow—"

Dorothy: "That's all still a blank. When I try to remember, just anything, it's like a flat white wall."

Katie took her hand. "Honey, I bet it'll come back. And now, would it bother you to have a little chat with Rick and the guys? We can do it in here or in the conference room."

"I guess we're going to talk about stars."

Katie laughed "Well, you sort of brought up the subject, last night."

"Can I wear those jeans again?"

Rick and Sir Alistair were joined in the conference room by all three Nobels, two astrophysicists and an arcane mathematician, plus the others. An aide brought in a big pillow and Dorothy climbed up onto her chair. Rick led off the interview. "Dorothy, our group here is sort of split. Some, I have to say, really don't believe you are a star. I do, myself, and therefore my first question, the obvious first question is, why did a star come to visit our solar system?"

Dorothy considered solemnly. "You are assuming purpose. A woman going to the store to buy something has purpose. In the universe there is no purpose."

"I *knew* it!" exclaimed one of the Nobels. Nobel number two started to argue but Rick shushed them.

Dorothy went on. "I guess I was just a little girl. But over the past few days I've become aware. Things just come in my mind, slowly. Names and things come up and I Google them. And I can read real fast now. Mr. Hawking explained about Newton and Einstein and some of the rest my star filled in."

"If I may ask a question," ventured Sir Alistair. "It's about that black hole. Why isn't it just sucking the whole solar system into it instantly?"

Dorothy thought again, scratched her head. "I'm trying to think of the words. "It's in, uh..., null entropy. It is in fact a star but at some, uh, location in spacetime it is, was, became a black hole. It escaped gravity and can be anywhere at any time. Mr. Hawking speaks of wormholes and wrinkles in spacetime. I think he got a bit beyond me." She gestured helplessly.

There was a round of "hmms," glances exchanged and adjusting of eyeglasses.

"So your vigintillion-pound gorilla can just waltz through space and time?" chuckled the mathematician. They all laughed.

Dorothy's frowned. "Vigintillion. That's 63 zeros. Actually my star has 72 zeros. I don't know the word for that." She rubbed her earring. "Anyway, it says that being here is just 'ex-ist-ent-ial.'"

"Existential," pronounced Sir Alistair. "The oldest alibi in the world. "Might he not be investigating one of what you call 'wrinkles' in space time?"

"Why do you call my star 'he'? After all, I'm a she." Dorothy looked over at Katie and grinned. "But you raise a good question. Why did the star choose me to be its...uh... spokesperson? Maybe there is a purpose? I don't know."

"None the less," murmured the third Nobel, a minute Indian man, "a mass more than twice that of our sun, just lurking around our neighborhood...you're sure there is nothing we should be worrying about?"

Second Nobel: I'm still working on the bit about 'escaping gravity.' You mean to say that gravity is not a universal field?"

Sir Alistair: an entity that can escape gravity can reacquire it. That mass could immediately destroy the solar system."

Second Nobel: "Escaping gravity... acquiring it! Little Miss, all these ideas are totally beyond any theories we know. Is there some force your star enjoys of which we remain innocent?"

Dorothy played with a strand of her hair, contemplating. "Well...there is always *nous*—"

"*Nous!?* What the—" the refrain went around the table.

"Of course, said the mathematician. She is speaking of *voῦς* in ancient Greek. Meaning *mind*, or a sort of cosmic intellect. First proposed by Anaxagoras in the fifth century B.C. as the force that started the universe moving—"

"Oh bullshit!" exclaimed the second Nobel and a round of similar, if more diplomatic expressions echoed through the room.

"Please, gentlemen," cried Rick, striking the table with the flat of his hand. "Consider the feelings of our guest!"

"No," said Dorothy firmly. "That was correct, what you said... about starting the universe moving. It was *nous* and is always *nous*. It's always there and...my star says it...uh, sort of *tunes* things, like a...like a musical instrument."

Rick, anticipating another explosion of scorn, broke in swiftly, "But Dorothy, everything we believe in science is based on observation, or prediction tested by experimentation. Can you, or your star suggest any evidence for the existence of *nous*?

Dorothy: "May I ask a question, Mr. Doulton?"

"It's Rick, darling. We're all family here. And ask away!"

"Okay. I know you have space vehicles in your company."

"Boy, do we ever! We have six shuttles out there in the pine barrens. We can put satellites in orbit, contract to shuttle folks up to the space station—"

"And he takes silly rich people up for an orbit or two and charges a few hundred thousand dollars." Katie spoke up for the first time. "Would you like a ride?"

"We've got a wedding going up sometime in the next few days, if they can come up with the check. But we can put them off for a bit. That vehicle can take four of us—"

The girl clapped her hands gleefully. "Oh! Oh, could we?" She looked round the room, assumed a bit more gravitas. "My star is saying there *is* evidence but we have to be out in orbit to... uh measure it."

"That's fine for you—." All three Nobels started protesting at the same time. Rick put his hands up. "No, no, wait! We're all set up in that vehicle to Zoom all observations right back here on the big screen. If there is some *nous*-inspired wrinkle visible or measurable, everyone here will be right on top of it, and with two-way communication."

"I hope you'll include at least one real astronomer," grumped Sir Alistair. "Of course," answered Rick. "You, me, Katie and Dorothy. I'll call the launch pad right away, set it up for day after tomorrow!"

Homer Spode was ranting away in that church basement. "Nothing! Nobody's seen that burglar. If that son of a bitch ran out with that jewel—"

"My guy inside says the girl still has the earring. Something happened to Persons. Cops found his car in a lot a half mile away."

"Think he's in custody, they're keeping it a secret?"

"Negative. Cops found the security guard he drugged wandering around in his underwear. They're still working on his story."

"That settles it! No more half measures. We're leaving for New Jersey. Deacon, you think you can steal an earring?"

The next day was a flurry of activity for Rick. His Spastek operation had taken over the old Fort Dix and all the pine barrens between it and the sea. Spastek could launch two shuttles a day if they had a NASA contract and they could arrange a civilian orbit, with TV and a wet bar in a day, easy. Dorothy had her head in the computer most of the day and the rest of the time picking out her clothes, once Katie told her that they would be Zooming live back to earth on cable news.

The scientists congregated in the conference room and snarled at each other, citing wormholes and singularities until they could barely agree on Newton and Einstein. A good dinner put them all to sleep well before Colbert.

The televangelist attack was sudden and vicious. Wearing New Jersey highway patrol uniforms, the Deacon and a massive ex-wrestler leaped out of a waiting van and forced a door, then sprinted down the hall. Dorothy awoke to find her head clenched in hard hands. The Deacon felt the tightness of the earring, swore a terrible oath and with his penknife simply made a little cut on the bottom of Dorothy's earlobe. Then they were out of the door and gone.

Dorothy's anguished cry woke everyone. Guards rushed to see a black van disappearing in the distance. Katie dashed in to find the nurse cradling the poor child in her arms, her hand over her ear, blood and tears streaming. A doctor hurried in, quickly applied a local anesthetic and bound the wound, but Dorothy couldn't stop crying.

"My star, my star! He took my star! He cut me! Oh, oh, oh!" The medic finally sedated her and she went to sleep in Katie's arms, Katie crying herself and trying not to mutter "Fucking bastards, fucking bastards," too loud as the place filled with police.

The televangelists had driven as swiftly as possible out of New Jersey and to a reserved suite on the 49th floor of the Times Square Marriott. Only there did they finally relax and examine their bloody trophy. "Cut that fucking meat off it, Deacon!" cried Homer Spode. "That's the holy jasper, first jewel of the temple!" They all agreed that the normal Baptist injunctions against alcohol couldn't apply at such a triumphant moment and ordered up a few bottles of Jack Daniel's, a decent Tennessee beverage. They finally all went into a boozy slumber, the "sacred stone," a small, silent very black stone resting in the center of a table, waiting.

Rick, Katie and the scientists were all standing around in the conference room early the next morning having coffee and doughnuts when Dorothy marched in, still in her nightgown.

"Darling, I've called off the launch—" began Rick. But Dorothy interrupted in a clarion clear voice that froze the group in mid-breath.

"No, Rick! Now of all times we must get out into orbit. We must! It's absolutely...it's— You will see something...*perceive* something so incredible—"

"But Dorothy!" cried Katie. You're still hurt...and your star... we have to get your star back! The FBI says—"

Dorothy shook her head calmly. "I'm not hurt. A tiny cut. And I know where my star is. It has told me. And it's too late... there's nothing that..." She stopped. "My star is now running things. Rick! Katie! Call Fort Dix again. If we can launch by...uh, 1030, we'll be in place by, let's see, about nine minutes and then... Let's say 1100. That will do."

Her voice was so hypnotic in its urgency and authority that no one thought to object, only the small Indian Nobel muttering, "She has the true performative function of speech...Barthes was right!" And of course, everyone desperately *wanted* to see whatever wrinkle of space-time Dorothy's star might be planning.

With not much more than a change of clothes—"*Warm* clothes! *warm* clothes!" Rick counseling—Dorothy, Katie, Rick and Sir Alistair were bundling into a R66 turbocopter and winging off to the pine barrens of Fort Dix. The launch was back on again, had barely started to stand down, in fact, and the ground crew helped the presumptive astronauts into the luxurious space capsule with its bubble canopy of aluminum glass, stronger than titanium and offering 360° visibility. The Zoom screen showed the tense faces of the scientists back at the Center.

"Get ready for three Gs," warned Rick. "We have to get up to over 17,000 miles an hour in under nine minutes." There was a howl of exploding fuel and Dorothy felt herself pressed back into her take-off pod by an enormous weight. The capsule quickly outdistanced its own sound and they were in the silence of space. In a few minutes Katie unbuckled Dorothy and then they were all floating around the bubble. Rick cautioned them all to find a mooring handle and Dorothy found herself able with just a little effort to keep a stable position with a great view of what looked like an ocean below her...or was it above? "This is so cool!" she marveled, now back again with her little-girl voice.

The televangelist-burglar brigade woke late and groggily. They ordered a huge breakfast and another couple of bottles of their Tennessee beverage and for a while ate silently at the big table, contemplating the tiny black stone in the center.

"Don't look like much. Sure it's jasper?" mumbled a bleary chap through a mouth full of pancake.

"This," orated Homer, "is the first stone of the temple. Men, Look on it and wonder at the glory!" He hurled the heavy curtains back and held the stone up to the rays of the morning sun streaming in the window.

The sunlight hit the stone. His hand burst into flame. The stone tore its way through his hand, fell onto his large stomach, continued down through it as it acquired gravity, then through the concrete floor and thence through forty-eight more floors, gaining speed, three garage floors, through the granite of Manhattan and started its descent to the center of the earth three thousand nine hundred and fifty nine miles away at a speed of several thousand miles per hour. Once there it bathed in liquid iron at a temperature of eleven thousand degrees Fahrenheit.

As her companions raved at the vistas of the earth passing before them Dorothy suddenly said, "Uh oh!" She quickly had their undivided attention.

"My star is loose," she said. It's got back gravity and is heading for the center of the earth." As they slid over Japan with its glistening cities in the night suddenly all the lights below went out.

"How did it do that?" Katie squealed. No one answered for a moment. Then Dorothy murmured, "It's two hundred years ago. No lights." Then they were in sunlight again and the earth glistened white. There were no cities. Another rotation and the earth turned green and brown, then white again.

"It's not possible," said Sir Alistair calmly.

"What's not possible? None of this is possible! What is—"

Sir Alistair went on: "Your star, my dear, has reversed time. Turned back the clock he did, she did, whatever. First the lights went out; they hadn't been invented yet. Then, speeding up, the glacial ages began. You saw the snow and ice. 'So we beat on.... borne back ceaselessly into the past.' as it were." Prompted by *Gatsby*, Katie added, 'That star has more piety and wit than Omar Khayyam counted on."

"It's not changing space," said Dorothy. "It's using all its energy to turn time back instead. It's going to fix the wrinkle by going back to when it started, then start over again." Drawn by the high shrill voice, all stared at Dorothy, who was now a toddler of three or so. "We're caught in the wavelength too!"

"My boobs, where are my boobs!?" They all saw a fifteen-year-old Katie clutching her quite boyish chest with both hands. Rick's youthful hair grew back and pushed off his tousled hairpiece, which went floating around the capsule.

"If you have a moment, do you have any idea what's going to happen to us?" Sir Alistair asked. "Is this the end of the universe?"

"This one, I don't know." lisped baby Dorothy, "There are others, you know, all together, like pages in a book—" and *blip*, she was gone.

The outlines of the others grew indistinct, and smaller, as the shuttle continued its journey. California sank below the waves; the Mediterranean opened at both ends; South America lurched across the Atlantic and nestled into Africa's gulf of Guinea; India tore off and headed south to join Antarctica as *nous* guided his star in fixing the tiny wrinkle, not in space, but in time.

In Barnswallow a woman leaned out the kitchen window of a bungalow. "Dorothy," she called. It's getting dark, sweetheart. Better come in for supper."

The little girl skipped in the door. "Mom, I just saw a shooting star! It was the coolest thing."

The asteroid hit the planet's atmosphere, turned bright red and burst into flames as it hurtled on westward into the sunset, where it finally splashed harmlessly into the ocean.

CHAPTER NINE

Spencer and Michael dropped off their wives at the Tolliver house back in Barigoule. They clustered by the terrace for a moment, conferring over the various food and drink shortages threatening both households. Spencer insisted he didn't need a list, but Nicole jotted a short list for Michael and added the items Rosalind wanted. Spencer never remembered garbage bags, she said. The men left for Apt to shop at the ATAC supermarket. Nicole unlocked the massive front door and turned off the alarm at the keypad inside the door. The sun had been beating down on the terrace outside and the two women stood for a moment in the great circular room appreciating the coolness.

"I'm mad with jealousy every time I see this room," said Rosalind. She and Spencer lived in a splendid modern farmhouse a kilometer out of town, a house they'd bought before considering older, quainter village houses.

"Sometimes I wish we could trade," laughed Nicole. "This old mill is fun, but it's been such a lot of work. And you have a pool. And all that land. Can I get you a drink of something cold?"

"The land. I know. And Spencer is threatening to actually grow something on it. Maybe a glass of wine? If you have some open? Don't go to any trouble. We've got the kitchen garden, of course, but he's thinking of real crops—you know, like tomatoes or peppers, asparagus or something. I know he'd love to have a stall at the market in Gordes on Tuesdays and charge absurd prices to American tourists. What's worse, he was talking the other day about raising animals."

"Do you mean chickens, or something?" The two women had moved into the kitchen, a step up from the old mill room and Nicole was looking through the refrigerator. "There's a Tavel rosé."

"Worse. Sheep, goats, and then of course he'd milk them and make cheese. Right! And I've had enough mess just with the olives. Rosé sounds marvelous. Just right after all that sun." Spencer had harvested the olives from their two trees last December and had spent two weeks brining them, changing the brine, adding garlic, herbs, and hot peppers, and putting them in bottles. They'd eaten a few dozen over the course of the winter and then for some reason the olives all turned moldy.

"Spencer is a good cook," said Nicole. "I wonder what went wrong with the olives?"

"He loves to cook. I just wish I loved to eat what he cooks. Everything cooked in gobbets of olive oil, and even butter added. And of course he loves the fat cuts of meat, the duck, the lamb chops. I love desserts, but when he's cooking I cut them out." She felt her hips with distaste. "Otherwise I'd be out of all my jeans. If I didn't run almost every day I would be. These are way tight already."

"Michael loves to cook too. But I know what you mean about men cooks. Will he do just a nice baked *pintade*? Or a vegetable soup? No. He says we're French now and we should eat traditional dishes, like—"

"Don't tell me, I've been through it too. Tripe, and andouillettes, any unspeakable part of the animal that normal people would just throw away!" They both laughed and poured some more wine.

"Maybe we could trade husbands at dinner. They could cook for each other and we could just have a salad—"

"Or just dessert!" They laughed again.

The two women moved back into the mill room.

"I have to order some more curtains," said Nicole. "But there are so many in the catalogs. Why don't you help me narrow it down a bit?" They spent over an hour walking around looking at the various windows and making check marks in the catalogs. Finally Nicole laughed.

"It never fails. Everything I checked is the most expensive on the whole page. Michael's going to say, 'Why not just order by price? It'll save you the time and it'll turn out to be what you wanted anyway?'"

"I hate sarcasam," said Rosalind.

"Oh, he's not sarcastic...he's right. You know, I felt like getting some fish the other day and I had just told the girl to weigh some *rougets* and Michael says, 'Look at the sign—the rouget are from Dakar. They're out of season here and the price is 28 euros a kilo.' I never look at the price."

"Why should we bother our pretty heads over such trivia," said Rosalind, laughing.

"Where are you buying your fish these days? I used to go to that new place in Apt but the last few times it's been smelly."

"It's farther to drive but I like Inter in L'Isle, or Leclerc in Carpentras. Actually Leclerc in Cavaillon is good too, if you don't mind the traffic...hullo?" Rosalind was looking out the front window at four men coming across the terrace. The bell rang.

Michael had just parked the car in his usual spot behind the post office. He and Spencer were walking up the street when they saw four figures at the door of his house. They were in shadow and the bright sunlight made it difficult to identify the visitors.

"Uh oh!" said Michael and began to jog up the steps to the terrace. Then the door opened and he could see Nicole and Rosalind standing in the entrance. The four men turned, hearing

Michael and Spencer approaching, and the tall stooping figure of Marius was now identifiable. Behind him was Jeannot, Richard, the village policeman, and a slender man, a stranger in a suit and tie. They all met at the door in a babble of questions and explanations. The stranger quickly cut off the talk, lifting his hands for quiet. He spoke quickly but clearly in French.

"I am from the police in Avignon. Who is Mr. Tolliver?"

"That's me," said Michael.

"And this is your house?"

"Yes, but—"

"Then I must ask you some questions. Do I have permission to go in your house?"

"Well...yes of course. But my friend here—"

"Was he with you earlier today?"

"Yes, the four of us were—"

"The four of you. Yes. Very good. You must all come in. And Bérard here," he said, indicating Jeannot. "You two may go," he told Marius and the village policeman.

"But this is a village matter, and I must—," Marius started to complain.

The Avignon policeman's voice was sharp. "This is not your business. I have the complete authority here. Do you understand?" The two backed up before his commanding tone.

"Thank you for your assistance in identifying Monsieur Tolliver's house, but there is a matter of security now and this investigation is private. Goodbye, messieurs." Marius and the constable turned away briskly as if it had been their decision all along, saving their grumbling for later.

The policeman led Michael and Spencer into the house and they all found chairs in a circle.

"I am inspector Dreyfus," the policeman said, waving off all offers of refreshment from Nicole. "I asked Jeannot here to stay and help if there is a problem with translation. I am sorry my English is not adequate and Jeannot is an old associate. I can trust him." Jeannot nodded but his usual cheerful face was grim.

There was a chorus of questions but Dreyfus put up his hands again.

"Please, this will go much faster if I just ask questions in the proper order and you reply, no more, okay? Will you all approve that we speak in French? Otherwise..."

They all protested that their French was adequate. Rosalind was obviously going to ask something but Spencer put his hand on her arm. "Let's just go along, sweetheart. We'll find out what's happening quicker."

Dreyfus took all their names, addresses, and passport numbers, plus routine information about present or past occupations and resident status. Finally he nodded and looked up from his notebook.

"First, let me establish: the four of you ate lunch at the restaurant Philip today with Professor Lebarbe. Is that correct?"

"Yes..."

"And the purpose of your meeting with the Professor?"

They all looked at each other, puzzled. Michael decided to be the spokesman.

"You see, I am writing a book, and Professor Lebarbe was very helpful in explaining some background about—"

"About religion?"

"Well...yes, but also—"

"Did you have an argument of any kind? Maybe about religion?"

Now Spencer protested. "That's ridiculous! We had a friendly lunch! What the hell do you mean...?"

Inspector Dreyfus sighed and exchanged a glance with Jeannot, who shrugged.

His voice now turned solemn. "I regret to inform you that Professor Lebarbe had an unfortunate accident this afternoon shortly after your lunch. He fell into the waters high up near the Fontaine and was instantly killed in the rapids. Please! Let me continue just a moment. His body—what was left after it passed over all those sharp rocks—was found stuck in the barrage just by the paper mill, you know the place?"

"Oh my God!" They were all stunned.

"That sweet man!" said Rosalind, her voice catching.

"But you say it was an accident," said Spencer alertly. "Why a detective from Avignon?"

Dreyfus looked up sharply, then turned to Jeannot and back, relaxing. "You are not familiar with French police procedure. Since you are American, I will explain a little."

Inspector Dreyfus continued with the story, as he had been able to reconstruct it. The moment the body was seen from the shore the word spread instantly through the shops and cafés up and down the tourist path. A daring fireman tiptoed out along the barrage and, being very strong, was able to pick up the cadaver and bring it to the bank. One of the staff from Restaurant Philip was leaving his shift and immediately recognized Lebarbe as the little Frenchman in a black suit who had dined with four foreigners. The local police and tourist personnel had evacuated the paths up to the spring and then searched along the banks for any kind of evidence. They were assuming an accidental fall, or perhaps a suicide, with a note left behind. But an alert and sharp-eyed policewoman spotted a flash of light reflecting from Professor Lebarbe's glasses. She was clever enough to descend the path carefully so as not to disturb any evidence. And there in the muddy spot where the professor had stood were his crushed glasses, ground into the damp earth by a large footprint, obviously left by a distinctive running shoe. Without going any farther, the policewoman called her superior and explained what she had seen. Alarm bells went off; they realized that foul play had possibly taken place and therefore the incident must be referred to the criminal investigators in Avignon.

By the time Inspector Dreyfus and his assistant arrived the local police had interrogated the staff at Philip. Yes, the victim had left with the four foreigners. They had been discussing religion, said one waiter. Who were these foreigners? English, said the receptionist. No, Americans, said the waiter, who had not talked with Rosalind. Dreyfus's assistant immediately asked, did they pay by credit card? Now they all looked at her. The locals of Fontaine de Vaucluse had been slightly surprised to hear the name of the inspector. Dreyfus. A Jew—and there were not many Jewish police. Now they noticed his woman partner and were intrigued. A woman almost Dreyfus's height, very feminine as to her figure, even in police uniform, and with the acquiline features and glossy black hair that were certainly North African in origin. An Arab woman in the police? And with a Jewish detective as a partner?

Now they remembered her question. The credit card. Of course! And the cashier woman at Restaurant Philip pushed her colleagues aside and made a search through the day's receipts in her drawer until—there was the slip, and the name...Tolliver. The Vaucluse telephone directory provided the address and the inspector had come immediately to question the victim's last known associates while the trail was warm.

"You are the four who dined with the Professor?" They all nodded, silent only because they were impatient to find out why they were there.

"I must now ask you if you have running shoes," Dreyfus asked.

Spencer was wearing his and held his feet out for inspection.

"They are the right size," said the inspector, "but a different marque." Michael brought his Reeboks downstairs but the inspector dismissed them.

"Too small. And your wives obviously have feet too small. The person who smashed the victim's glasses had large feet and was wearing...was wearing a certain brand, still unknown, but we will identify it. That person may not actually have killed the victim but we assume he was on the spot and may have witnessed the incident. Before you left the village did any of you see a large person wearing running shoes?"

"These days everyone wears shoes like that," said Nicole.

"You know...there's something in the back of my mind, nagging me...something I remember seeing that I thought was funny. It's driving me nuts, right on the tip of my tongue..." Rosalind's face was tense with concentration.

The others began to offer helpful suggestions but Dreyfus interrupted, directed his attention to Rosalind.

"For the moment, may I take down some other information? What is your full name?"

"Rosalind Bereford Sullivan, but—"

"Excuse me. And where do you live?"

"Outside the village. On the road to the Col."

"And your husband's name?"

"Sullivan, Spencer Sullivan."

"What is the color of your car?"

"Sort of a silver gray..."

"Where did you see running shoes?"

"There was this nun...Bloody hell! How did you do that?! Of course! The two nuns, all in black habits, you know, but they were wearing very bright running shoes, blue, I remember, and yellow, maybe some red. How did you make me remember?"

"It is a standard technique of interrogation." Inspector Dreyfus permitted himself the tiniest of smiles. He excused himself while he tried to use his cell phone.

"They won't work up here," said Michael. "No relay near enough." So Dreyfus borrowed the house phone and made a quick call, then was all business again.

"We will, of course, pursue the shoe business, although in France we do not normally suspect sisters of the church of murder. Now the important questions I must ask you: did Professor Lebarbe seem worried, distracted, or even fearful in any way?"

"It was our first meeting," said Michael. "I would say that he was charming, at ease, and answered all my queries at length and most usefully."

"And these questions were about religion?"

"Yes. Well, first, he told us about the geology of the fountain. After that it was all about the persecution of the Vaudois during the wars of religion four hundred and fifty years ago."

Dreyfus looked aside, appeared to be thinking. "Ah, yes. The Vaudois. I remember from university, but not very much. Now, you were asking anything about religion today, these days, about controversies in the Catholic church?"

They all voiced their objections. "Not a bit!"

"We never discussed anything modern!"

Dreyfus shrugged. "I must ask these questions about the deplored victim's state of mind, possible controversies he might have been involved in. Tempers can run high—"

"In the Catholic church?" Spencer was startled. "Leading to violence...or murder?"

"There have been cases, of course. Not highly publicized, because it is sensitive for a Catholic country." He adjusted his glasses." I myself am a Jew and look at these things objectively. Now permit me to ask each of you individually some questions."

The inspector then spent over twenty minutes asking the four of them the same questions over and over: how long have you known the professor? Why did you ask him to consult on these interests? Did you personally detect anything unusual in the professor's manner? Did he mention any concerns or fears? Did you notice anyone watching him? Was anyone paying too much attention to your conversation? To this last question, three of the group answered in the negative, but Spencer spoke up.

"You know, I thought the waiter was hovering a bit. Then when I wanted something he was talking on his cell phone. I thought it peculiar." Dreyfus jotted down something in his notebook. Then he smiled his little smile and turned to Jeannot. "My friend, I think we may leave these good people at liberty, don't you?"

He got up to leave. "Please accept my sympathy for the loss of your friend. I will no doubt be back to ask more questions as our investigation continues. Should you remember any further details, call me immediately at any time at the number of my *portable*." He handed out cards with his cell phone number and other addresses.

After Michael had shown him out of the door they all sat for a moment in silence.

"I'm just devastated," Nicole said finally. "Such a nice man. And I just can't believe anyone would *kill* him. My God!"

"If they did, the police will get him," offered Spencer with a sigh. "This is France and they clear a hell of a lot more crimes than we do at home. Isn't that right, Jeannot?"

"Dreyfus will get them, all right. He is without mercy, never stops. I've seen him working before."

"How do you know him?" asked Michael.

"And he let *you* stay and kicked out our local lout of a cop and that busybody Marius! Did you see their faces?" said Rosalind with a harsh laugh.

Jeannot looked at them without smiling. "He is an old-boy. A rugby old-boy. I played against him twice. I wanted to tackle him and crush him but I must say, I was closer to him this afternoon that ever in those two matches. He was so fast. Anyway, I have seen him talk to the little *voyous*, the young gangsters who steal cars, car radios. He talks to storekeepers, everyone, asking, who was around. Only one name he needs. He finds him at his mother's house...these little *cons*, excuse my language, all still live at home. And he questions them there, quietly, not down at the station yelling, like most *flics*. So friendly, even the mother brings some cake for this nice man being gentle with her son. Before he goes he has the names of the others and the promise of the young man to appear at the tribunal tomorrow to admit his crime. Now he has been promoted to detective. Right now he is going after your waiter, I can tell you."

Dreyfus was taking matters one at a time back at the Fontaine. He told a policeman to get the name of the waiter who had served the professor's table. Then he joined his woman partner who had been interviewing visitors to the Fontaine early that afternoon. The local policemen had been watching her every move. Her name was *Leyla Abdelaziz* and they had never seen an Arab woman in a French police uniform. But they had to admit she knew what she was doing.

"Many people saw the two nuns," she said. "And they all remembered, 'one big one, one little one.' And they were wearing running shoes. Some schoolchildren talked to them, said they were nice, laughing and joking. The shoes—"

"A distinctive pattern. Do we know the marque?"

"Not a famous one, Nike or Adidas. The sergeant thinks it is the house brand of Carrefour."

"Yes. A discount brand. Cheap. What a nun would buy. Twenty euros rather than fifty. And they sell tens of thousands of them. So we don't look for shoes...we look for nuns. Make a note to call every order of sisters in the department. Nuns have to check in and out—I think. What two sisters went on a little excursion today to the Fontaine de Vaucluse? Ask them."

Now the sergeant came running up with the address of the waiter, Jacques Borie, who lived with his parents in L'Isle-sur-la-Sorgue. The inspector phoned and spoke with his mother, who was in great distress. Her son Jacques had returned from work, packed a bag and left, obviously disturbed, not answering questions. This, finally, was enough of a suspicious event to call in the criminal investigation facilities of the national gendarmerie, and Inspector Dreyfus made the call.

Michael and Nicole were eating a modest supper of leftover roast duck, with a salad of radicchio. The mistral had come up and was battering their house on its western exposure. They were still subdued from the news of the death at the Fontaine.

"If I were writing an old-fashioned detective novel, it would go exactly this way." Michael was mopping up the oil in the salad bowl with a crust of bread.

"What do you mean?"

"It's the formula. The detective is looking into some deep, dark crime. As soon as he finds the first real clue leading to the apparent suspect, he goes to accuse him and finds him dead. Usually gets knocked on the head at the same time. Happened to Philip Marlowe all the time."

"But who would care about a secret four hundred and fifty years old?" Nicole was irritated. She poured herelf another glass of Seguret. "And what secret could it be? We know the local militia killed everyone they could find back then, all over the Luberon. What is there to hide? They were all bastards!"

"What is there to hide, and why are they hiding it? That's what I have to find out.If I were Philip Marlowe, or Spenser or somebody like that the next thing would be some heavy coming around and warning me off."

"Great! Just what we need. I admit I'm curious, but why do you *have* to find out, Mikey? Maybe it'll be something simple, like local families still owning land they stole from the Vaudois, and feeling ashamed of it."

"According to Spencer, most of the land changed hands during the Revolution. We know the local baron of Barigoule had his head chopped off. Most of the big landowners did. No. I think it's something deeper. And you know, I've just only started the book of documents. Maybe I'll work on that after supper. Something to take my mind off poor Lebarbe, anyway."

The testimony given before the learned jurist Jacques Aubery in 1553 was organized to demonstrate the growth of the Vaudois heresy in that part of Provence north of the Durance river which included the hills of the Luberon and the valley and foothills farther north. The Vaudois were known to be hard-working, having improved the lands of every landowner for whom they had worked. They were also remarkably free of vice, obedient, and devout, even if they were also given to preaching from the Gospels in a tedious manner at every opportunity. On the rich lands of Provence they prospered, and enriched the landowners who had been smart enough to take them in as tenants.

But their preaching became a problem. They insisted that nothing that could not be found in the Gospels was worthy of worship. The only sacraments were baptism and communion. Prayer to the Virgin and to the saints was useless. There was no such thing as purgatory, therefore no one should have to pay corrupt priests huge sums to shorten their time in purgatory.

Worst of all, many local clerics were supporting the Vaudois, either secretly or openly. The rumor of heresy in Provence had brought judicial experts from the Inquisition to the larger cities of the area and they had begun to collect information. In Cabrières there were nineteen households, all heretics; in Barigoule, sixteen; in Merindol, all were of the Vaudois heresy. Lists were made, followed by appeals to the royal authority. For the Vaudois were pious and devout, but they were not pacifists. Local attempts to menace them were met with force. A body of militia sent against Roque d'Antheron was battered and fled to a local abbey where they were besieged for two days. Finally, the king of France, François I, who had many more important things to worry about, was talked into an edict of "execution," against all the households and villages said to be in error. Immediately influential supporters of the Vaudois counterattacked. A famous legal scholar pointed out that a massacre of rats in one town had been called in question because of the lack of due process in persecution of the rats; if even rats had the defense of law, should not pious French peasants deserve the same consideration. King François suspended the edict for what turned out to be five years.

But now began the campaign of slander initiated by the young baron of Oppède, Jean Maynier. The baron was fanatic in his hatred of heresy. When he found the royal authority uninterested and slow to act, he created the rumor of a vast conspiracy against the crown. There were at least fifteen to twenty thousand Vaudois, he said, all armed. Worse, he had discovered that they were plotting to take Marseille by storm and make it into an independent state, ruled by vile Protestant law.

Conspiracy theory is easy enough to spread in the most modern countries of the twenty-first century. How much easier then, in an era with no journalists and virtually no records, when it took almost a month for a courier to go from Marseille to Paris. Maynier and his supporters convinced the king that his original edict should be put into force and reluctantly the king agreed.

The testimony about the massacre of innocents was relentless, punishing, finally nauseating. Baron Jean Maynier of Oppède had mustered his own troops, those of other loyal Catholic towns, and mercenaries from the Piedmont who were waiting in Marseille to take ship for the English war. Coming from the south they had taken Merindol first and burned it to the ground. Merindol lay with its back against the steep southern slope of the Luberon, riven with gorges and secret ways. Most of the men escaped, as did all the women who had an inkling of what could happen when large bodies of men were given license to do what they would. The priest and a congregation of faithful Catholics remained behind to greet the host that came to punish heresy. Alas, no one had thought to instruct the excited army of the faith. The priest was struck down by an arrow before he could say a word of welcome. The mercenaries were astounded to see a village full of women, undoubtedly heretics, therefore deserving the most extreme indignities and abuse that the faithful could devise.

Leaving a ruin of smoking cinders and hacked, dismembered women and children, the avenging army swept onward to the other villages of the southern Luberon. Cadenet, Villelaure, Lourmarin were all sacked, the pathetic inhabitants unable to flee were massacred. Those suspected of concealing wealth were tortured, an old woman was put head first into a bakery oven. All pretext of punishing heresy was forgotten as the mob, now out of control, surged across the pleasant countryside.

To the east, a broad valley spread between the massif of the Luberon and the Durance river to the south. These were the lands of the Dame de Cental, administered for her by her son and grandson. These fields were among the richest in Provence and had been farmed by industrious Vaudois tenant farmers. Baron Maynier, whose fief of Oppede perched on the northern, hardscrabble slopes of the Luberon, thirsted to possess these lands under the cover of extirpating heresy. Tour d'Aigues, Cabrières d'Aigues, all the villages fell to his troops, aided by local volunteers settling old scores and taking whatever land fell conveniently vacant.

With the lands south of the Luberon ravaged and depopulated, the armies of the Lord swept northward toward the stronghold of Cabrières d'Avignon, whose master occupied a fortified village that had easily repelled police actions in the past. There was a siege of several days. Finally, the lord of Cabrières negotiated a surrender. He would open his gates on the condition that all inhabitants be spared. Alas, the theologians who accompanied the royal troops explained that sworn oaths given to a heretic might be broken without sin. The flames of Cabrières mounted into the sky, taking with them the smoke from the roasting bodies that had been herded into the church before it was set aflame.

Finally, on the 20th of April, 1545, the weary troops looked northeastward toward the remote village of Barigoule. All there were thought to be Vaudois and the order of execution specifically mentioned Barigoule. The village lay uphill, along a long and narrow road, and many of the baron's allies were spent, more interested in a good meal and the casks of good wine they had liberated at Cabrières. But some papal troops had recently joined the slaughter and valiantly declared themselves ready to finish the work at hand. Up the hill they marched, burning a few farms and houses around Gordes, whose castle walls were too thick and well guarded to tempt men at arms used to easier conquests. Eight kilometers away across the hills lay Barigoule.

By this time, anyone with any brains in Barigoule had devined the reason for the columns of smoke mounting across the valley below, and what they couldn't guess refugees had explained to them in gory detail. Every able-bodied person in Barigoule took to the hills. The heights of the Vaucluse to the north are full of wild valleys and gorges, and there the men waited, hoping that papist troops might venture into an ambush.

The women and children of Barigoule tired of the climb after a few kilometers. Besides, they knew of the grottos, hidden down a long, brush-choked path. The main grotto was supposed to be holy, blessed by St. Gens himself, who had rested there while plowing the surrounding fields with his wolf. The grotto of Saint Loup, the holy wolf, some of the old witches said. There they waited silently.

The testimony received by Judge Aubery said only that the women and children were betrayed, and not by whom, but it is believable. In a small village there are always bitter feuds, and religious disputes can be irrelevant. The papal troops, led by Captain Mormoiron, were led by someone to the grotto. The captain shouted that all should come out...that they would be spared. But there were a very few survivors from Cabrières among the women and they knew very well what the word of Holy Church was worth. The captain was enraged. He ordered his men to fire arquebuses into the narrow opening of the grotto. But it became obvious that the interior of the cave was too big; refuge from those primitive weapons was easy.

The end was quick. Brush was gathered, logs were heaped upon the fire, and for a whole day the conflagration burned. When the ground was cool enough, one could look in and see only lifeless bodies, suffocated by the smoke and lack of air. Here the testimony concerning Barigoule ends.

But there was no relief for the little village of Lacoste, southward across the valley of the Calavon from Barigoule. The baron of Oppède had been fully occupied at other sites, but he now sent troops to Lacoste and orders to the local magistrates to open the gates.

The troops arrived first and the sensible magistrates closed the gates against even the friendliest entreaties. The soldiers had to content themselves by rounding up whatever local women they could find and violating them in the gardens that lay outside the walls. Then, enraged by the continued stubbornness of the magistrates, they destroyed all the trees and three centuries worth of careful and artistic plantings in the gardens. Finally the orders arrived and the seigneur had no alternative but to open the gates. In poured the soldiery, thirsting for victims and booty. Poor Lacoste suffered the familiar atrocities of the other Luberon villages. Mothers offered knives to their daughters and begged them to kill themselves to avoid violation. Some tried to hang themselves, but it is said that Heaven would not suffer the holy ban on suicide to be broken and caused the ropes to break. One young woman threw herself from the walls, unfortunately not killing herself completely. Some soldiers noted that she was not dead and raped her mangled body.

"My God! I can't read any more of this awful stuff," Nicole complained. "Are we sure that it isn't exaggerated?"

Nicole and Michael were sitting in Jeannot's café relating what they had found to the burly proprietor. A hot day had turned cool as banks of clouds were coming up from the south and blotting out the sun from time to time. An idle breath of wind chased a plastic cup across the terrace and under their table.

Michael was trying to soften the impact of what they'd been reading.

"Well...compared to what we've seen the last few years—Bosnia, Ruanda, Iraq—this is pretty mild stuff. What was it? Three thousand dead and six hundred sent to the galleys?"

Nicole was about to protest but Jeannot held up his big hand. "And—very important when you think of our civilization here, four hundred and fifty years ago—the only reason you know these things is because of the inquiry and then the trial in court." He turned and shouted into the interior of the bar. "Gaby! Bring monsieur Mike another *ballon*." A Dutch couple sitting at another table looked at the darkening sky and started searching for coins to pay their bill.

Michael started to say something, but Jeannot went on. "Humans can turn to animals, it is true, and there are massacres, rapes, pillage. But here in Europe there is a small, how do you say, *couche...*"

"A layer?"

"Yes, a layer of civilized obligations. The government knew something was wrong. Important people complained, so they had a trial. This man Aubery, you quote him, he was a just man, and he investigated all the crimes. You know, of course, the massacre at Oradour sur Glan?" The wind now swirled from the other direction and the plastic cup went back out into the street.

Michael and Nicole were silent for a moment. Then she spoke up. "Of course! The Nazi massacre at Oradour. But what has that to do—?"

Jeannot smiled, grimly. "Yes, what has that to do? Well, our partisans killed some German soldiers. It was stupid! The war was lost and the Germans knew it. They were already packing up, ready to leave. And then some angry young men among the partisans fired on the troops. So the commandant was furious. And he massacred the whole village. The same thing, packing the people into the church and burning it. But there, after Oradour, the Germans themselves had an inquiry. It was allowed to kill ten French for every German murdered, as they said. But the commandant had killed far too many. And you know how the Germans are...exactly this, exactly that! He was tried by his own German courts. There is your proof of civilization, if only a tiny one. There was crime, yes, but it was investigated, and it was punished!"

"He's right," said Michael. "We can't hold our heads up. Look at El Mozote, in Salvador. The troops we trained massacred over nine hundred people, mostly women and children...what was it, twenty years ago or more? And what Jeannot said. There was never an investigation, trial, anything! In fact, everyone in the government lied in their teeth, trying to deny it. So where does that leave us?"

"I don't know," said Nicole. She was shaking her head, looking glum. Now she hugged her bare arms, feeling the chill of the wind.

"So you see," went on Jeannot. "What happened here in Barigoule was nothing, compared to the rest of the Luberon. You can write a book like Monsieur Rousset, about Lacoste, but no one will believe it. Will they publish such a book, or even make a movie?

"Oh, they'd make a movie, all right," said Nicole, bitterly. "A rape movie. Tits and ass and lots of blood. Wouldn't even bother to show it in the theaters, just go right to video and advertise it on all the kinky internet sites."

Jeannot looked mystified.

"Unfortunately that's how it works in our version of capitalism," said Michael. "They think they can figure within ten thousand dollars or so how well a movie will do in the movie houses. Showing movies in theaters is expensive. So if the accountants don't think the movie will break even in the theaters, they just make videos and sell millions of them in video stores."

"And they say in the ads, 'Too powerful for the big screen.'"

Michael translated. "That means, too much sex and sadism for the audiences of mainstream theaters. Do you understand?"

Jeannot was nodding his head. "Yes. You could sell this movie in France too. But it would have to be, how do you say, artistic?"

"Oh yeah!" Nicole said, laughing mockingly. "You mean, with clowns running out of the fog and disappearing again?"

Jeannot roared with laughter and smacked his massive thigh. "Oh yes, clowns in the fog. Symbolism. French cinema. But not so much now. The young people are now the market, and they want action, car chases, much shooting, sex. Sometimes I miss the clowns in the fog."

Now a splatter of huge drops came down. Gaby was coming out with Mike's glass of wine but stopped dead in the doorway, looking up at the sky. It seemed best to retreat indoors.

In the end, Michael had to explore the gorge of the Veroncle by himself. They had all agreed that the episode of the mills would add an exotic touch to the grotto story. But Spencer absolutely refused to go and Nicole was hesitant.

"The mills...Mike. They're from the same era, okay. But...but I'm just a little worried about climbing down a deserted gorge. After what happened to the professor, you know? And what does it have to do with your story?"

Michael was shaking his head. "I don't know. I just don't know. But Jeannot was so descriptive...I've never seen him so animated. You'd think he'd seen the dam being built. So I guess I'm just pointed in that direction for the moment. Maybe I'll have some inspiration. The book's not going all that great so far." He gave a frustrated laugh. "So how about tomorrow?"

The next day was beautiful. But Rosalind's hairdresser in Apt called to say there was a cancellation and she could fit her in and Nicole as well. Michael stubbornly filled his small pack. A bottle of water. A geologist's hammer. A half baguette and a piece of sausage. At the last moment a digital camera. Nicole was worried, talking to him leaning halfway out the front door with Rosalind waiting for her in the car outside.

"Now be careful, okay? And there's fog down in the valley today. So if it starts coming up the gorge you better turn around."

Michael kissed her. "Go on. Have fun in Apt. And you know I've been all over the hills here by myself."

"Yeah! And almost killed by boars?"

"A one in a million thing. Go on. I'll see you after lunch. Where are you eating?"

"Rosalind says the Bistro de Paris has a new spring menu. Anyway, Henri there is always dependable. Bye..." She sprinted out the door as Rosalind honked impatiently.

Michael reached the first mill by ten. Now he found himself whistling Jeannot's little tune, couldn't get it out of his head..."One day you will see...we will meet once again..." So he concentrated instead on the various bird songs, finches and sparrows overhead, robins in the brush, a blackbird in the middle distance, and the usual cuckoo in a tree top somewhere. The first mill came into view, the old bones of the structure showing through the spring foliage. The waterfall was muted, beginning to taper off in the dry days of early summer. Here he had stood with Jeannot and then turned back. He took a quick shot of the first mill and its waterfall with the camera, then struck off downhill on the well marked trail. Little blue and yellow spray paint slashes on trees and stones marked the way. At intersecting trails, he could see yellow Xs on prominent trees, proclaiming "not this way."

In some ways France is too civilized, he was thinking. It would have been nice to cut his own trail, backtracking when wrong, following up leads. And he remembered. Several years before he and Nicole had gone climbing up trails in the Pyrenees. The day had started out foggy and they had meant only to wander up to a small waterfall promised on their map. But halfway up, the sun had emerged, burned off the fog and they could see the entire Pic du Midi rising to their left. So they had climbed much further than they had planned, having only a half *ficele* sandwich bought below and a plastic water bottle, Michael wearing only sandals. They climbed past tiny lakes, past the tree line, planning to come down on another trail on their map. And there, at the top of the trail, was a small *buvette*, a refreshment stand built of logs, serving plates of bread, *paté*, salads, and of course, wine by the glass. They had collapsed in laughter. "France!" they chorused. "Where else but France!"

At this point Michael realized that the blue and yellow markings had given out. He was standing below the third mill, admiring the thirty foot revetment, all dry stone walling, hundreds of years old, and wondering where the path lay next. No spray painted line appeared on the surrounding rocks and he took off his sunglasses, which seemed to be misting up. In fact, he noticed immediately that the warm sun he had been enjoying on his back had disappeared and that the outlines of the gorge were beginning to look fuzzy. The fog in the valley below had started to creep up the gorge so gradually as to escape notice, and being compressed by the high limestone cliffs on each side had thickened. Michael considered the wisdom of creeping down uncertain paths above deep drops in a thickening fog. But one clear path was obvious, and being a male animal, he struck out. For two years he had watched the fog develop in the lower basin of Barigoule, and sometimes rise in great banks to cover the entire hill with its chateau, and he knew that the fog was a weak, ephemeral thing, likely to evaporate in seconds, leaving observers to wonder where it had gone.

The path was still muddy from the rain a week before, having no chance to dry under the canopy of oak and pine that ringed the gorge. Michael was wondering if he should have brought a walking stick. There were three sturdy ones he had cut from hard wood and trimmed...all standing next to his front door back home. Good luck! So he took out his geologist hammer and used it as a hook to get a grip on a tree or a branch as he descended steeper slopes. He'd gone almost a mile now, and hadn't seen the forest service markings. Was he on the right path?

But he could tell he was right in the middle of the gorge, and where else would a clever engineer put his mills?

As he hesitated to think out his next move and check his surroundings he suddenly heard a sound coming from back on the path he had been following, the sound of a small stone crunching underfoot. He strained to see through the fog, but the visibility had decreased to a mere twenty yards or so. Another lonely hiker?

He remained motionless, straining to hear another footfall. But the silence in the gorge was total. And now he noticed that even the bird song was stilled.

No hiker appeared and he decided to continue, stopping suddenly from time to time to listen for his phantom follower. Once he thought he heard a rock skittering off the path, but it sounded distant and he decided to stop worrying. Now the trail forked, one branch straight across a flat, bare rocky outcrop, the other splitting off to the right and uphill. Michael took the obvious trail across the outcrop, searching for its continuation in the underbrush ahead. The gorge had become quite narrow now and steep. The stream could be heard far below to his left but the fog had thickened to the point that he felt relieved when an obvious opening in the trees appeared in the haze. There finally was a paint stripe on a small oak and he realized that a mill must be just ahead. He almost kicked the red tin sign lying in the path where it had fallen from some tree, saw it just in time, and picked it up. DANGER! it said simply, leaving all specifics to the imagination. And then Michael could see the path continuing on a narrow stone ledge leading to what looked like a rectangular cave in the cliff ahead. Next to the path and parallel to it, he could make out a channel carved in the rock. This was evidently one of the conduits created long ago to carry water to a mill wheel. The channel led directly to the opening in the cliff. Michael peered in and felt a moment of vertigo because the hole in the cliff plunged steeply down, a tunnel, almost vertical, laboriously cut into the solid rock and leading into darkness below, twenty, thirty feet..? He judged it as more than the drop from a three story building. Here the water would have come rushing hundreds of years ago through the channel and into the tunnel, picking up vast speed and power as it dropped down the hole to spin some mechanism below. No wonder they had put up a DANGER sign. And then, still leaning into the tunnel, he heard a rock crunch under a footstep again, but this time right behind him.

He whirled around in terror and there before him in the mist he could make out the shadowy shape of a strange man...a pale face and a thin figure dressed in dark clothes. The figure had been moving toward him but now froze in place. Michael instinctively raised his hands to protect himself and realized that he was still holding the geologist's hammer in his right fist. He had a sudden image of Professor Lebarbe, stalked and hurled to his death in the slashing waters. So now his terror turned to anger and he started toward the figure, in his fury forgetting any words of French.

"Hey you! What the hell do you mean creeping—"

But the shadowy man turned quickly and sprinted up the steep hill, disappearing suddenly in the fog. Michael darted after him, intent on identifying the phantom. He stumbled a bit on the rocky slope, as he had running from the boar, but was still able to scramble along, gravel pelting down from above and revealing the route taken by his target. He reached a more gentle slope with better footing and started running as fast as he could with the hammer cocked back in his hand. And then suddenly he was above the fog and could feel the sun on his head. Above him...too far above, was the shadow man, leaping from rock to rock like a mountain goat, about to vanish into a patch of pines. Michael suddenly remembered his camera. He snatched it out of his pocket, aimed and clicked just as the figure vanished into the trees, the pale face looking back. On the camera monitor he could just barely make out the man outlined against the trees before the screen went black again.

By the time he reached home again Nicole was back. He toned down his description of the day's adventure, not wanting to make it too alarming, but Nicole was terrified.

"Mikey! You have to call the inspector! This...this could have been like the professor...he could have pushed you down...Jesus! We'd never find you! Maybe this was like what you were talking about, your detective plot. You know...when the heavy comes around to scare you—"

"I don't know. It's too flimsy to take to the cops, the story. And it could be just that we both scared each other there in the fog. And it was thick fog, Hollywood fog. Let's have a look at his photo first."

But when they downloaded the photo onto the computer screen it showed only a distant grove of trees.

"I swear he was still in the open when I shot the picture...in fact he was on the monitor!"

"Come on, Mike! You know that dumb camera's never worked right. Go on like this and we'll start thinking it was a vampire, won't show up on a photo." Nicole was trying to laugh it off, without conviction.

"Well...anyway it wasn't a nun. Maybe I scared some hiker with my hammer. But he sure didn't look like one, a real hiker, you know?

CHAPTER TEN

The glorious full sun of Provence poured down over the valley of the Calavon. In the villages of the Luberon diners in the outdoor cafés were finishing their wine, their coffees, looking over their bills, thinking about a nice nap at home until the sun started to set and the day became a bit cooler. It was a Sunday—the first Sunday in three weeks that it hadn't rained—and everyone in Provence had found somewhere to go out of doors.

Particularly in Barigoule the villagers were happy. The annual *concours de boules* had been scheduled for today, and although *boules* could certainly be played in cold or damp weather, it was much better when the sun was out. The good players from all the surrounding countryside would come and the bars and cafés would be full, as well as the traveling concessions that would always sprout their stalls and canopies any place large groups of French people assembled. Two small bands had arrived, and after a brief argument that almost came to blows, they agreed to take opposite ends of the *boule* pitch: the banjo, clarinet, and bass player to the south, and the singer, saxophonist, and accompanying cassette player-boombox to the north.

The various *boules* teams who had registered many weeks before were now playing elimination bouts. It was a sudden-death tournament: if your team lost, you were out and could start drinking—or just continue drinking at a faster pace.

The players tossed their steel *boule*s up and down gently, from hand to hand, concentrating. The game was one variation of the universal game of bowls, like *boccie* in Italy. The player on the line was trying to roll his ball as close as possible to the *cochonet*, the little plastic ball that was the target. Then succeeding players would try to roll their balls closer, or simply heave a ball at the opponent's closer ball to smash it away and improve their teammates' position. The only ball that counted was the closest to the *cochonet*. If a teammate's throws had also come closer than any of the opponents, his balls also counted. But generally, at this level of play, out of eight balls thrown by four players on two teams, only one ball would lie closest; the next nearest would be an opponent's.

Some of the teams were the usual old men, cloth caps on their heads, cigarettes clenched firmly in their mouths, crouching, aiming, and arching the heavy balls toward the *cochonet*. But there were also younger men on the teams, more enthusiasic, more physical, more inclined to violence against opponents' balls than careful placement. The leading team at the moment was led by an old man wearing *bleu de travail*. His partner was a younger construction worker with a flair for knocking opponents' balls out of the way. With the old man's accurate placement and his partner's kamikaze attacks on rival balls they were now in first place and had only two more teams to play.

Into this fray innocently ventured the Tolliver-Sullivan team. Michael and Spencer had been trounced so thoroughly every time they played against their wives that they had agreed to put up Nicole and Rosalind as a team. Weeks ago the team had been registered: Tolliver-Sullivan—and it was only now that the *boule*s players of Barigoule were realizing that the team in third place was composed of two women. The general reaction was *merde!*

Women didn't play *boules*! Well, sometimes on a picnic, with their husbands and children. But not a serious *concours de boules*!

The appearance of a competitive team composed of two females had already aroused a certain degree of merriment among the women of Barigoule, who were accustomed to the role of spectators, or listeners, having to endure after every match a replay and long account of all the treacherous maneuvers that had deprived their mates of a certain victory. Now the mothers, wives, and daughters of Barigoule were watching two women, who at the moment were beating the crap out of the local *pompiers*—the firemen. Many of the local men and boys were cheering on the Tolliver-Sullivan team, having noticed the fine figures of the two women, well set off by the skimpy clothing dictated by the weather. Nicole was the more robust, filling out her white blouse and jean shorts to good effect. Rosalind was wearing a wispy blue cotton tank top and black cycling shorts. Too thin, said the owner of the Tapounado to his friends. Maybe, but observe the movement in those black tights, advised the grocer. That one could wear you out.

The firemen were taking their defeat with good humor, trading insults with Nicole and Rosalind after every throw, and finally applauding themselves when the two women managed to place all four of their balls closer to the *cochonet* than any of theirs—a whole four points, or the equivalent of a grand slam home run. That finished the match and the captain of the firemen ran out with bottles of champagne in both hands to pour a tribute to Nicole and Rosalind, who stood there smiling grimly, tossing their *boules* from hand to hand in a calculated manner.

It now turned out that the final match of the day would be between these surprising women and the old man in the *bleu de travail* and his hulking partner. There had already been some grumbling among the older men in the crowd, and now Marius made an appearance to question if the two women were actually eligible to play in a Barigoule championship *concours de boules*.

His announcement was met by scattered applause and a much louder wave of hoots and whistles. Jeannot reminded Marius that by law, permanent residents of every village or commune enjoyed all the rights of every other resident, whether French citizens or not. Nicole and Rosalind, with permanent resident status, could not only vote in elections, he said, but even run for municipal council, should they wish, under the French constitution. If they could be village magistrates, could they not be village *champions de boules*? The logic convinced the crowd and once more they hooted down Marius and started shouting for the final match of the day. The old man in the *bleu de travail* and his partner had not taken part in the demonstrations and now they just looked at each other and nodded, the old man with the briefest of smiles and the younger man grinning broadly. His name was Denis and someone in the crowd said loudly that Denis knew how to play all sorts of games with women and always win. There was a chorus of laughter and a look on Rosalind's face that should have warned her opponents.

The old man was called Anselme. He had a small plot of land just outside the village and did odd jobs for everyone to supplement his income, which was very small. He was not a friendly sort, everyone said, but reliable. Now he presented Rosalind with the little pink *cochonet*. The two women were the challengers and therefore could spot the *cochonet*. Rosalind always liked a long pitch, so she took careful aim and threw the light little ball a good forty feet down the *boule* pitch. Some of the spectators whistled. That was a demanding length. Now Nicole stepped up to the line and sighted carefully down the length of the pitch. She then lobbed a ball that looked wide to the right but that gradually rolled almost in front of the *cochonet* and a little to the right. Like most of the human race, most *boulistes* are right handed and this ball was a good blocking shot for opponents throwing right-handed.

Old Anselme gave her a guarded glance. He then tried a knock-away shot, to get rid of her ball entirely, but his throw was not violent enough. His ball struck hers, remained exactly in place, but Nicole's ball, instead of flying out of play only rolled forward a bit to a spot only inches behind the *cochonet*. The crowd murmured. That was a very strategic spot. It was now the turn of Denis. He tried a delicate shot that gently hit Anselme's ball and knocked it closer to the *cochonet*. Now the judges had to go out and measure the relative distances. If one side were closer, the other side could throw. It turned out that Nicole's first throw was still closer, therefore the men could continue. Both Anselme and Denis tried to knock their previous throws closer and on the last of their tries, Anselme's ball was nudged closer to the *cochonet* than Nicole's first ball. Now Rosalind stepped to the line and for the first time most of the spectators realized that she was left-handed. Standing to the left corner of the line, she carefully rolled her first ball down the pitch. Down, down, down it rolled, seeming to be far off to the left. But at the last moment it began to veer and finally hit the *cochonet* itself gently, nudging it right up against Nicole's ball. Now the women had two balls closer to the *cochonet*. Rosalind still had one throw left and she just threw it away, not risking the loss of any points. They were two points up. Many in the crowd began to cheer and then retreat quickly to one of the bars to get a drink before the next round.

A game of *boules* ends when the first side reaches fifteen points, so there was a lot of playing to go. Anselme and Denis were seen conferring, with the usual aid of numerous and often *conflic*ting suggestions from onlookers. Michael and Spencer refrained from any advice and simply poured their wives a glass of wine.

Now that their opponents had taken their measure, Nicole and Rosalind no longer had the advantage of surprise. Anselme and Denis were as wily as they, and stronger, able to smash a ball into a crowded space and leave an open alley for the last shot. Game succeeded game with varying success. Under the shade of the chestnut trees in the afternoon sun a minor waft of mistral teased the ground, foretelling a full-fledged windstorm the next day.

The score stood women 13, men of Barigoule 14. Rosalind and Nicole were laughing with their husbands. "Do you think we should just tank?" asked Nicole. "I don't want the whole village to hate us."

"Are you out of your mind?" burst out Rosalind. "We've got them on the run now! Only two more points!"

"And most of the village seems to be rooting for us," put in Michael.

"Probably because we spend more money here than those two," added Spencer.

"Okay, let's get'em, girl," said Nicole bravely, and the two women walked out to the pitch.

The mens' art had failed them. Their first three throws were miles away from the three balls that Nicole and Rosalind had placed in a neat circle around the *cochonet*. Anselme and Denis spoke quietly, then signaled Marius, who listened, startled, then nodded, patting his hands downward. He came in front of the pitch and announced. "The team of Anselme is employing their substitute player."

There was a great noise in the crowd.

"The next ball will be thrown by Lomu."

Now there was consternation, some spectators laughing and applauding, others shouting imprecations at Marius. The Tollivers and Sullivans were just looking at each other and shaking their heads in wonder.

According to the rules, every team could have alternates, who could substitute on any throw. But this afternoon, after so many friendly games, hardly any alternates had been called, except to take a throw in a losing game. And almost no one had ever seen Lomu play *boules*.

The crowd parted with a murmur as the hulking youth shambled onto the *boules* pitch, his mouth open in a soundless laugh. He walked right up to Anselme and the old man reached up, grabbed his ear and pulled his head down to his own level so he could whisper something. Instantly Lomu's face changed from a vacant smile to furious concentration. He walked over to a pile of *boules* and picked one up. He looked over at the two women, standing now by their husbands, and then at the setup on the pitch. Without even approaching the line, he wound up and threw the heavy steel ball overhand as hard as he could at the collection of *boules* at the end of the pitch. The throw actually missed all of the balls except one of Denis's outlyers. It sent it hurtling down to the end of the park while Lomu's ball itself ricocheted up into the air and hit a child on the shoulder. She fell screaming to the ground.

The entire crowd began to rush to the wounded child and only Michael stood staring in wonder at Lomu. It was a lucky moment, because Lomu, not even paying attention to the child he had hit, or anything else on the pitch, stooped, picked up another *boule* and without hesitation threw it directly at Rosalind.

Michael had just time to yell, "Hey!" as loud as he could. Then he leaped to deflect the heavy ball. Catching a half-kilo steel *boule* is not like a softball. It tore through Michael's hands, missed Rosalind, and hit Nicole directly on her cheek just in front of her ear, as she had turned away in horror to watch the little girl. Nicole fell like a rag doll dropped from a child's hand. A few others in the crowd had also looked back and had seen Lomu throw at Rosalind. Now they saw him shriek something savage and charge right at Michael, his hands scrabbling in the air as if eager to rip something apart. Michael stood firm, enraged, intending to hit Lomu as hard as he could. But Jeannot was faster. The big man slanted out of the crowd and tackled Lomu hard right at knee height, putting his shoulder and full weight behind the tackle. There was a sharp crack, Lomu screamed and fell writhing to the ground.

CHAPTER ELEVEN

Nicole was wandering. She remembered vaguely that she had strayed up out of town and was now walking along the road north toward the hills, between the broad fields that stretched for hundreds of meters on each side. Here on top of the plateau the wind was blowing the wheat and sending waves billowing through the supple green blades. Nicole knew she was all alone and stood for a moment looking around in a complete circle. Swallows and swifts were wheeling over the fields as the sun was dying in the northwest. But then came a sudden premonition that she was being followed. She whirled, but the dark grey road between the fields was empty to the horizon. The hill of Barigoule was prominent, with the crenellated battlements of the old castle silhouetted against the yellow sky. Had someone come out of the castle? From the movement of the tousled wheat thrashing back and forth she could tell that a strong mistral was blowing, yet she could feel no trace of wind. All was silence and calm. She turned back northward and started to walk the familiar road to Rosalind and Spencer's house, just over the next rise. But when she could look down the slope she was horrified to see an empty ruin, roof gone, blackened timbers, scattered masonry blocks, and tall weeds sprouting from every crevice—many weeks of growth.

A terrible sadness descended upon her. Rosalind and Spencer were gone. But where was Michael. For some reason she knew he was up the road, he would be waiting for her up the road. And once again she felt the follower behind her, not daring to look back, so she increased her pace, almost running past the Sullivan house, the ruin, the swimming pool she could now see dark green with moss and vague shapes hulking beneath the surface. She was running now, up the hill, past the last few houses outside Barigoule, and up the road the led to...where did it lead? The answer was clear in her mind, but she could not put a word to it, and to distract her, came the sound of footsteps behind her, harder and harder, faster and faster. So she ran, ran like the wind...and came to the path off to the left that led to the...what was it? The words wouldn't come to her mind. But Michael was surely there waiting. So she ran up the path, trying not to trip on the stones and branches, calling now, "Michael! Mikey! Please, please, please help me!" But her voice made no sound no matter how loud she cried. And it seemed to her that she came to a brushy slope on her right and ran up it, light-footed, and came to...a hole in the cliff. Behind her the footsteps accelerated. The only safety was in the hole, so she threw herself down and crawled into the hole.

Suddenly there was a cold, cold feeling in her head and she know that Michael was not there, that she had been fooled, that she had been lured into the grotto of Barigoule, and she heard a soft voice somewhere in her head calling to her. "Nicole, Nicole..." A warm friendly voice imploring her to rest, calm down, be quiet, give up her struggle.

"Nicole. Listen to me. I want you closer, closer. Relax, Nicole, I love you. There is no more trouble." And a warm lassitude crept over Nicole, lying there in the darkness of the safe, safe hole, and she curled up in the comfort she was feeling.

"Yes, yes, Nicole. Rest, rest, poor thing. Your head is hurting, but soon it will go. Sleep, sleep, deeply, deeply, deep...deep... deep." And Nicole felt the voice become something physical, creeping into her warmth and comfort, not disturbing at all...

almost inviting, and she started to give in, to give herself up to the presence of the voice.

But then, just as she lost consciousness, she felt her eyes almost forced open. Blinking, there in the cave, she was looking directly at the stone overhead. And there she saw letters—clearly, as if drawn with a charcoal crayon—words that looked reasonable, looked like French, but she couldn't make sense of them, and now the voice returned, almost angry, saying "No, no, no, close your eyes—don't worry, don't worry." But by now she felt more awake, just as the letters faded out to grey and she heard another voice, Michael, faintly calling her and she started to rouse, wondering where she was, where Michael was. And the voice suddenly became harsh, demanding..."Come back, come back, you fool! You must...you must..." And it was almost like claws on her body, the pain she felt, but she must leave, flee, go back to Michael's voice calling, "Nicole, Nicole..."

"Nicole, Nicole...," Michael was crying, there in the hospital room in Cavaillon. Her eyes opened and immediately there was fierce pain on the entire right side of her head, bright light darting into her eyeballs. But she recognized Michael and reached out, defying the pain that stabbed down her neck and arms, reaching for his arms, and then he was clasping her and sighing, "Oh, Nicole, my God, Nicole...I thought they'd lost you..." He was crying, which Nicole had never seen before. A man in a white coat was standing behind Michael and he gestured to a nurse, who approached with a hypodermic. And it seemed suddenly that the last thing she wanted was a needle, to go back to sleep, to go back to the grotto and the sneaky voice. So she held up a hand...

"Non! Je ne le veut pas! Me laissez reveiller!" Above all things she wanted to know that she was out of her dream, that Michael was actually here with her, that she was safe.

The doctor and the nurse conferred briefly with Michael and then she was alone with him. She sank back with relief into the pillows and just smiled at Michael. Then she frowned.

"But...but what happened? Did I fall? or something?"

And Michael had to explain that big Lomu had gone deranged and had thrown a *boule* at them, that he had tried to stop it but it had hit her in the face.

"They did an X-ray. They thought maybe your cheekbone was fractured. But it's okay. You can't see yourself, but there's a terrible bruise all over the right side of your face."

Her hand flew up, expecting bandages.

"No, they want to leave it open. There's just a bit of broken skin over your cheek, but they put an antibiotic on it. The doctor says your face will be completely well in a two weeks, maybe less. He's worried about damage to your neck, your vertebrae, he said that your head probably snapped back. But they can't test it until you're in a little better shape. Oh my God! Nicole. You can't believe—"

"Lomu?" She had trouble comprehending what he'd said. "You said Lomu threw a *boule*?"

He shook his head. "It was crazy. He just went nuts. He threw that one *boule* at our balls out there on the court. It was much too hard and almost hurt a kid when it bounced off...do you remember that?"

She shook her head dreamily. "No. Actually I"m thinking hard. I remember us playing the firemen. And I don't remember how it came out. Did we win?"

"Right. You beat the firemen. Then you played that creepy old guy, Anselme? And the big guy Denis. And you were beating them when they got Lomu to make the last throw." He grinned. "You won, you know, the whole thing. You and Rosalind are the *championnes de boule*s of Barigoule." He was trying to laugh, but tears kept rolling down his cheeks.

Nicole gazed at him, feeling her heart almost breaking to see the depth of his grief. Then suddenly she wondered.

"Lomu? What happened to him? Is he still loose out there somewhere." She was suddenly terrified.

"Don't worry. Actually as soon as he threw the *boule* he rushed over to attack us, you, me, who knows? But Jeannot tackled him, almost broke his leg, and all those big louts standing around, firemen, policemen, they all jumped on him, finally got the cuffs on him. He's in the prison ward of the hospital down in Apt. Everyone says he'll wind up in the loony bin. His aunt was crying, saying he's a good boy, he just forgot to take his medicine." Michael rolled his eyes.

"Who knows what set him off. If I had to guess, I'd say that the old bastards in town were talking behind their hands about how terrible and shameful it was for women to play *boule*s. If he heard that kind of shit over and over he probably thought it was okay just to attack us. Anyway, that's over for him."

Nicole sank back, tried to take it all in. It seemed too much to comprehend...on top of the awful dream she'd been having, what was it about? And she clutched Michael's arm as she remembered being stalked along the empty road, the wheat on both sides, the presence behind her and then...

Her eyes opened wide and she stared at her husband.

"Michael! I was there...in the grotto! I had to hide and I crawled in there and someone...something tried to, to take me over. It was horrible!" She saw his face puzzled. "I mean, in my dream. Just now, before I woke up. God, it was so real!"

She had his arm now with both hands. "Darling, when can I get out of here? I feel fine. Really I do. And I'm scared to be here alone. I'm scared I'll go back to sleep and be in that dream again."

Michael leaned over and kissed her, held her as well as he could, leaning over the bed, trying not to hurt her.

"It's late Monday now. You've been out almost a whole day. I'm sure they won't let you out until tomorrow...till they're sure everything's okay." He put up a hand to still her protest. "But I'm going to stay here tonight. I'll pull the chair up closer and you can hold my hand all night. The grotto...I don't know. Maybe we should give the grottos a rest for a bit."

"But you said you were just getting started...what—"

Michael tousled her hair, kissed her ear on the unhurt side. "I think you should sleep some more. Then we can get out of here tomorrow. Don't worry, babe, I'm here. Always."

And she slept again, and again she dreamed of the grotto, but this time she felt at peace, and when a voice came into her head it was calm...not pretending to be friendly or anything...just telling her, *look at the ceiling, see what it says.* She looked up into the dark and it began to clear away and she could see the writing there, unfocused at first, but then, like a slide projector coming into focus, the letters became sharp and she read,

veramen vous lou dise niadaqueli quesouneici—

But it didn't seem to make sense and she felt herself getting tired, dozing off, when the voice said again, *remember His words. They keep us safe*— And she was out like a light, this time in deep, dreamless sleep.

The next morning she woke clearheaded, almost no pain in her head, and Michael had news.

"My editor called, anyway. Robbie. Couldn't raise anyone at the house so he called my cell. For once I had it turned on and he had to kid me about that. Then I told him what happened and where I was and he was like in shock. He wanted to fly you home in a chartered jet. I told him you were tough and ready to fight the doctors if they won't let you out today. Anyway, Robbie says the publisher wants me to do a book tour for the paperback edition. We haven't been back to the States for a while. Maybe this is a good time. I want to have you looked at by Baker at the clinic back home. Think you could bear flying around to big cities this summer?"

PART TWO

CHAPTER TWELVE

The valley of the Calavon river roasted in the late summer sun. Three days of mistral had fanned the plateau of the Vaucluse, making the sun almost bearable, then it had died and the heat just settled. The river itself had slowed to a trickle under the Pont Julien. Spencer and Rosalind were standing by their parked car just across the bridge, arguing.

"I told you to remind me about the camera! You knew I wanted a good shot of the bridge!" Rosalind was fuming.

"My dear, I distinctly told you, just before I had to go to the bathroom, put the camera out. What the hell? We've got all summer to get a good photo, with this weather."

The bridge itself, having been built by Julius Caesar, as its name indicates, and being the only complete surviving cut-stone Roman arch bridge in Provence, had probably heard more significant discussions. It had survived every single major flooding of the Calavon for well over two thousand years. Caesar had made his engineers dig down to bed rock, then carve deep footings for the masonry blocks that formed the foundation. The elegant arch across the river had been built entirely with dry stone but so well was it cut and fitted that it had outlasted a score of modern concrete bridges closer to Apt, their foundations washed out by the rare but huge floods that swept down the valley after unusual rainfall. In the winter of 1944 an angry German general radioed the local engineer battalion, just ready to evacuate, and ordered the bridge dynamited before they left. The bridge actually had no strategic value; there were two other modern bridges on either side, on main roads. The general was just following his Führer's instructions to destroy all cultural monuments in the hated land of the French and to leave a wasteland in his rear. A captain of engineers took his staff to inspect the bridge. They had all looked it over and admired it many times. *How much dynamite will it take to bring that beauty down?* asked the captain. His sergeant knew what they all felt, looking at an engineering miracle, two thousand years old. *We have almost no blasting material left, sir. May I suggest we save it for an emergency?*

And the bridge remains, insulted only by a nearby drain outlet that had been situated by later French engineers with fewer sensibilities.

"Let's go," said Spencer. "That drain really stinks in this weather."

The Sullivans were on their way to Lacoste for an exposition of pottery. They had little hope of finding a pot or two that would add to the pieces scattered around the house. Rosalind had made a foray into Italy several years ago and had gone through the shops in Deruta like a whirlwind. Local potters were just not in the same league with Deruta majolica but Rosalind kept trying.

The Peugeot climbed the slopes toward Lacoste until both sides of the road began to be filled with parked cars. The usual argument started again.

"Might as well park here, while we can," said Spencer.

"Christ! We're miles away. And I didn't wear the right shoes to walk. Drive up to the walls of the village at least. Maybe we'll find someone leaving."

Spencer sighed and let in the clutch. His wife had run five miles that morning and had bragged about it. Now she couldn't walk up a hill. They continued up the slope, slower and slower as the route began to fill with pedestrians coming and going, some laden with ugly pottery. He was about to counsel a difficult turning around and going back when Rosalind shouted, "There! Reverse lights on! Dutch Beamer. Quick, block the road, there's another car backing down the road trying to get in."

Spencer managed to block the road against the rapidly reversing Audi with Paris plates, but he also prevented the BMW from backing out. An exchange of hand signals indicated that he wanted their place. The Dutch smiled, backed up into the small space he left them, and departed. Spencer slid into the vacated spot and waved apologetically at the fuming Parisians as they continued down the hill.

"If it was anyone, I'm glad it was Parisians," said Rosalind. Parisians were widely hated for their arrogant attitude toward the provinces and for their general incompetence as drivers. In the city of Paris, one rarely wants to drive because of the virtually stationary traffic; there is no opportunity to cultivate the normal driving skills of the French provinces, where locals whizz along rural roads at 110 kmh or more.

Spencer and Rosalind walked up the short stretch of road to the entrance through the old medieval walls of Lacoste. The potters had set up stands on both sides of the street and within the town square they had occupied two large concentric circles. The Sullivans circulated, Spencer his hands clasped behind his back in an attitude of mild curiosity, Rosalind busier, darting to look more closely at a large purple bowl here, a yellow and orange lamp there .

"Awful, awful," she was muttering. Spencer had paused before a plain terracotta sculpture of a tiny village surmounting a hill, surrounded with cypresses, the little houses meticulously finished, tiny tiles on their roofs, little streets winding their way bewteen the buildings.

"This isn't bad, you know," he offered.

Rosalind looked it over noncommitally. "It's rather nice, you're right. But where would we put it?" They nodded politely to the proprietor of the stand, a tall, thin woman in jeans and a T-shirt, who was pretending not to listen, and moved up the street.

Expositions of pottery, paintings, or anything else are not exclusive in Provence. Anyone who gets there early enough can set up a stand to sell almost anything. Along the route was a bookstand, presided over by a small old man in a black suit, now arguing ferociously with what seemed to be a older German couple. Rosalind could understand his French.

This is true history of Lacoste! To understand you must read our local histories, the older times!

The large man explained himself in halting French. *But I read many things before. I was here a long time ago, in the war? I always love Provence. We come back many times.*

The little man stared with disbelief at someone who would actually admit that he'd been here in the German army of occupation. He seemed to be swelling with a retort, but out of the corner of his eye he caught Spencer and Rosalind, and instead completely ignored the Germans and turned to his new customers.

Bonjour, m'sieur dame. I think I've seen you before? Maybe in Bonnieux?

They continued to talk in French as the Germans drifted away. Rosalind had not met this bookseller, but had heard Michael and Nicole's stories about his awful book.

"Yes, Monsieur, we were in Bonnieux, maybe it was a month ago? Our friends bought your book."

The little man's face split into a smile and his eyes lit up the square. "You read my *roman*? And how did you like it?"

Spencer was diplomatic. "Actually, I've only looked through it. It seemed very...powerful. But you know...we've been studying the history of the Vaudois. And in university I did my *doctorat* on the reign of Henri IV...a great man."

The little man had been trying desperately to interrupt.

"But...but at any rate, you know what happened here at Lacoste?"

"Yes, we read the testimony in Aubéry. It was horrible. And your *roman*—"

"My book, yes. I wrote a fiction, of course, with a *romance*, but you know, the cruelty was real...the rape, sometimes of children ten years old...this was real. People tell me no one wants to read that stuff anymore. And around here? The Nazis were here four years and in some ways they were worse. Machine guns, systematic torture to create terror...and they did not just pillage and rape, get drunk, and go away again. They were here four years!" He paused. "So you can see that people think my book is ancient history. The wicked baron, the papal troops, all gone, all gone. Forget it."

The little man had shrugged, almost stooping, when suddenly he stood upright, looked right and left and took Spencer by his sleeve.

"Monsieur! They are still here! Not the baron, maybe, but his people. I risk my life to tell you this, but...but after I heard about my friend Lebarbe—"

Now it was Spencer's turn to be excited. He leaned forward and almost shouted, "You knew Lebarbe?"

Several people passing by turned, attracted by what seemed to be an argument. Rosalind caught Spencer by the arm and shushed him. She spoke quietly to the little man.

"We are very concerned about this, about what happened to Monsieur Lebarbe. He was our friend, and we had just had lunch with him before he died—"

"Before he was killed!" The little man held up his right hand, waggling a finger. Two older French men, looking like locals, paused to stare at him. Spencer, excited, feeling on the verge of discovery, started to answer, then realized there was a small crowd forming.

He looked around, smiled at everyone, turned back to the little bookseller. "Maybe we should go have a coffee? It is my treat, monsieur. And we are very interested in what you are saying. I just wish my friend Michael were here."

They sat in a cafe where they could see the bookstall. Rosalind was worried someone would swipe a book. The bookseller was amused at the idea.

"My *roman*? They won't even steal it! All right, maybe it is exaggerated, too...how should I say...dramatic? But I kept to the outline of the actual testimony. I only invented characters...the boy, the girl who loved him, how they were killed. The baron I made an ugly, loathsome man. You know... actually he was handsome and young, Jean Maynier was. But he was a fanatic against the Vaudois, and he didn't mind enriching himself on the lands of those who protected the Vaudois."

Spencer managed to break in. "Yes, I've read all of Aubéry, the testimony. But you seem to know more. Did you make up some of the details in your book?"

A young girl came and took their orders. Spencer had a plain coffee, Rosalind a *noisette*, and M. Rousset, as he had introduced himself, ordered a *café marc*.

"Pardon monsieur?" asked the girl.

"A *café*, and with it a glass of *marc*." He was smiling and shrugging. "Against the chill," although the day was simmering. And he hugged himself in his black wool suit.

"They don't know anything these days," M. Rousset commented, after the girl had left. "Twenty, thirty years ago, no one drank a coffee without a drop of something in it. But now, I must tell you, you who know of Henri IV, our greatest king, that there is more information, more testimony."

Once again he looked all around, as if the Nazis were still there, then leaned across the table and spoke with greater intensity.

"You see, Henri had been a Protestant. But he had to make a deal to become king, otherwise the nobles, the people, everyone, would never have allowed it. So he became a Catholic. You know what he said...'Paris is worth a Mass.' But he nursed in his heart a hatred of certain elements within the church. Especially the Dominicans, who administered the Inquisition. He himself knew of many cases in which the inquisitors had cooperated with certain nobles to condemn rich people as heretics in order to apportion their lands with their corrupt friends. After the heretics had been burnt alive, of course," M. Rousset chuckled sardonically.

"So King Henri commenced a secret investigation into the misdeeds of the Inquisition. Testimony was taken. Many inquisitors were punished. Many lords had their lands condemned. This happened in 1595, exactly fifty years after our massacre here."

Two older men, wearing the caps and stained short-sleeved shirts of the typical village farmer, pushed their way through the crowded café and stood directly behind Monsieur Rousset.

"Is it possible to share your table?" one of them said, looking directly at Spencer. He was about to tell them "of course," but Monsieur Rousset became animated.

"No, no. I am sorry. It is crowded, I know, but with too many people, I have asthma attacks." And he held up his arms and waved them in circles, showing the amount of space he needed to avoid asthma. The two men backed away, one of them mumbling, just as the little girl arrived with their coffees.

"I could never mention these things I know with other people around," said Rousset, pouring half of the fiery marc into his coffee. "Particularly these local types. There are people watching, watching, you know. And listening."

Spencer and Rosalind looked at each other, but neither felt like expressing disbelief. They had become too intrigued with what Rousset was about to tell them about the inquest of Henri IV.

The cigarette smoke of a crowded café wafted across their table, but the asthmatic Monsieur Rousset didn't seem to mind. Rosalind waved a menu to disperse the smoke and the old man continued his story.

"You see, Henri appointed a tribunal of his old supporters, some of them from La Rochelle, the stronghold of the Protestants. They conducted an investigation in secret, with the power to subpoena anyone who might know something. And you know what? There was a transcription of these investigations."

"But fifty years later!" Spencer broke in. "What would anyone know or remember? People didn't live very long then. Was anyone still alive who remembered the massacres?"

Monsieur Rousset smiled a thin smile, once again looking around to see who might be listening.

"Monsieur, Madame, I have almost never told anyone... but I sense your interest, also that you might do something! The proceedings of King Henri's tribunal were faithfully kept by his advisors. Then, as you well know, affairs of state and impending wars took his interest. He spent years on his grand design...what was it? Scholars still argue. To create a European Union, maybe? Four hundred years ago? Maybe. His plans were secret. But the testimony about the massacres lay there in the archives, lying silently, waiting for the right strategic moment."

"YOUR HEALTH MONSIEUR!" Rousset raised his voice and proposed a toast just as three old men shuffled behind their table, as if looking for a place to sit.

Spencer and Rosalind were startled, but returned the toast willingly, looking around to inspect the crowd. Looking closely at the faces behind them they both believed the old men seemed familiar, one of them almost certainly owned a cherry orchard near Barigoule. They were now convinced conspirators and they leaned across the table to hear what Rousset would say next.

"Yes. A precaution. I trust no one around here. Especially these old men.

"Where was I? Yes, in 1609 powers within the church were conspiring to obstruct King Henri's grand design, and he decided to bring out his evidence against the church...to weaken them, throw them off balance. And what happened then?" He pointed triumphantly at Spencer, the French historian.

"Well, it was the next year, right? A Catholic fanatic shot and killed the king. And there were many rumors about how many noble families were close to, to...what was his name?"

"Ravaillac. An insane monster. Maybe. He was tortured for days to reveal his accomplices. And he roared only that he was God's emissary and had worked alone. Then finally he said that if a priest would give him extreme unction and forgive him, he would make a statement. The next day the cardinal of Paris announced his refusal to give final unction and they immediatly drew and quartered him. End of all statements." Rousset made a washing motion with his hands and nodded his head with satisfaction.

"But the testimony?" exclaimed Rosalind and Spencer together. "What happened—?"

Rousset held up his hand. "Monsieur, madame, I hesitate to speak of these things in this crowded room. Perhaps, if we were to walk around the square?"

The merchants were beginning to pack up their pottery, to fold their display tables. The vans and small trucks they had come in were now maneuvering for room in the square, trying to get as close as possible to the piles of heavy ceramics. Monsieur Rousset led them to his table, covered with ranks of old books, spines up, and a display stack of *Blood and Steel on the Land,* garish covers to the front. Rousset began to pack books into plastic cartons under his display table.

"I will tell this quickly," he said, looking around once again, his head swiveling on his thin neck almost without effort, like a bird's.

"The investigation of Henri IV was discovered almost fifty years ago in the darkest corners of the Bibliothèque Nationale. The scholars who found the manuscript had been working very quietly for fifteen years...since the end of the war. Quietly, because their predecessors, in 1940, had made too much show of their investigations, had announced certain findings to the newspapers before they actually found anything. But in June of that year the Bibliothèque was closed, in order to store the most valuable materials before the war everyone knew was coming. You remember?"

Spencer and Rosalind looked at each other, and he began to speak.

But Rousset broke in. "Of course not. You are both too young. But you know your history, correct?"

"I know this part very well, monsieur," said Spencer. "I wrote a paper in university on the French...uh, the French...uh, response to the German invasion."

"The response, you say. Yes. You didn't want to say 'collapse' or 'humiliation.' *Hein*? Never mind. You are right. The whole nation was rotten, some actually hoping for fascism, the rest defeatist. *Quand-même*... Anyway, The library was closed. Our scholars are excited, on the brink of discovery. They think they know the actual shelves in the basements where these documents might lie."

Spencer and Rosalind were engrossed, leaning forward to hear the next words.

"BAM!" Rousset's hand struck the table and their heads flew backward. "Killed! Both of them. One day apart, in accidents in the streets. But the Germans were streaming through the Maginot line and no one cared. No one paid attention. Bombs were falling." He shrugged, spreading his hands wide.

"But...but how...?" Spencer was desperate to know the end of the story.

Two old men drifted like dark shadows by Rousset's table, began looking at the few books that were still stacked on the table. They were solemn and omi*nous* and even in the heat of the afternoon they seemed to exude a curious chill.

"I'm sorry, messieurs," shouted Rousset. "I am closing up now. I just have to give something to monsieur 'dame here."

He whispered to them. "It is dangerous now. These imbeciles are not interested in books. I can find you in Barigoule, yes? Tomorrow, then?"

At six that evening Rosalind phoned the Palo Alto number Michael had left them. An answering machine came on and Nicole's voice spoke. "If this is the sixteenth, we are in Santa Barbara. Lunch with Sue Grafton. Book signing this afternoon, four o'clock, at Chaucers. We're at the El Encanto." She gave the number.

Rosalind looked over to where Spencer was reading today's *Figaro*. "For God's sake, Spencer. You won't phone so I have to. Michael hates recording the answering machine so Nicole has to. What is it with you men?"

"Sorry, my dear. I'll make the call to Mike—"

"The hell you will. I've done all the work, I get to talk first, I've already dialed in fact...hello, Nicole!...

Yes. I figured you'd be up but not out yet. How is Michael? ... No, I don't want to speak to him yet, and Spencer is lunging at me, trying to get the phone... Bugger off, I said! No, not you, darling, Spencer. At any rate, here's our news! We spoke with Monsieur Rousset today... yes the little man with the dreadful book. But listen, he actually knows a great deal! He said there was a follow-up royal investigation of the massacres fifty years later and he has a transcript or something of the proceedings... Yes! ... But all sorts of sinister chaps, local peasants, kept trying to listen in, so he's coming over tomorrow, bringing us some documents... Yes, of course, we'll call back.

CHAPTER THIRTEEN

On a hot Monday afternoon the mistral had picked up again, splaying the warm, dry wind across the Vaucluse and the Luberon. At two o'clock in the afternoon the landscape was as still as in the depths of the night. Only the wind moved across the vineyards and the bare fields from which the wheat and colza had long since been cropped. Otherwise Provence was sunk in after-lunch torpor and only the restaurants and cafés in the towns and villages were full of fully relaxed diners. Now and then a hiking party of Belgians, Dutch, or Germans would go striding down the street, to the amused head-shaking and clucking of the French. The temperature stood at 32° Celsius, or about 90°F to the few Americans who were still interested in anything but finding a cool, dark room in which to nap.

In Lacoste Monsieur Rousset quietly let himself out his gate and climbed into his twenty-year-old tan Citroën CV 2. Under his arm he carried a stout leather folder from another era, cracked and stained, bursting with papers. The engine caught on the third try and he let the old car roll down the slope out of town. Once down on the plain, his route lay along narrow farm roads, crossing the trickle of the Calavon on the Pont Julien baking in the sun, and thence in the direction Joucas, where he would ascend the hill to Barigoule. The CV 2 ambled along at its prudent 50 kph along deserted roads. At the intersection to Roussillon, Monsieur

Rousset noticed a large construction truck idling, dusty, full of large rocks. The driver seemed to be leaning out and yelling something to a little old black Citroën AX 10 just hehind him. Curiously, the Citroën seemed to be full of nuns.

Alarmed, Rousset stepped on the accelerator and the old CV 2 spurted down the road to Joucas. Now in the rear view mirror he could see the truck making the turn and then coming up behind him, roaring in a middle gear, then shifting into high and coming up hard on his rear. Rousset desperately floored the gas pedal and the old car reached its top speed of 90 kph. Not enough. The truck was almost upon him when he thought to pull over and let it pass. But the road was barely wide enough for the two of them. The second he started to pull over the truck turned as well and smashed into the rear of the frail Citroën. Rousset made one frantic attempt to turn back onto the road, but the car went plunging off the road and into the four-foot-deep drainage canal that lined all the roads here on the bottom of the valley. The little car crashed with a scream of metal and stood on its nose in the canal, coming to a sudden halt. The great truck didn't slow for a second but sped off toward the Gordes intersection.

Calmly, the AX 10 rolled to a stop and a small nun got out of the passenger seat. She scampered to the side of the wrecked car and leaned in, reached a black-clad arm through the window and brought out the leather folder. She ran to the passenger window and gave the folder to a very large nun wedged there in the driver's seat of the small car. The large nun inspected the documents carefully, swore a terrible oath, and tore two pages from the back of a stapled stack of pages.

She handed the folder back to the small nun. "Put it back beside him. Nothing else should be missing." The little nun was turning away when her partner yelled out the window.

"Is the bastard dead?"

The little nun giggled. "His head went through the windscreen. His throat is cut like a lamb at Easter. So much blood for a little piece of shit."

"Good for him! Come on, let's get out of here." And they rolled away.

Few creatures were stirring abroad on that hot afternoon and no French people at all. But it so happened that a painter of *acquarelles*, water colors, an Englishwoman, had been painting the glorious expanse of the valley from the heights of Joucas when she heard vehicles approaching at high speed. Being also a bird watcher, she had a pair of binoculars at hand and had them to her eyes just in time to see a large truck obviously bumping and running a much smaller car off the road. At first she had thought it an accident, but then she clearly saw a car stop, a nun get out, and take something from the wrecked car. Her first thought was that the nuns were going to go for help but when she clearly saw the two of them laughing, it seemed to her so bizarre that she grabbed her cell phone and dialed one-seven, the universal emergency police number in Europe. She was connected to the gendarmerie in Gordes.

The men on duty in the gendarmerie in Gordes were not pleased to be disturbed on a hot afternoon during a televised rugby match between Toulouse and a visiting South African side. Nevertheless, once they were firmly convinced that serious injury or death had occurred, they sent a car. As a matter of routine, the watch commander passed on the details to the office of the *police judiciaire* in Avignon, including the curious event of the laughing nuns. Nuns and fatal accidents. Such a coincidence might never have attracted official attention except that Dreyfus just happened to be in his office and heard a clerk asking someone, "Were we looking for nuns, or something?"

Dreyfus was out of his chair in a flash, looking so grim that the terrified clerk stuttered as he recounted everything he'd heard on the phone. On his way to his car Dreyfus ran into his superior, a large and cynical detective named Barbu.

"I've got to go to Joucas! There are nuns killing people again!"

"Not more nuns! You have no idea what shit we took over that last incident, at the Fontaine! Are you sure?"

"The gendarmes are there now. I must arrive before they fuck up the evidence."

"Go then. But take Abdelaziz."

Dreyfus was about to protest, but Barbu held up a hand.

"You know the policy. It is so rare to have a woman, an Arab woman in the *police judiciare* that she must succeed. And that means as much experience as possible. You know what the papers would say if she failed, or resigned? They would say we drove her out, sabotaged her."

"But some other detective could—"

"No. I want her with you, Dreyfus. You are my best investigator, best teacher. She will do well. Her father came from Morocco as a boy and he was a policeman all his life in Marseille. She worshipped him. Now hurry up and solve this case for me."

Rosalind was out watering the garden in the early evening when the dark blue Renault pulled up in front.

"Uh oh," she said to herself. The Renault reversed to point back out the gravel driveway. There were two figures in the car and they seemed to be having a discussion. Then the doors opened and she recognized Inspector Dreyfus in his usual impeccable grey suit. From the passenger door emerged a slim woman dressed in a khaki uniform. She had long black hair pulled back into a ponytail and at the moment a severe, bad-tempered face focused on Dreyfus.

Rosalind had moved under the willow tree in their yard, avoiding the last hot rays of the sun from the west.

"Madame Sullivan." Dreyfus approached her, his face stern. He suddenly seemed to remember the woman beside him.

"May I present my deputy, Mademoiselle Abdelaziz? She is a probationer in my department and is learning our methodology." His expression did not give the impression that she was learning very quickly.

Rosalind stepped forward and shook hands awkwardly with the young woman, who had hesitated, wondering whether she should shake hands or not.

"Monsieur Dreyfus. Something is wrong. What is it?"

Dreyfus looked around, sighed. "Is Monsieur Sullivan here?"

"I believe he is still in the bath," lied Rosalind, seeing in her mind the snoring figure in the recliner in front of the television, oblivious to the tennis match at Wimbledon in which he had expressed such interest an hour ago.

"What has happened? And...and why are you coming *here* again?"

Inspector Dreyfus nodded his head silently, agreeing with some decision he had made. He looked sideways at Abdelaziz, as if to attract her attention, if nothing else, then spoke.

"I am sorry to report that Monsieur Rousset, of Lacoste, has had a very bad accident. We believe that he was coming to visit you. Is that right?"

Rosalind was flustered. "To visit us? Well...yes sometime, he said. An accident? How is he?"

Once more Dreyfus looked at his partner, as if making sure she would agree with what he said."

"I am sorry to say he was killed in his car. Driving into a ditch."

"Oh, Jesus!" Suddenly Rosalind felt as if she would collapse. She started to slump and Dreyfus moved forward, but the woman was faster, darting forward, grasping her by the elbows with startling strong hands and guiding her to a rude wooden bench beside the tree.

"Take five deep breaths," said Abdelaziz. "Then take a deep breath, hold it for five seconds and let it out slowly...*slow-ly*, I said."

Rosalind was not functioning, except to follow orders. She did exactly what Mlle. Abdelaziz said and felt the blood flowing back into her brain. In her field of vision she saw Spencer, woozy from his nap, come stumbling out the front door.

"Hullo! What's up, love?" he asked, seeing her slumped, held partially in the arms of a kneeling woman. Then he noticed Dreyfus and the car.

"Uh oh! Inspector! Now what's happened?"

Dreyfus suggested that they all go inside into the cool and out of view of any curiosity seekers who had seen his obvious police car traverse the village. Once there, Abdelaziz refused to allow questions until she had brought Rosalind a large glass of water and had made sure she was not still in shock. Then she stood up, addressing Spencer in clumsy English.

"Monsieur Sullivan. Is it true that you expect a visit from Monsieur Rousset?"

Dreyfus started to say that they should all speak French, but she withered him with a look.

"I...we...that is, yesterday we met Monsieur Rousset by chance in Lacoste and he said he wanted to give us some documents," said Rosalind, in French.

"And what documents was that?" Abdelaziz continued stubbornly in English

"About the massacre...you know? The massacre in the grotto?"

"Aha!" Abdelaziz expelled her breath in triumph. "You are telling about a massacre? When? And you were there?"

Dreyfus cleared his throat, spoke so rapidly and quietly in French that neither Spencer nor Rosalind could understand a word and Abelaziz clamped her mouth shut. Then he turned to them, still speaking in French, but slowly and clearly now.

"Monsieur Sullivan. May I ask you to explain to deputy Abdelaziz the massacre of 1545, and why exactly you are seeking information about it. I was unable, on the way here, to clarify the connection between these two crimes, five hundred years...let us say, four hundred and fifty years apart."

For the next twenty minutes Spencer told the story of the massacre at the grotto, explaining just how his friend, Michael had become interested in writing a book. From time to time, Rosalind would add a remark or offer a correction on some point. Abdelaziz's eyebrows kept shooting up with surprise at certain revelations, her eyes narrowing in suspicion at the narration of dubious details.

Dreyfus then took the floor.

"You must know, we never found any nuns to connect to the murder of Lebarbe. In fact, our supervisor now says we must declare accidental death. He says if the blah blah blah media—I spare you the adjectives, madame—hear about nuns who murder, we will all be in the...in trouble. But now—"

"It's obvious!" Spencer was on his feet now. "It's what Mike was saying. Everyone who wants to give us information is getting killed. Just like detective novels!"

Dreyfus and Abdelaziz looked mystfied.

"Detective novels! Even French ones. In the beginning of the plot anyone who knows something about the crime gets killed. You've read..." he scoured his mind quickly for French crime novels... "some of San Antonio? His books?"

Dreyfus and Abdelaziz both laughed sarcastically. "San Antonio, yes," said Dreyfus. "Simenon too, and his inspector Maigret. We read San Antonio because he makes us laugh, he is so crazy. But even San Antonio never wrote a detective story in which they kill people to conceal a crime five hundred years old, *hein*?" Spencer spread his hands in frustrated agreement.

Dreyfus went on. "Then, let me ask you. You are not writing a book about the massacre. That is Monsieur Tolliver. But Monsieur Rousset was bringing you some document. If you looked through these papers, do you think you would know what he thought was most important?"

Spencer and Rosalind leafed through the papers in Rousset's old leather portfolio. Most of the papers were faxes of articles from what seemed to be evangelical French publications, detailing crimes against Protestant martyrs. There were a very few reviews of Rousset's *Blood and Steel*, so devastatingly critical that they wondered why Rousset had kept them. Then finally they found a copy of an actual scholarly article from a journal that looked to have fallen on hard times; the pages had been photocopied from badly typed camera-ready typewriter copy. It was a 1973 issue of *Bulletin de la société des études vaudoises*, the second issue of the year, published in June of that year. The title of the photocopied article was "*Document inédits: Temoin de Jean de Moulin en 1595*," that is to say, the testimony of Jean the Miller in 1595."

Spencer only had to read the title and he rapped the pages with the back of his hand.

"This is it! This is what Rousset was talking about. An investigation of the massacre fifty years later!" He handed the pages to Dreyfus.

The detective leafed rapidly through the photocopy, then looked twice at the last page. He examined the staple and his face was somber.

"I will have to read this article," he said. "But I can tell you right away that at least two pages have been torn out. See here?... the last page, number 56? The sentence is incomplete. And look here at the staple." Spencer and Rosalind looked closely. There were obviously two tiny bits of torn paper under the staple. They looked at each other, mystified, then at Dreyfus, who was explaining to the Abdelaziz woman, who looked uncomprehending.

Finally Dreyfus looked back at the Sullivans. "I am forced to conclude that someone has murdered a man and mutilated a document in order to conceal something about a crime four hundred and fifty years old. To me, this smacks of fantasy."

Abdelaziz muttered something, too fast for the Sullivans to understand.

Dreyfus cut her off. "Abdelaziz, would you please bring Madame Sullivan another glass of water. I don't want her to faint again." And as the young woman went off into the kitchen, he said quickly, "Her father was one of the first Moroccan police officers in Marseille. He was a legend! And so his daughter followed him. But she tends to make everything difficult. Leyla just said that it is ridiculous to spend valuable police time on a craziness like this, when there is violent crime every night in Avignon. In a way, I have to agree with her. Nevertheless, a man has been murdered... two men, so far, with nuns involved, and this investigation must go forward."

Leyla Abedlaziz came back with a glass of water for Rosalind and looked at her partner suspiciously.

He drew himself up. "M'sieur'dame. Thank you for your information. I will read this material directly. And now we must leave."

Rosalind sputtered, "But can't we read the article too? I mean, Michael spent so much time on this...we should send him the information too! Don't—"

Dreyfus held up a hand. "Madame, I am sorry. It is not the practice of the French judicial system to share evidence with the public, no matter how concerned they may be."

Perhaps sensing that he was being abrupt to the point of insult, he paused, and a tiny smile emerged on his thin lips.

"Madame, Monsieur Sullivan..." He made shushing motions with his hands to ward off interruptions.

"I have often read your English detective *romance*s when I was a boy, when I decided to become a police. Always, I remember, the nice people who were not police, the old ladies of a certain age, the priest, the nobleman a bit—how you say—sissy? These are the people who solve the crime, while the poor stupid police misinterpret all the evidence, are getting ready to hang the wrong person...but forgive me—I go on too long. I just say that in France we do not invite good people, intelligent people like yourselves, to help us, and nevertheless our—how shall I say—conviction rate is almost eighty-four percent. Much higher than in the country of Mr. Holmes and Miss Christie." He closed M. Rousset's folder with a snap. "Now, we must go," and he gestured to Abdelaziz, who had been alternately staring at him with hostility or sighing with boredom.

The detectives from Avignon marched out into the evening light, rosy in the west, deep green in the east, a chorus of cicadas saluting the end of a hot day and the forecast of another one tomorrow.

CHAPTER FOURTEEN

"Michael! Grab a pen or something!" Rosalind had luckily caught the Tollivers at their hotel in San Francisco before they went out to lunch.

"First, some bad news. Monsieur Rousset, who was going to give us some documents? Yes, yes...let me go on. He was killed today...yes *killed, killed,* on the way here—" She paused to let Michael protest, exclaim, then went on.

"Yes. He was coming here and was murdered on the road by a huge truck, and two nuns, coming up behind, took something out of his car... Right, nuns again."

She told the story in bits and pieces as Michael, and now Nicole on the other phone, kept breaking in with incredulous comments.

"Now. Here's the important part. The document was missing the two last pages and that Dreyfus prick insisted on hauling it off to Avignon. But Spencer remembered the title of the journal. Ready, Spence?"

And Spencer was on the phone. "It's an obscure journal, privately printed, I'm sure, on a copy machine. But the title is *Bulletin de la société des études vaudoises.* Got that?"

Spencer listened a moment. "Yes. And I thought, only crazy American libraries, with all their money and frenzied acquisition, will have bought this strange Vaudois *Bulletin*. What?...Yes. You're absolutely right. You're in exactly the right place to start a search for any *Bulletins* that might be in America. You're right there in the Bay Area. Go directly to the UC Library in Berkeley, they'll have a copy. And then ask their interlibrary loan department to locate every other copy in the US...Of course you can do it. You're a best-selling novelist with a book they're making a movie of... Never mind, lie! Tell them Anthony Hopkins and Brad Pitt are going to be in it.... Look, I've worked in that library, among many others. Librarians would die to help work on some project that's really interesting. I know them. And when are you guys coming back?"

Michael hung up the phone, sitting on the side of the bed in the San Francisco hotel. He was studying the notes he'd taken.

"Berkeley," he said to Nicole. "What are we doing this afternoon?"

"After this lunch, you mean?" They were due at the St. Francis to meet a columnist.

"I'd like to hit the library right away. Now I *really* want to see that article."

"I have my hair at three. But that's okay. Take the car. It's been sitting there in the parking garage at thirty-three dollars a day since Monday. Might as well have some use out of it."

The lunch was predictably boring, as Michael was pestered, one more time, to explain how he had decided to write a novel about the *Babylon*ian Captivity, and what did he know about the Middle East in the sixth century B.C., and was he Jewish, and if not, why did he decide to write about Jewish history, and¬¬ once again¬¬ he was asked to give his opinion about the current situation in Israel. This was always the point at which Michael could smile and shrug his shoulders and say that there were more knowledgeable people who could answer that question. He and Nicole were hoping for a lively item in the column that would promote better sales in the Bay Area, which had been soft, so they were polite and insisted on splitting the bill with the newspaper.

The columnist, a slim, handsome man, who didn't really resemble the photo next to his byline in the paper, laughed and said what a pleasure it had been. And by the way, how was his present book going?"

Michael held up a hand, smiling back. "I'm sorry, that's a question I never answer till the book's at the publisher. You understand?"

"Of course. I've heard that from other authors too."

"Actually, I'm still doing research. One of the reasons we're looking at libraries around here."

"Michael had a great tip about this article we've been looking for," said Nicole. "Just deep background, of course. He's going to check the Berkeley library this afternoon."

"Is that right? Well, good luck! It took me two hours finding a place to park last time I had to go over there!"

It only took Michael an hour. He walked up the hill, almost a half mile, from the lot the parking guard had allowed him to share for only $3.50 an hour, and entered the cool precincts of Bancroft Library, one of the largest and best in the world. He was told that access to the stacks was limited to cardholders and legitimate researchers with a signed permit from the librarian. But once he was able to talk to a supervising Librarian, all turned out as Spencer had predicted. Ah, yes, the Library did in fact have copies of his last three books, in the American literature section. And yes, they would do everything they could to assist in his research for his next novel. What was the name of the journal?

At exactly that moment an older woman teaching in the French Department received a call on her cell phone. She left her office immediately and strode off to Bancroft Library.

At almost the same moment Nicole was getting ready for her hair appointment in her hotel room and heard her phone ringing.

"Hi, Mrs. Tolliver?"

"Uh, yes?" She was trying to think who actually knew they were staying in this hotel.

"Hi. This is Jay Friedlander...from the *Chronicle?* We had an appointment with your husband for lunch and and I wonder if we got our wires crossed?"

Nicole had to take a deep breath. "Mr. Friedlander? Didn't we just have lunch with you at the St. Francis?"

To his stunned response she quickly described the man they had been talking to, described Michael's plans for the afternoon, answered a few additional questions, and then agreed with Mr. Friedlander that law enforcement should be sent to the Berkeley campus, to the library, to find Michael in case someone was actually gunning for him.

Michael found the floor where obscure journals had been stored. It was very dark, but he soon discovered that each row of stacks had a light switch on the side, and he made his way slowly to the section where old journals of French religious history were shelved. He finally found the *Bulletin de la société des études vaudoises*, a very few tattered copies in a heavy cardboard box for preservation, which, according to the library computer, were all that had ever been published, from 1969 to 1974.

He held his breath, looking at the bound journals. Yes! 1973 was there. And there was the number given him by Spencer. Michael opened the volume reverently, looking for the table of contents. And there it was..."*Temoin de Jean de Moulin.*"

He was turning the pages to reach the article when a women from the library staff came down the narrow aisle. She was pushing a book cart and looking up at the stack opposite him. She smiled apologetically

"I'm sorry, excuse me a minute."

Michael scrunched up against the stack he was standing by, to let her go, his finger holding the page in the journal that he was looking for. He was looking down at the page, making sure he had the right page, when the lights went out.

CHAPTER FIFTEEN

The cab carrying Nicole Tolliver screamed across the Bay Bridge. She had run in front of three couples waiting for cabs outside the St. Francis and had thrust a hundred-dollar bill at the driver.

"Bancroft Library, UC Berkeley...and don't stop at the gate. It's an emergency and the police will be there already."

The driver found her explanation convincing and left a parking attendant fuming at the main entrance to the Berkeley campus as he streaked up the road to the library. As Nicole had predicted, there were police cars and an ambulance outside the Library, plus a huge crowd of students and other onlookers. She rushed to the side of a detective in plain clothes who was talking over a radio.

"Please...my husband? Michael? What's happened?"

The detective put his hand over his mouthpiece. "Just a minute...You say your husband?"

Just then Nicole saw two attendants and a stretcher coming out the main entrance and she took off running. Michael was on the stretcher, his face pale as a sheet, but his eyes were open and he smiled to see Nicole, as she almost threw herself at the stretcher. The attendants were forced to stop.

"Michael! Oh my God! What happened?" She burst into tears, leaning forward, trying to cradle his head.

A few minutes later, in the shade of large trees, with the crowds at bay and surrounded by curious police from several jurisdictions, Michael was able to sit up, sip some water, and recount what he remembered.

"There was this woman with a book cart...looked just like a librarian. I couldn't describe her more than that for a million dollars. Anyway. I sort of turned to let her pass me and...I'm not sure whether the lights went out first, or maybe I just got hit and went out. But...but I remember waking up just as I was being dragged on my stomach by the feet along the floor. And the lights were all out on that floor..." He stopped to take a deep breath and a paramedic leaned forward.

"Maybe...maybe you should just lie down and—"

"No, no!" Michael protested. "I want to get all this down while I still remember it. Like it's so clear in my head right now. Okay?"

"Yeah, let him go on." The police wanted to know who to go looking for.

"I was still real groggy, seeing stars, and then I stopped being dragged, and I saw a light to my left. So I turned my head that way. And I was looking down the space in the middle of the staircase... you know what I mean? Maybe six flights up, but the space in the middle goes all the way down. So I was looking like *way, way* down, sixty feet or more, and then I realize someone is trying to roll me under the railing and down—"

"Oh my God!" Nicole caught her breath. "Mikey...!"

"But then ... I'd been feeling paralyzed—you know, like in a bad dream, when you can't move—but then I suddenly could get my arms going and I grabbed the railing above me, trying to get up, and I heard this woman say, *'Merde!'*——"

"Mare?" asked the nearest police detective.

Michael laughed, then flinched and grabbed his head.

"Ouch...remind me not to laugh."

"The person said 'shit' in French," said Nicole, angrily. "It was some fucking French woman trying to kill my husband. How hard could it be to round up some suspects, huh? A French librarian carrying a blackjack or something?"

The detective made soothing noises. "Okay, okay! We're already going there, who's in the Library this afternoon, middle of the summer. Now we can narrow it down. French."

But it didn't narrow down. Anyone with a library card could enter the stacks, and during the summer, with a skeleton staff, no one remembered an older woman who might or might not have been French. Furthermore, once Michael and Nicole had been taken to a more comfortable faculty lounge and the local police had had an opportunity to inquire about the background of the attempted murder, Michael and Nicole were asked the same incredulous question that Spencer and Rosalind had earlier.

"You mean, someone is trying to cover up a crime four hundred and fifty years old?" The detective was well dressed for Berkeley. He was a lanky redhead with clean jeans and a Hawaiian shirt. Meanwhile a short, dark doctor was examining Michael's left temple.

"There is no abrasion, but a puffiness. If I had to guess, I'd say she slugged you with a soft blackjack of some kind...lead shot in a leather sheath. Not like a hard cop sap."

"Whatdya know about cop saps, doc?" asked a uniform, laughing. He was a large black man, thumbs tucked into his equipment belt.

But the doctor was serious. "No, officer. I mean it. Give me your sap." And he took the little weapon by the handle. "You see this? Meant to in*flic*t paralyzing pain on a shoulder joint, or elbow, or wrist. End of discussion. But not to the head. Too hard. Dangerous. And always leaves a mark." He gave the sap back to the policeman, who whacked it into his cupped hand a few times and returned it to its place on his equipment belt.

"As I was saying..." The detective was trying to get their attention. But the doctor went on.

"When I was still in Pakistan they had longer leather tubes, with lead shot more loosely packed. And the police hit for the head, every time. Very effective for knocking you out."

"You got that right, doctor," said Michael. "Now am I going to be concussed, or something?"

The doctor explained to Michael and Nicole the symptoms they should watch for. "Twenty-four hours in a dark room, drink water, take aspirin for pain. You'll be fine."

But Michael protested. "First, I want to answer the detective. Yes. Someone *is* trying to cover up a crime, a multiple murder, four hundred and fifty years old. If you'll talk to French police in our area, they'll tell you that two different old men who were going to give us information on this murder were killed almost as soon as they contacted us."

Michael started to explain, but Nicole broke in.

"Look, I want to get my husband into that dark room and resting. But there's this article he was looking for—"

"And had it in my hand when I got coshed...," added Michael.

"And now there's no trace of it?" A thin Asian serials librarian shook her head. "Mr. Tolliver asked me where it would be in the stacks. I went to check after the attack and that year is missing."

"Okay, I think I can function just until we check Interlibrary Loans," said Michael, rubbing his eyes. "They should be able to locate every collection of the *Bulletin de la société des études vaudoises* in the country. It couldn't take five minutes."

And a wheelchair was provided and Michael was wheeled up the path to the Bancroft Library. The staff was agog with wonder that a serious researcher into ancient massacres could be assaulted to conceal information about the crime. There was a large crowd of library staff around the computer where a small pale youth, the acknowledged master of Interlibrary Loan software, was seated, strumming his fingers across the keyboard, Horowitz preparing for Liszt.

The Asian librarian read from the sheet of paper Michael had printed for her, pronouncing it clearly for the man at the computer.

"*Bulletin* de la société des études vaudoises, maestro. Hit it! Or shall I spell out the French?"

He gave her a withering look and his fingers flew across the keys.

"Any idea how many units we got out there?" he asked, waiting while his computer whirred and clicked.

"Couldn't be many," said Michael. "We're not talking *National Geographic* here."

Almost immediately titles accumulated on the screen. It seemed that the Vaudois journal was held by Brigham Young, Notre Dame, the Eastern Arkansas Institute of Bible Studies, and no other library in the United States or Canada.

Michael looked puzzled. "Two of the biggest religious schools in the country, and Arkansas?

"Okay, Mike. Now let's get to that dark room."

"But...how will we know if—"

The Asian woman spoke up. "I am Wei Ling. I will contact those libraries immediately to check on that volume, what was it, 1973? Mr. Tolliver, you go rest. I can do this faster than you anyway. Call me tomorrow." And she gave Nicole a card.

CHAPTER SIXTEEN

It was early evening in Barigoule. Summer was running out of steam. The heat of midday began to evaporate around mid-afternoon, and twilight began to creep over the hills from the east by the time Danielle was pouring the first of the evening drinks in Jeannot's café. As the shadows descended, three men left different tables in the square and casually walked up the narrow, cobblestoned street that led to the church.

In the broad *place* under the tall trees in front of the church a Dutch couple had lingered to take sunset photos of the hills to the west. The three men dispersed and loitered until the Dutch had left. Then they pulled open the heavy church door and entered.

A large person was facing them and showed impatience as they all dipped into the font and crossed themselves.

"Come on, come on. This is important!"

"But—"

"But nothing! This is the Lord's work we do. Listen!"

And he seemed to swell, to gain in size, a giant dark man in the shadows as he spoke.

"The heretics were killed, all of them, and it was good in the sight of God. But now, so many years...centuries later, people are poking their noses into what happened."

"But...it is all known! In the writings, in the report of that Aubéry—"

"Yes. Most of it is known. The commission of Henri II, all the testimony. And what does it say about Barigoule?"

His listeners were not readers. They looked down at the stone floor of the old church.

"It says merely that the women were caught in the grotto. That the captain Mormoiron ordered the great fire built in the entry of the grotto. That the women were all suffocated." The big man hesitated.

"But then, fifty years later, another French king, another cursed heretic, Henri IV, reopened the inquiry."

The three men looked at each other, at their feet, back at the big man.

"Most people don't know about the inquiry. There were only a few hearings in 1595, then the blasphemer Henri was distracted by wars and politics. It was one of us who got him, you know," he added.

"Ravaillac," said one of the other men. Everyone knew that Ravaillac had died, unshriven, after days of *peine forte et dure,* insisting to the end that he had no associates in the murder of the king.

"Ravaillac. Yes. A man who should have been sainted, not torn to pieces with red hot pincers. Be that as it may, the inquiry into the massacres here was printed, the pages went into forgotten archives to molder away. Until..."

"Yes? Until?" The men leaned forward as if pursuing the end of a great story at a café table.

"Until some goddamned busybodies of Vaudois so-called religious historians found some bits of Henri's inquiry...twenty, no more than thirty years ago, in the Bibliothéque Nationale.

Actually, looking for something else, but they found these terrible pages and published them."

"But...but...," the men protested. "You say the pages were published! What did people say?"

The big man forced a sarcastic laugh. "No one paid attention, and those who did just called everything superstitious fantasy, the researchers fanatics. The thing is, a mystery has two ends, maybe three, like a rabbit warren. You go in one end...empty tunnels, nothing, so you get bored and give up. But if someone goes in the other end, later, then they figure out the mystery, close off the ends and they catch the rabbits."

"Just like me, the other day!" said the youngest of the other men. "I was out near——"

"Shut up, you imbecile!" The big man was furious and there was complete silence for a moment.

"No one paid attention in 1973. Now someone is looking down a different hole, and if they figure out what the 1973 people were thinking, they will finally know..." He did not complete the sentence.

"If they should talk to the 1973 people—," one of the other men ventured.

"They all had accidents." The dark interior of the cathedral suddenly seemd much colder.

"But their publication is still out there. Not many places. But it only takes one."

CHAPTER SEVENTEEN

icole burst into their hotel room. Michael had slept the night through and was now sitting groggily on the edge of the bed.

"Wei Ling sent a fax over. Notre Dame said they couldn't find the journal. But Brigham Young had it and faxed her a copy. How are you, poor baby?"

"I'll live. Actually, I feel much better. I think mostly because we didn't do the cat scan thing."

The doctor yesterday had suggested that if they were at all nervous Michael should have a cat scan, to make sure there was no subdural bleeding in his brain. Michael and Nicole had just stared at each other, realizing suddenly that they had no medical insurance in the United States and had never expected to need any. When the doctor quoted a median price for an MRI or cat scan, they had just laughed.

Anyway, I didn't even look. Wanted you to get first read." And she handed over a sheaf of amateurishly photocopied pages.

In the court of instruction ordered by his Catholic majesty, Henri, on the 21st day of November, 1595, the testimony of Jean of Barigoule, known also as Jean le Moulin, son of Jacques le Moulin, of that town.

"I swear by Jesus Christ, God the father, and the Holy Spirit that my words are truth. I am an old man now, but I remember every moment of those days as if they were yesterday. The court has asked what happened on the 20th of April, fifty years ago.

"In the dawn, the word came up the hill: that soldiers were coming to Barigoule from Gordes. All the men that were left in town took parcels of food and fled to the hills. Having injured my foot in the mill the day before, I was left behind. I was always a true believer in the holy church, in the Virgin and all the Saints and I felt no fear. Our priest, a good man, assembled the women and children and put them in charge of Madame Serre, whom many thought was a witch. I knew her to be a follower of the Vaudois beliefs, as were many in Barigoule, but the most Godfearing woman and a saint to many.

[At this point the court put a question to Jean le Moulin]

"As to the Vaudois, my lord, many in Barigoule professed to their faith. I myself saw nothing wrong that they preached the Gospels, led a life of poverty, and counseled against sin. But I was ignorant of these matters, my lord, and for that matter, I know nothing of the fine workings of the church, having all my life simply made confession and attended holy mass, as is required. And more—"

[Jean le Moulin is asked to continue his testimony as to the day in question]

"Yes, my lord. Well, Madame Serre took the women and children up the hill out of town. She did not say where she was going, but those of us who stayed believed she would go to the grottos, maybe an hour away, to hide until the soldiery left town. After all, we had all heard the stories about the previous week, the slaughter of men and boys, even priests, and the violation of women and girls, girls young as eight years old. My lord, it was hard for us to think of this as a matter ordered by holy church. Some old soldiers, who remembered the wars earlier, before they left for the hills they said it was always the same, when soldiers were let loose. They would willingly slay, torment, and

violate the holy Saints themselves whenever their officers gave them liberty to do so. I was afraid and hid in a storeroom of the mill.

I heard the troops arrive and from the noise¬¬, whooping and laughing¬¬, I knew they had found Roland's wine shop and I hoped they would get drunk and sleep. But no, some one was ordering them to go house to house to find the heretics, and the treasures that the heretics had supposedly hidden, although I knew no one in Barigoule village had two groats to rub together. And then they found me and threatened me with beatings, asking where the women had gone. I said I knew not, but they had a priest with them who came and told them to put my feet to the fire and he told me it was God's will and the will of Jesus and Mary and all the saints in heaven that I deliver the heretics. And¬¬

[Jean le Moulin lost his composure and was allowed to take a short rest]

I knew I should obey a priest and yet I feared for the women and children. They put me over the millstone and burned three fagots under my feet, one after another, each time asking me where the women had gone. And finally my whole world was nothing but pain and they had brought out the fourth fagot and I could not help, I told them the grottos, and they said, 'Good, and we shall take you to the grottos. If you have lied we will burn you alive, bit by bit.' So up the hill we went.

"Once we reached the big grotto, the one with the cave in front, it was obvious the women were inside. It had rained a few days before and their footprints led right to the cave. The Captain Mormoiron declared in a great voice that they should not fear, but come out, that they would be protected. But, my lord, some poor women from Cabrières had escaped to Barigoule a few days before and told of their repeated violation and torment...even an old woman put live in the village oven, so the women of Barigoule knew better than to come out. Then the Captain ordered a man at arms to crawl into the grotto and drive the women out. And, my lord, he feared to go, all could see, but obeyed and started to crawl in when he stopped and lay down. Some

others dragged him back, and lo, his head was almost severed from his body and we could hear the witch, Madame Serre crying out, saying that they might be women but they had swords and knew how to use them. At that the Captain was in a rage and he commanded the arquebusiers to fire their weapons into the cave. But it seemed they were only hitting the rock; the cave was deep and wide. So the Captain ordered brush wood to be brought in great quantity and heaped in the cave. And it was I who told him that the grotto was a deep one and that the heat would not go in, hoping that he would desist.

'Do you want me to toast your feet some more?' he asked me, using curse words I cannot repeat. 'The fire will not burn. But it will suck all the air out and the heretics will suffocate on their way to Hell.' And he gave the command to light the fire. It was a huge blaze and burned for hours. The soldiers cooked their dinner over the coals for they had killed most of our cattle and goats and sheep and the fire helped to make a good dinner for them."

"Oh for God's sake!" said Nicole. She had been reading the narrative to Michael under the only light in the darkened room.

"What's wrong?"

"This is wrong!" And she waved the last sheet. "It ends there. That can't be right!"

It was later that day when, with Wei Ling's assistance, they were able to speak with a librarian at Brigham Young University.

"I know it's strange," she said. "I never noticed when I photocopied the article. I don't know much French, but I reached the last page and the facing page began a different article so I figured it was the end."

"But—," Michael started.

"But I'm looking at the journal right now and I can see that there is a whole two pages missing. And down at the spine I can see that someone cut them out, maybe with a razor." Her voice became indignant. "I'll report this immediately! We can't tolerate mutilation of library materials."

"Do you have any record who checked it out?" asked Wei Ling on the other phone.

"Oh no. These journals don't circulate. Someone must have done it in the stacks. I...maybe I should notify Professor Tobin in French Studies. He might know who would have been interested."

Nicole sat glumly, reading the surviving pages, after they had hung up.

"Brigham Young has 36,000 students," she said

"That should narrow it down," commented Michael. "I was thinking of contacting Professor Tobin myself but then I thought, what if he winds up under a truck or something. With what's going on I wouldn't wonder."

"So. That leaves—"

"Right. Eastern Arkansas Institute of Bible Studies. And since our book tour is going to New Orleans...I wonder where I can find a road map, see how far, let's see, Orbit, Arkansas is..."

It turned out that Dallas was a little closer, so they decided to fly to Dallas, rent a car, and visit the Bible Institute on the way to New Orleans. In the meantime, Michael managed to find the number of the institute through information. He was expecting to be routed through a switchboard and was pleasantly surprised when the man who answered the phone turned out to be the director.

He laughed when Michael expressed surprise. "Eastern Arkansas Institute of Bible Studies is not exactly UCLA," he said. He also had an unmistakable French accent, so that Michael could cut through a lot of the complicated explanation he had been composing in his mind and just state his main concern.

"I hesitate to name the document we're trying to locate, Doctor...um...Boisset?"

"Please call me Henri. I have lived in Arkansas for over thirty years. In this town we don't even know last names. We have all adopted American ways now. But go on."

"Yes. Henri. And I have to admit that while we have been trying to find this document certain people who were trying to help us were...uh, assaulted."

"Ah! Not seriously, I hope?"

When Boisset was told that two had been killed and that Michael himself had been knocked out he was silent for such a long time that Michael wondered if the connection was broken.

"Hello...?"

"No. No, I am here. Mr. Tolliver, hearing you say this, I have to confess immediately that our institute of Bible studies is, in fact, a center, in fact, the only center primarily devoted to the study of the Vaudois movement in the United States...I should say, the western hemisphere. We are, I admit, in a remote location, but no matter, scholars visit us all the time, either in person or on our website, and we have an exchange agreement with the Religious Studies department of the University of California at Santa Barbara, one of the first departments of its kind."

"I apologize for not having learned about you...sloppy research on my part. But then you know all about—"

"About the massacres of 1545? And those of the preceding century, in Piedmont, in Prague, in Apulia? Of course. I myself concentrate on the beginnings of the Poor of Lyons, but my colleague Marie Hartman has collected a mass of material about the Luberon killings. Would you like to speak to her?"

It was decided that they would all meet the following week. In the meantime Michael warned the director that someone was systematically destroying the obscure journal they were trying to locate.

"If you have a good safe, it would be best to lock the 1973 journal up as soon as possible."

Boisset sounded amused. "I will find the journal immediately, Mr. Tolliver, if just to satisfy my curiosity about this secret. But I assure you, this is a small town and a stranger would immediately become obvious. Also, we have a security fence around our buildings and two reliable dogs."

CHAPTER EIGHTEEN

Pirate was the name of the older male Rotweiller. He was really too good natured to be a guard dog, having been raised by very kindly Christians. He was also overweight, as Christian kindliness had run to excess rations whenever he asked for them, which was often. His mate, Francine, however, was suspicious by nature and she was the first dog that afternoon to lift her head, crinkle her nostrils, and charge barking and snarling to the deserted northeastern corner of the Bible Institute property, where only a few scrub pines grew. Pirate followed her, dutifully, and only out of the corner of his eye saw a figure entering the rarely guarded front gate. He was about to return when he smelled smoke in the direction to which Francine was running, so he began barking too and ran heavily toward the little stand of pines where he could now see flames licking around the roots of the trees.

From the back entrance of the library Henri Boisset came running. He was a lean old man, but a daily runner in the streets of Orbit, and now he was running hard. As soon as he saw the flames, he backtracked and grabbed a hose at the side of the building. Turning it on full blast, he ran back toward the fire. The hose reached its end quite a bit before the corner of the property, dragging Boisset back on his heels, but he was able to elevate the nozzle and was relieved to see the spray falling all over the fire zone. White smoke and steam began to rise, while Boisset commenced to curse the imbecile cigarette smoker who had undoubtedly tossed a careless cigarette butt into the weeds at the edge of the property.

But Francine and Pirate had by that time been diverted to the opposite corner of the northern fence and were barking even more furiously, seeing some threat in that direction.

Dr. Boisset watched them curiously, still directing the spray from his hose onto the smoking remains of the fire. Then he heard the unmistakable clap of a shot from a firearm and Pirate sank to the ground. Francine stopped barking immediately and ran to the side of her mate, sniffing and whining. Boisset was joined by librarian Marie Hartman, a woman who could have been his sister, spare and elderly.

"Here, Marie! Hold this hose on the fire! Something has happened to Pirate!" And he left the woman with the hose and ran to where the dog lay motionless. He gave a loud cry.

"Oh my God! Pirate is dead. He's been shot." And indeed it was obvious. Blood flowed in a steady stream from the dog's big chest and his open eyes were glazed.

Abruptly Francine stopped whining. Her head went up and she streaked back toward the main building of the institute.

Boisset's puzzled gaze followed the dog and then he jumped to his feet himself and began to run, hearing screams and shouting coming from the building. As he rounded the entrance he saw a confused mass of figures in the foyer. There was the familiar form of Mrs. Mabel Williams, an elderly black woman who worked as general housekeeper. Mrs. Williams was slapping with her apron at Francine, who was growling furiously atop a twisting body on the floor.

"Stop! Stop her! Please!" Mrs. Williams was screaming. "She gonna kill him!"

But the figure on the floor slowed and was now motionless, and Francine, still growling, lifted her massive head. Blood and slaver hung in loops from her jaws.

Dr. Boisset could only stare in disbelief as it slowly dawned on him that his dog had, in fact, just killed the man on the floor, ripping at his throat in a fit of rage. Only then did he notice the red gallon can of gas on its side, gasoline slowly trickling from its spout. He quickly picked it up and shouted to Mrs. Williams.

"Mabel! There's gasoline spilled! Quickly, get a towel or something. If there's a spark or..." Francine, the hair still up on her back, stalked out the door toward her dead mate, encountering Marie Hartman just coming in.

The Orbit police were as puzzled as everyone else. Crime in this town on the Mississippi river valley flatlands ran to weekend drunks and an occasional fight down at Elsie's Roadhouse. Chief Larkins was a large brown man. He had come squealing up in the town's only police car, followed shortly by a running patrolman from the other direction and the local firetruck. Within a few minutes the crowd was swelled by an ambulance from Mercy Hospital in a bigger town ten miles away and two deputy sheriffs from the Phillips county substation. Rarely used yellow crime scene tape had finally been located and strung around the foyer of the institute, and an indignant Mabel Williams had been banished before she could try to clean up the mess.

No one present had ever seen the dead man before. He appeared to be Caucasian, medium height, thin, possibly mid-thirties. He was wearing black jeans and a blue work shirt. It seemed obvious that either he, or an accomplice, had set the fire out in the pines as a diversion and that he intended to sneak into the building and set it on fire with the gasoline. According to Mrs. Williams, she had heard the commotion outside and had been coming from the pantry and saw the man heading for the library. Just then Francine had come barreling in the door on the attack.

The man had cursed and kicked at the dog, but the big Rottweiler brought him down and started savaging him.

"I never saw that dog even growl at anyone," Marie Hartman was saying. "She was the sweetest thing, wouldn't even bark at the garbage man."

"That's right," added Boisset. "UPS drivers or anyone. Those dogs were too friendly to be guard dogs."

"But she killed that man like...like one of them dogs in San Francisco I read about, tore up that woman," Chief Larkins was saying.

"I think she must have known that he killed Pirate," said Boisset. "Or just the shock of Pirate being killed. And then she must have seen him sneaking into the building and...and her instincts took over."

The group automatically looked out toward the yard where Francine was still disconsolately standing over the dead Pirate.

"You gotta excuse me, Doc," said Larkins, "but I have to ask, why in the world is anyone gonna try to burn down a Bible institute? Muslims or such? That there Al Qaeda? Is there something I don't understand here?"

"Oh my God!" exclaimed Marie Hartman, her hand over her mouth. "Do you think it could have been that article...?"

She was interrupted by the uniformed patrolman, who had been inspecting the dead man's clothes.

"He don't have no wallet, nothin' I can find. Not even car keys."

"He didn't walk all the way through town carryin' that gas can, a white man," said Larkins. "Local people would'a been spooked for sure." He looked over the crowd, which was growing larger every moment, townspeople coming to find out what was going on. "Hey you there, Bill, LaVar, some of you, he'p us out here. Start goin' round the neighborhood, look for a car or truck parked got the keys in it, out of town license, somethin' like that."

But two hours later, with the unknown John Doe hauled away to the morgue, and with every witness questioned over and over again, the locals had wandered all streets within a half mile of the institute and had reliably reported that every vehicle in sight was accounted for.

Henri Boisset was looking sadly out at the back lawn, where a handyman was digging a grave for Pirate. The light of day was fading and a breath of air was beginning to part the dense humidity of eastern Arkansas. Two large black men with shotguns were walking perimeter around the property to make sure no madmen would try another assault. They had been joined by Francine, who plodded along in front of them, growling softly now and then, her head swiveling from side to side. Marie Hartman came to stand beside the director.

"You know, Henri?"

"Yes, Marie?"

"I was going to tell all about the article to the police. The article that the writer wanted, what was his name?"

Boisset straightened up, slapped his forehead. "I don't believe...I forgot all about it. I was just about to locate the journal when the dogs... Do you suppose...?"

"I thought suddenly I shouldn't tell the police. It would make everything so complicated."

"You are very right!" Boisset jumped to his feet. "If that man was trying to burn our library there must be something terribly, terribly important in that article." He started off to the library. Marie Hartman stopped him.

"Henri, I just looked. The whole volume for that year is missing."

Boisset almost staggered with the shock. "*Merde!* How can this be? We don't lend...Nobody could have... That thief! If someone had stolen it already, who would he—?"

Marie put a hand on his arm. "The only thing I can think of is that peculiar French woman who came last month. She was doing research on Vaudois and she spent a whole afternoon in the library. You remember her? Marron was her name?"

Boisset struck himself on the side of the head. "But...but she was a distinguished scholar. She knew her field completely. It is impossible that Madame Marron would have taken one of our journals."

"It could have been innocent, Henri. She had masses of her own notes and was writing, writing. The journal is very thin...she could have just gathered it up."

Boisset looked at her sternly. "Marie. Can you remember anything about that journal article? Mr. Tolliver was certain it was about the massacres in 1545. And that is your field, *hein?*"

The heat and humidity had returned to the lower valley of the Mississippi. Michael and Nicole, fresh from the cool sea air of San Francisco, were stifling, sitting out on the back lawn of the Institute for Bible Studies, drinking iced tea with Boisset and Marie Hartman. The attack on the institute had taken place while they were in the skies over the western desert. Landing in Dallas they had phoned ahead and learned about the arson attempt. In frustration Michael had broken all speed limits in two different states getting their rental car to this placid corner of eastern Arkansas. The shady streets and almost somnolent calm of the town of Orbit made it hard to imagine the violence of the day before. Dr. Boisset and Miss Hartman had welcomed them to institute, shown them the embers of the decoy fire and the ughly scrubbed foyer where the unknown assailant had met Now Francine lay on the grass in front of them, her head ws, staring mournfully into the distance.

"My poor, poor dog!" Boisset was saying. "And there is a state law requiring quarantine and possible destruction of a dog that kills."

"Chief Larkin says he's going to forget about it unless someone reminds him," said Marie. "In this part of the South a guard dog that kills an invader, an arsonist even more, will never be harmed. It is part of the culture."

Nicole fanned her face. "It's just incredible. We've had people killed to prevent us from reading that article. And now someone completely different has walked off with it."

"Actually, I have read that article," said Marie Hartman. Today, in spite of the heat, she was wearing a long-sleeved navy dress that hung loose on her angular frame. "I was telling Dr. Boisset the day of the attack."

She had everyone's attention immediately.

"But I hope I won't disappoint you. I'm afraid I have no photographic memory. I'm trying to remember the exact testimony of the miller boy Jean, and I know it had to do with some curse. You see, the research I was doing at the time was less on the massacres than on witchcraft and sorcery and that was what drew my attention...some curse that Jean heard."

"Sorcery?" asked Nicole. "They were trying to fight off hordes of brutal soldiers with curses?" She sounded outraged.

"I know it sounds crazy," said the librarian. "Allow me to explain."

The villages of Provence, she went on, like those everywhere in sixteenth-century Europe, looked not only to clergy and local leaders for answers to everyday problems. Every little community had at least one or two persons, usually female, usually elderly, with a reputed knowledge of spells and simple magic, sometimes assisted by charms or potions. Although so-called witchcraft was condemned by the church and could be punished by the stake, minor remedies passed beneath the notice of the authorities always alert for heresy. Every one of the holy Saints, after all, could be persuaded to intercede in mortal affairs if one knew the proper prayers.

"My research involved the combination of Christian prayer and—how shall I say?—traditional magic that certainly goes back to pagan times. You pray, for instance, to St. Jerome, to help you find something lost. But the old woman who lives next door tells you that while praying you must tie a yellow thread around your right wrist to help your hand remember where the object was put. You can imagine even the nearsighted village priest asking an old woman with a reputation for such gifts to help him find the house key he misplaced somewhere."

Michael and Nicole laughed. "I can just see it," Nicole said. "But—"

"I was compiling a data base from old anecdotes, tales from all over Provence, in which prayer to various saints was combined with popular spells in order to deal with everyday problems."

"Rural Catholics in Europe still do that...," started Michael.

"Catholics, all Christians except the most austere, Jews, Muslims, everyone in the world looks for some kind of supernatural help," said Dr. Boisset. "It is common to mankind. And now may I intercede with Mabel to bring us some more iced tea?"

Marie Hartman paused to fill her glass, then went on.

"The Vaudois are special, you must remember. For them the Gospels were so vital to their lives that many of the older people had actually memorized them."

Michael looked startled, but Marie went on. "It sounds incredible, I know, for uneducated people, but remember that many ancient Greeks had all of Homer to heart—so much longer than the Gospels."

As she explained it, the elders of the Vaudois community were revered for their ability to quote specific passages from the Gospels in response to problems confronting people in their villages.

"And, you will remember, what is it that takes up so much of the Gospels?"

Michael and Nicole looked at each other and spoke at the same time.

"Miracles!" Michael exclained. "We've already heard this, from our friend Professor Lebarbe, who was murdered, probably for telling us."

Marie Hartman looked stricken. She looked at Dr. Boisset and spoke rapidly in French. Nicole started to tell Michael what she was saying, but Boisset put up a hand.

"Forgive us! We know you understand French. But Marie was so startled—the name "Lebarbe" of course has a special meaning to Vaudois. *Barbe* means "guide." In so far as the Vaudois had a clergy, it was the selected elders—the *barbes*— who preached the Gospels and led the congregation."

Marie Hartman had recovered her composure. "Lebarbe! Of course. There are still Vaudois, everywhere there are Catholics, as I am sure you know. And believe it or not, there are still...persons who want to destroy them. When the French owned Louisiana, the local bishops persecuted certain communities suspected of Valdisme. Many of them moved north and tried to start communes, just to be left alone."

Dr. Boisset explained. In the wilderness of the lower Mississipi in the late seventeenth century only true believers would try to establish a self-sustaining community. The poor pilgrims didn't understand the crops that would survive, they didn't know the weather—blistering heat in summer and crop-destroying deluges in all seasons. And to the west were Indians. But in the town that came to be known as Orbit...

"A community of Vaudois survived here, we believe, because of strong leadership," continued Boisset. "And the town became a refuge for Negroes, which is why it is almost completely black today. The Vaudois, of course, had no racism." He smiled. "You will not find racism in the Gospels, you know. Then, a benefactor created this institute, to continue the study of Valdism, its spirit, you understand. We are a hundred and fifty years old here."

Michael and Nicole looked at each other. "But you are both French?" asked Nicole.

"I am French, of course. Marie is Canadian, but she was born in France too, near Avignon."

"You could call us Vaudois," said Marie, "although we are both modern and live in the world of the present. We respect the... purity of the original Vaudois beliefs and continue the collection of data about their lives and their complex system of shared traditions. Not only the Gospels, but—my specialty—the accretion of spells and rituals from pre-Christian mystery cults that were attracted to Valdisme and helped to make it a target of the conservative Catholic majority. It is hard to believe, I know, in these days of Jews and Arabs, that old obscure beliefs are still... But no matter. About Professor Lebarbe, from what he told you, you must know. The Gospels are a collection of stories about miracles. Every saint of the church could perform miracles—in fact, it is a requirement for canonization, as everyone knows. Miracles? Witchcraft? How could villagers of the late Middle Ages distinguish between prayers drawn from the Gospels and the advice of local *mascoun*, if I may use the Provençal term, to pat a black cat, to burn a pile of chestnut leaves, to leave a bowl of milk by a lightning-struck tree? You see what I mean?"

"But the curse," interjected Michael, coming back to the main subject. "You read about a curse? Up at the grotto?"

"Yes. As far as I can remember. Maybe you didn't know, but when they pulled the bodies out of the cave, suffocated, there was an old woman who was still alive, just barely. And she cursed the soldiers...I am so sorry, I was in a hurry and I was looking for some familiar magical chants or spells and what she said was meaningless...so I don't really remember. And a few sentences later the paper was eaten away. I meant to go back sometime and copy the passage, but I was in the middle of some intriguing connections between St. Gens and St. Veran and at the moment it didn't seem relevant. Now...I wish—"

"An old woman...a curse...," Michael mused. "We haven't read anything like that so far."

"This is the first we've heard that there were any survivors," said Nicole. "What happened to her?"

"Oh! The captain Mormoiron—a terrible man—was so angry he ran her through with his sword right away. I remember that part from Jean's testimony, it is so clear in my mind, his rage...and he shouted something, *est-ce-que tu veuls...* I cannot remember. And then she spoke this curse and he stabbed her. That is what was so shocking that I must have ignored what she said exactly... all I saw in my mind was an old woman, dirty, ash-covered, barely alive, and this soldier bastard—you must forgive me—about to slaughter her!"

The four of them sat silent, shaken by the blossoming of that one moment, outside the grotto of Barigoule, a moment that seemed to be so minor, in the midst of a full-scale slaughter of innocents. Only twenty-five had died...but what was so different about their sacrifice? What was there that could possibly be covered up?

Mrs. Williams appeared through the french doors, behind her a large brown man in uniform pants and a tan, short-sleeved shirt with sweat stains. Chief Larkin did not have very helpful information. The dead attacker was still unidentified, except that he was white, in an Arkansas town where almost everyone was African American. An older maroon Toyota Camry had been found parked behind the roadhouse on the outskirts of Orbit. This was a town where every car was known and the strange car's presence was soon reported to the police and the plate number was phoned in to the state highway patrol. The number rang a bell right away; the car had been stolen from a hospital parking lot in Shreveport two nights before.

"Lady is a sixty-year-old nurse," said Chief Larkin, sitting down now to cool off with an iced tea, wiping his forehead with a large blue bandana. "Say she always forgets to take the keys." He looked at Boisset. "That dead man? He had no ID whatsoever. Sent his prints to the FBI but who knows when they gonna get 'round to checkin' them. Car was wiped clean. But what I figure, they musta been two guys. One start the fire and shoot the dog and t'other run in the door soon as the doc and Miz Hartman run out. Dog was shot with a .22 varmint rifle, which everybody in Arkansas got one somewhere, so you not gonner track that one down any time soon. Dead man not carring a fire arm. So there you are. Good thing you got two dogs. These fellas prolly didn't know you had two of 'em, found out the hard way."

The chief leaned down and patted Francine. "Oh. And the docs say that the victim, guy who ran in here? He died of a heart attack. Dog just chewed him a little. Just terrified him to death. So I told the state we quarantined your dog. I figure we can quarantine her right here, let ever'body forget about it."

Boisset and Marie Hartman watched the Tollivers drive away.

"I am still disturbed that someone took that journal," said the director.

"No one took the journal," said the librarian. And then, seeing his shocked face. "I lied to you, Henri. I read the testimony three days ago. And now I know what happened. But it is a thing that should be hidden. It is not for their world to know. The journal is locked away in the fireproofed safe. But now, I will show you."

CHAPTER NINETEEN

nselme hung up the phone in the cafe and walked outside to join two other old men at a table. There were four tiny empty coffee cups spread around an ashtray laden with cigarette butts. The skies over Barigoule were leaden and a soft breeze blew from the southeast, foreboding rain very soon. Chestnut leaves blew down the street in brown swirls. The old men had been arguing about the recent sale of a superstar footballer by the Marseille club for unbelievable millions, but they stopped quickly. Anselme looked all around, leaned forward and spoke rapidly.

"The two who were hired failed. The driver got away but the other was killed by a dog before he could light the fire."

"Killed by a dog? What shit!"

"And the Tolliver man? Did he—?"

"The other man, the driver...he came back and sat in the bar that night, just listening. He is a *noir*. Nobody noticed him there. Everyone was talking. There is a *femme de menage* at that damned institute. It is a town like this. No one can fart without everyone knowing in what key, and if you had cabbage for lunch. She told her nephew that the people were worried about a document...but the woman who runs the library says the document is not there.... it was stolen!"

"Stolen! *Quel connerie!* And do they know what was in the document?"

"This housemaid said the librarian can't remember. Said they were all sitting around with long faces. So maybe—"

"Maybe, maybe...," grunted Anselme. "Too many maybes. We have to talk to the big one, find out what we should do now. The Sullivan man and his wife are still here, still looking around."

"Maybe it's time for something to happen to the Sullivans?"

"No! Idiot! Then the police are down on us, full strength. Just now...they lose interest. But that Jew bastard, Dreyfus, he worries me. They tell me he is looking up old archives in the Palais des Papes in Avignon."

"What can he find there?"

"If we knew what he is looking for, we could get there first. But this is not an American library, you know, everything organized, easy to find. The archives in the Palais are a *pagaille*...a mess. You fight the spiders and the moths to find anything...a ten-watt light bulb to see by, and a bitch of an old librarian to watch you every second. Maybe easier to find the Jew."

Dreyfus closed the large folio he had been reading, blowing a cloud of dust over the old harridan of a librarian who had been shadowing him all morning, unimpressed with his police credentials. She snarled in fury, waving her hands at the motes in the air.

"Thank you for your patience, Madame," he said, scribbling some notes on his pad. "I must go now, but I look forward to our future happy collaboration." And ignoring her angry mumbling he made his way out the many tunnels into the gloomy overcast noon of the courtyard of the Palais des Papes. The monstrous edifice of the corrupt fourteenth-century popes loomed over him, gray and threatening. A biting wind was blowing from the north and the great square was almost deserted. A few derelicts huddled in corners. A couple of vendors were packing up their portable displays of tourist junk. Anyone who was French had flowed out into the adjoining street and its row of restaurants at the very stroke of twelve o'clock. A mime was still trying to amuse a handful of Dutch and Belgian tourists, who seemed more concerned by the threat of rain.

The mime had on an old black suit, with no shirt under it and all his visible skin was powdered dead white except for his blood-red lips and blackened eye sockets. He seemed to be miming a drunk trying to find his way home and running into walls, which made his black top hat fall off, although he always caught it. Dreyfus paused to watch for a moment, impressed to see the mime mimicking clumsy forward and backward motion and stumbling sideways while keeping his feet always in the same place. Now the drunk ran into an invisible wall in front of him and his hat fell off behind him, but with a spavined lurch, he bent forward, reached backward through his splayed legs and caught the hat at the last moment. He bowed to the little group and held out the hat. Even the bored tourists clapped and two of the men threw some coins into the topper.

The first drops of rain began to fall and the square rapidly cleared. Dreyfus ducked under the awning of the nearest café and ordered a coffee. The mime had disappeared somewhere. A talented one, he thought. Why was he wasting his time outside the Palais des Papes on a rainy day?

He was on his way to the underground parking when he passed the public *toilettes*, and his recent cup of coffee made him decide to pay a visit to avoid urgency later. It was a cold, squalid little room, dirty white tile and with a smelly urinal, overused and undercleaned. As he unzipped, Dreyfus as usual was glad that he didn't have to touch anything here that wasn't his. He was also glad he wasn't a woman, having to use the closet next door, no seat, probably, and normally out of paper. And then...as his urine splashed into the basin, full of brown water and a cluster of cigarette butts, he was suddenly aware that someone had entered behind him.

Spencer had been napping in his big armchair when the phone rang. He waited for Rosalind to pick up, then remembered she was working in the garden. He stumbled across the room, wondering, as usual, why he hadn't had a phone jack put in next to his chair.

"Allo?" he said, woozily.

"Spencer? It's Mike...hello?"

"Yes, yes, hello! Michael, where are you?"

"The airport lounge in Miami. We've got a flight to Paris in an hour. We—"

"But the book tour, I thought—"

"We decided to skip the rest. Only a few cities, and a lot has happened here." He filled in Spencer on the Arkansas attack, cutting off his more and more insistent questions.

"I'll explain everything when we get back. But...no, listen...I want you to phone Dreyfus and, yeah, probably, Jeannot as well. We'll get into Marseille tomorrow and the day after I want a conference, figure out what's going on and whether or not we're actually in a lot of danger."

"Danger...? I—"

"I know, I hate to leave you with that thought, old pal, but somebody is serious out there. So lock the doors tonight. After the thing with the fire in Arkansas, Nicole finally told me that when she was in the hospital, you know..? after that maniac hit her with the *boule*, she had a nightmare that involved your house...she was running along a road trying to find help there and your house was a wreck, all burned down."

"Burned down? My God, Mike! But this is a dream, right? Don't scare me!"

"Okay. A dream. And we are rational people. But what's been happening to us isn't rational, right? So...if I were you, I'd get someone from the village, someone with a dog, come and stay for a few days, maybe Jeannot. And now Nicole is signaling that they're about to board. *A tout à l'heure!*"

Dreyfus had risen through the ranks of police in Avignon. As a Jew, his progress had been slower than most because of the invisible, always denied, hard-core anti-Semitism in the country of his birth. Long years in uniform, assigned to the highest crime districts of Avignon, having to make countless late night arrests of dangerous car burglars, had made him a survivor. A normal male civilian, threatened in the normal vulnerable posture before a urinal, will first tuck his member into a safe place. But a sudden overwhelming feeling of menace made Dreyfus whirl, his hand darting to the small Beretta automatic under his arm instead of his naked penis, which whirled with him, spraying a few last drops on the tile floor as his sphincter clenched. He saw clearly the apparition of the mime from the square, moving swiftly, his face now snarling, his arm high in the air.

And now the arm came down before he could avoid it and a heavy object struck him on the side of his head, a glancing blow because he was able to flinch at the last moment. His last memory was the ear splitting blast of his pistol there in that tiled chamber, as he managed to free it from its holster under his arm and squeeze off one quick shot at the black suit in front of him. Then everything went black.

"Rosalind!" Spencer was calling out into the yard. It was another overcast day in Barigoule, with the tops of the hills to the north tucked into the bottom of the clouds streaming overhead. A chill wind was blowing from the north with a few drops of rain landing now and then on Spencer's face. He couldn't see Rosalind, and his voice rose to a shout as he rushed out into the yard where she'd been raking leaves just a few minutes ago. Around the corner of the house he found her sprawled on the ground.

"Oh-my-God, Roz!" It was almost a shriek into the wind.

To his immense surprise Rosalind leaped to her feet.

"Good fucking Christ, Spencer! What in the world…?"

Leyla Abdelaziz had been looking for her partner. She'd been down to the parking under the square of the Palais des Papes and found the dark blue police Renault. Instead of waiting down there in the caver*nous*, echoing parking levels, she decided to find Dreyfus up on the surface. So she was on the last few steps to the surface when she heard a shot.

She sprinted to the top, loosening her own automatic in the hip holster. She had just a glimpse of a black figure, coat swirling in the wind like batwings, hurtling away and around a corner. She was set to chase the fugitive but as she passed the public toilet an unmistakable waft of gunpowder smoke emerged, visible in the cold air. So she paused and looked into the restroom, immediately seeing a prostrate body, an outstretched arm with a Beretta still clutched in a rigid fist. Leyla looked regretfully after the fugitive who had disappeared, then darted into the toilet. Her partner was lying there unconscious on the dirty tiles. But what brought a gasp of horror to her lips was the sight of a naked penis emerging from the fly of his trousers.

Leyla Abdelaziz was a thoroughly moral Muslim young woman. Although in weak moments she had twice allowed treacherous lovers to lure her into the bed of sin on the promise of virtually immediate marriage, she had never actually seen the instrument that had done the dirty deed. Now she stood, pistol in hand, staring in shocked disbelief at her partner, whom duty insisted she aid and assist without hesitation, paralyzed by the sight of ten small centimeters of pale, male flesh…a tiny, insignificant part of the male anatomy, but one that she believed was at the bottom of every debased instinct of the masculine sex. And she had never seen one before.

But Leyla was a police officer and made of sterner stuff than the girls she knew on the streets of her youth who had fondled, dandled, and done unspeakable things to the bit of male anatomy she was now looking at. Two swift steps took her to the side of Inspector Dreyfus and a swifter kick adjusted the hanging folds of his raincoat to cover his shame. Then she knelt to feel the artery in his throat. It was beating strongly. So far as she could see there were no open wounds on his body.

She was gingerly feeling his head when she felt him wince, then he cried out softly in pain. His eyes jerked open and saw her face poised anxiously above his. He cursed and tried to climb to his feet. But almost immediately he realized that an aspect of his grooming needed attention.

Leyla, seeing the recognition in his eyes, leaped to her feet and rushed to the door of the toilet, turning her back.

"He's gone! I saw him running!" she exclaimed, hearing a quick zip behind her, and when she turned slowly, indeed Inspector Dreyfus was once more on his feet, and completely in uniform, so to speak.

"Goddam! That bastard hammered me with my prick out in the—." He looked at her intently. "You didn't—"

"No, no, no!" she almost screamed. "I just saw you lying...I thought you were dead at first."

Spencer fell back, stunned. "Roz? My God! I thought you—"

"Bloody hell, Spencer! You come racing round the house screaming my name! What the hell did you think?"

"I saw you!" he expostulated. "I saw you prostrate on the ground and I thought you were dead..."

Her face softened and she came up and put her arms around him. "Oh, Spencer, old bear! How could you think...just because I was lying on the ground? I saw two of my irises were gone and was listening for gopher noises...like at home."

Spencer expelled the breath he had been holding.

"Gophers? There are no gophers in France. Why do you think I moved here from California? No. No—," and he cut off her objections. "No. Michael just called with frightening news. Somebody tried to firebomb this place in Arkansas. That had the journal article? And then he said Nicole had had a dream that our house was burned down. It frightened me. And then I saw you—"

Rosalind kissed him. "I love you, fat bear. But we must do something now. Call Jeannot? And the detective?"

"Dreyfus? Do you think he'd come about a dream?"

Dreyfus and Abdelaziz were conferring about the attack of the mime. "Should we report this at all?" she was saying. "They will harrass you about being attacked. And by a stupid mime."

"That was no stupid mime. That was a malin, a clever criminal, and an attempted murderer. But...I am tempted to let it go, as you say..."

But they changed their minds, following the route followed by the fleeing mime. There was a spot of blood, then two or three, then gouts and spurts making a track toward one of the other underground parking entrances.

"He is hurt!" Abdelaziz yelled. "Maybe we can catch him." And she ran off quickly, just as quickly turned back as she saw her partner hobbling wearily after her.

"Dreyfus? Can you make it? I'm so sorry I forgot—" She clasped his arms, looked deeply into his grey eyes.

Dreyfus felt a sudden stab of sorrow, remembering the last time a lovely woman had looked so deeply into his soul. He reached out and patted her shoulder, the lightest of gestures. "No. I can follow. Just not so fast. And keep me with you. This man is dangerous and you...you have a pistol?"

She showed him her Glock .40 with pride, narrowed her eyes with a grim smile. "Just let him try..."

The blood trail, although copious, ended at a vacant parking slot on the first underground level. They stared at each other.

Dreyful sighed. "Now we have to report it. I wounded him, maybe badly, and they will have to get his DNA. And notify all the hospitals."

"But if he dies, maybe, in his car? On the way...?"

"The shooting was justified. You were the witness. And look at my head, the bruise. It hurts like hell..."

Abdelaziz looked uncertain. "True, a logical story. But the way they treat you...and me..."

"Yes. A Jew and a Beure. If we agree on something they have to believe us." He grunted something that was almost a laugh and took out his cell phone.

Leyla Abdelaziz felt the churning of conflicting emotions. She had immediately hated Dreyfus when assigned as his partner. A Jew? But she was clever enough to see that someone evil in the department had arranged this, perhaps hoping to provoke a confrontation and get rid of both of them. But only a few days with Dreyfus had confused her. He was so competent, so polite to her. And he was not handsome, but...she often wanted to comb his hair the right way or straighten his jacket. He needed taking care of, that was sure. And then she blotted the thoughts from her mind, thinking what her father, now retired and back in Morocco would say.

CHAPTER TWENTY

A small man wearing shapeless woolen pants, a brown sweater under an old field jacket, and a cloth cap stood by the bar in the Air France arrivals lounge at Marignane airport outside of Marseille. He was just an anonymous older Frenchman waiting there at the airport, typical, from the cigarette he was smoking nervously—to the pastis in front of him, which he hadn't touched. Several gendarmes on security duty had strolled around the huge building since he had arrived, and somewhere in the vicinity of these uniformed cops everyone knew there were the *flics* in plain clothes, watching the people watching the gendarmes. If you were a North African Islamist planning to plant a bomb or otherwise kill many people violently, you might be surprised to find yourself suddenly handcuffed by the woman going around emptying the waste cans.

Nobody gave the old man a second glance. Maybe the bartender wondered why he wasn't drinking his pastis. And then the tone sounded and the arrivals bulletin board announced that the AF 1615 flight from Paris had arrived and was disembarking. The old man now fixed his attention on a couple waiting outside the gate. The man was well fed, standing with his hands clasped behind his back, eyes riveted on the gate; the woman was thin and agitated, talking to the man. It would be at least ten minutes before the arrivals collected their baggage and started to emerge. Why don't they relax? thought the old man.

When finally the expected couple came out into the lounge, pushing a baggage cart, looking around, then falling into the arms of their waiting friends, the old man didn't hesitate. He drank half of his pastis, gestured at the barman to save his place, and walked quickly to a rank of telephones. His call was answered on the first ring.

"Yes?"

"They are all here. They can't be back to Barigoule for at least an hour. And going through Cavaillon this time of day—always traffic."

"Good. Thank you for the call. We'll prepare the welcome."

Out of an alley up near the chateau in Barigoule a figure emerged, carrying a canvas tote bag. He could have been the twin of the man at the airport, older, dressed in an old windbreaker and a cap. Surely he was one of the many residents in the hamlets outside town, going home after a few rounds in the village café. He walked steadily along the narrow road leading north from Barigoule. He was on top of the plateau here, an almost treeless expanse. The few trees along the road were black skeletons against the sky, burdened by huge, swollen masses of mistletoe. Broad fields stretched away on either side, featureless brown dirt, recently plowed and ready for the sowing of winter wheat. Fog was beginning to drift across the plateau in the late afternoon and the traveler was almost invisible. As he approached the Sullivan house he could see headlights coming slowly his way so he crouched quickly behind the *genet* lining the road. No other cars came in either direction so he sprinted the last few yards to the Sullivans' wrought iron gate. He had a key, but curiously, the gate was unlocked.

What idiots! He thought. *Now they will learn something.* And he took a five liter *bidon* of gasoline out of his tote bag.

Spencer's Peugeot waited in line at the Cavaillon exit and toll station. One could drive from the airport to this point on the autoroute in twenty minutes at 130 km per hour—or much faster if one needed to save three minutes. But then one had to wait at the toll gate, snake around an endless access road behind lumbering trucks to cross the Durance river, then drive through the big town of Cavaillon, often quite quickly, but never possible between five and seven in the afternoon. On the bridge over the Durance, Rosalind turned to Michael and Nicole in the back seat.

"I'm sorry, I know we all want to get home, but I just thought, I've been putting it off, but I really have to get just a few things at Leclerc—would you mind awfully?"

Spencer started to protest but Nicole responded. "It's okay, Spence. We don't have a thing at home to eat. I can pick up some bread and a barbecued chicken, maybe some lettuce for a salad."

"Better idea," said Rosalind. "Get your chicken and salad, bring it over and we'll all eat together. It's been so long."

"Sounds fine to me," echoed Michael. "It won't take a minute." And they turned off the roundabout into the parking lot of the big supermarket.

The shadowy figure moved swiftly through the Sullivan garden. He was looking at the big picture window that they never shuttered and thinking, *I'll just break it all in, jump inside, throw all the wood furniture in the one room, then soak it with my gasoline.* But in the fog he didn't see the low stone bench, caught it at mid-shin and sprawled on the ground, cursing and grabbing for the gas can. One of his arms was up in the air. Suddenly he was shocked out of his wits when out of nowhere a huge tan dog appeared and clamped down on his arm so viciously that he thought he could feel the bone crack. He screamed and fought the dog's jaws, but the creature looked to be well over fifty kilos and wouldn't budge.

"*Lâche!*" said a voice near him, and the dog let go. He grabbed his injured forearm with the other hand and looked up, eyes wide.

A giant man was standing, back to the west, silhouetted against the sky. He tried to get up, but the man suddenly kicked him so hard in the side that the pain made him retch, and then heave and heave to get his breath started once more.

"Tell me at once! Who sent you to do this? You tell me, or I break every fucking rib in your chest." There was a softer kick, but right on the first spot and agony made a red curtain in front of his eyes. He held up a hand, gasping for breath in order to speak.

"It was...the big one. Someone came from the service station and gave me the can..." He pointed at the red gas can, slowly spilling its contents onto the lawn.

"Who came from the service station?" The foot hovered above his ribs, threatening.

"No, no! Please! Stop!" He described the young man, and the man who had attacked him thought for a minute.

"Yes, I know him. And what did you think this would accomplish...all of you imbeciles?"

The man on the ground now showed a bit of temper.

"It came down from...from on high. The big one. And you should look out, Jeannot. You are getting in the way!"

Jeannot chuckled, kicked the man softly again in the ribs. "'Getting in the way.' Maybe getting in the way of having headlines in *La Provence*, maybe even national papers, or TV. You know the local police investigate nothing, unless there is news in the paper. Then they make a show, send some Paris types down to be on the *télé*. So far, you people killed a professor, then an old man with a harmless book, then you attack my friend Tolliver in a library in California, then in some way you try to burn down a building in America, in a state I can't even pronounce. What do you think? If you burn down this house, it will be just a coincidence? *Hein*? Stupid, stupid! There are no geniuses there in Avignon, the police.

But give them enough to put together...they will start thinking of the publicity they will get and Barigoule will be swarming!"

"But, Jeannot...the big one...?"

"He is insulated. Out of touch. For once, let me handle things. Right now I don't even know what to do with you. *"Simba!"* he called, and the dog standing over the man began to growl.

"An African dog, bred with a mastiff. She can't bark. You'll never hear her coming, but she can kill you in ten seconds. Maybe less. Shall we test it?"

"No! No, no, no, Jeannot! Whatever you say! I will tell the big one—"

"You will not speak with the big one. I will. You...you should go away for a week somewhere. Let this blow over. Understand? Or the dog..."

The man was silent for a moment, then... "You know, my daughter and her husband live up in Drome. Maybe I should visit...they always ask me..."

"*Bon!* It's settled then. And careful, don't move too fast. The dog is nervous."

Spencer's Peugeot stopped in front of the wrought iron gates and Rosalind got out to open them.

"I've got to get an electronic gate opener," Spencer said to the Tollivers, "But here in France they don't seem to have them, like just ready-to-buy in hardware stores. You ask for them and get referred to security companies who will install them for five thousand euros, on condition that you also subscribe for twenty thousand a year to their complete protection program."

"It's like...," started Nicole, but then the gate was opened and there was Jeannot welcoming them, a large tan dog by his side. They got out of the car wondering, the dog prancing around wagging its tail, trying to lick their hands.

Later they were all sitting around the big table in the Sullivan's kitchen, finishing the chicken, and a third bottle of Cairanne. Simba had volunteered to dispose of the bones.

"It's no problem," Jeannot said, watching the dog, grinning and scratching his three-day-old beard. "She knows how to eat chicken bones. And anything else too. Henri left her with me for a while...you remember him, from the team? He's picking up some money, playing thirteens in Bayonne for a few matches."

"We're grateful you came by," said Spencer. "I know it was silly, just based on a dream, but we worried anyway."

"Well. No problems. Not a soul came by—"

The phone rang and Rosalind went over to answer it.

"I wouldn't want to mess with Simba—," Michael started to say, but then Rosalind shushed him, her hand over the phone. She looked wild.

"It's Dreyfus. He says he is on his way over. And some people from the National Police. Something happened yesterday in Avignon but he wouldn't talk about it on the phone."

CHAPTER TWENTY-ONE

TO:Minister of Interior

FROM: Juge d'instruction, Avignon

RE:Certain suspected homicides; relationship to attempted assault on police officer; possible relationship to events in the United States.

On 30 May Professor Lebarbe, Jules, University of Provence, retired, either fell or was pushed with fatal results into the Sorgue river emerging with great force from the Fontaine de Vaucluse. His glasses were found at the edge of the chasm, superimposed by a footprint subsequently identified as a Runnerman sports shoe, a brand marketed by Carrefour stores by tens of thousands. A witness, Sullivan, Rosalind (v. infra), claimed to have seen such a shoe on a nun. A witness to the presence of Prof. Lebarbe, Mme. Sullivan, and others, at lunch, one Borie, Jacques, a waiter, was questioned at the scene, but later disappeared and is still missing. Inspector Dreyfus, David, was ordered as an agent of the Police Judiciaire to pursue the investigation. Inquiries were made as to the location of nuns from conservative orders in the vicinity (the sister was in full habit), with no results.

On 26 August M. Rousset, Jean Claude, was en route from Lacoste to Barigoule, supposedly to show some historical documents to M./Mme. Sullivan. On the Joucas road M. Rousset was ostensibly forced off the road by a truck and killed. A witness (Fothergill, Anne,

English) from a distance of over two hundred meters claimed that a car driven by nuns stopped and examined the wreckage, then drove off. Inspector Dreyfus heard of the reference to a nun and investigated. Local inquiries as to nuns in this vicinity were also without result.

On 25 September M. Tolliver, Michael, (with spouse Nicole), a resident of Barigoule, acquainted with the Sullivan couple and the deceased Prof. Lebarbe, was engaged in a promotion for his book in the United States. He was looking for French historical documents in the library of the University of California at Berkeley in that state when he was supposedly attacked and knocked momentarily unconscious. He claims that the document he was looking for was stolen or mutilated. He subsequently traveled to the state of Arkansau (?) to find a copy of this document and arrived at a so-called Institute of Bible Studies to find that a madman had tried to set a fire but had been killed by a dog. The Federal Bureau of Investigation of the United States was informed, as it appeared that the two crimes were connected.

On 10 October Inspector Dreyfus, after consulting records in the Palais des Papes, was attacked in a public convenience by a mime, who knocked him unconscious, but not before he was able to fire a shot from his firearm. His partner, corporal Abdelaziz, Leyla, arrived immediately at the scene. They followed blood spots to the underground parking of the Palais des Papes, where the trail ended, obviously when the assailant took his car and left. Inquiries to hospitals and clinics have had no result.

The juge d'instruction ordered an investigation and interview of all persons involved.

Everyone was clustered in the Sullivan living room. Dreyfus had arrived with a bandage around his head and a shockingly pale complexion. He was accompanied by a uniformed gendarme with epaulets denoting high rank and a tough-looking middle-aged man, tan and fit, wearing a leather jacket, jeans, and running shoes.

"I present my superior, Commissaire Barbu," said Dreyfus speaking in French in a pained voice, nodding to the jeans-clad man. "And Lieutenant Francès, from the national police. Commissaire Barbu will conduct the questioning. I would like Jeannot to stay to attest some details, also to help translate if there is a difficulty.

Barbu evidently felt no difficulty. He began immediately in almost perfect English.

"I had a very strict course in English at Aix, ladies and gentlemen, then I attended your FBI Academy at Quantico. If I make some mistakes, I hope you will forgive me; I was not speaking English a long time. Okay?"

They all nodded, still stunned by the sudden descent of major French police authority.

"Very well." He looked around, made eye contact with everyone in the room. "I will describe the events that have taken place and will ask some questions about details. Please do not interrupt until I am through. Please do not venture information I have not asked for. You will have a chance to explain other matters afterward. Understood?" He set a tape recorder on the coffee table and they could see the little spools unwinding.

They all agreed. There was a knock on the front door and the policemen turned, startled. Jeannot was on his feet like a big cat and opened the door to reveal Marius and the village policeman standing there. He was about to say something, but Lieutenant Francès stood quickly and fired some angry French at the newcomers, who sheepishly backed away. Francès barked an additional command at the village policeman and the two men disappeared into the night.

"I told your local policeman to stay here and patrol the grounds to keep other curiosity seekers away," said the lieutenant. "I hope he enjoys the weather."

Barbu went quickly over the various incidents, the two killings, the attacks in the U.S., the attack that afternoon on Dreyfus. He asked each one of the Sullivans and Tollivers if their memory of the event was the same, and several times he turned to Jeannot for a rapid conversation in French. Finally, he sighed.

"I notice your impatience. But this is our method. First of all, collect the data. Description. Only then do we go to analysis, in this case, *why are these violent attacks happening?* Mr. Tolliver. You have been squirming so long. Now will you please offer your analysis."

So Michael began with the story of the massacre. The grotto. The curiosity about the events of April 1545. The decision to do serious research. Professor Lebarbe had been most helpful—but then, immediately, he was killed. Michael explained the basic suspense thriller plot: the device by which every person who seemed to have an answer to the mystery was found dead. Lieutenant Francès frowned in disbelief, but Barbu nodded, smiling.

"Yes, yes. I read those books. Raymond Chandler, Agatha Christie. But also of course our own immortal Simenon and his inspector Maigret. A formula, of course." He turned to the gendarme lieutenant. "You are shaking your head, Pierre, because in our work we deal ninety-nine percent with stupid, stupid people. The burglar who gets drunk and falls asleep in the bar he has broken into. The husband who bludgeons his rich wife to death, then sends his clothes to the cleaners, where we recover them spotted with her blood."

He turned to Michael. "This is our normal work. So we are surprised to see someone actually clever, covering tracks...if that is what is happening here." He turned to Spencer. "And Monsieur Rousset?"

Spencer obliged, recounting their visit to Lacoste, the chance encounter with Rousset, and his promise to bring them some revealing documents. Rosalind came out of the kitchen and refreshed all the coffee cups. Spencer went on.

"And you know, the funny thing, the whole time there at Lacoste, you know? When he was trying to talk to us? He kept breaking it off because these old men were obviously trying to get close and listen. I thought at first he was paranoid, but then, you know, every time I looked around there was some peasant in a cap trying to sit down at the same table. Right, Roz?"

"Yes, and I know I've seen some of those faces...maybe here in Barigoule. A cherry farmer for sure. That creepy man we played *boule*s against. And then the next day—"

"Yes. The next day. That was when Rousset was on his way over here and was murdered."

"And you learned of this...when?"

"Well. The report went to the gendarmerie in Gordes, then Inspector Dreyfus here heard about it...the connection between a murder and nuns, and next thing we knew he was here, telling us about it."

Dreyfus nodded, looking down at some notes. "Yes. I hear about a suspected murder, and some nuns, and it is like an alarm bell. We came immediately, I and corporal Abdelaziz, and received the information about the document."

"And this document?" said Barbu. "I heard the name before in a report, but could you tell me again?"

"Yes...," said Michael and Spencer at the same time. They looked at each other and Michael went on.

"The document was an article in the *Bulletin de la société des études vaudoises* for 1973. It contained testimony taken in 1595 from a young man here in Barigoule⌐⌐—actually in 1595 he was an old man—but anyway, a man who had been forced to tell the papal troops where the women were hidden. The testimony continued to the point when the great fire had suffocated all the women in the grotto...and then, just as the witness was telling about an old woman, still alive, the last pages of the article are missing. The article in the library at the University of California in Berkeley, the article from the library of Brigham Young University—all have been mutilated."

"And don't forget Rousset's copy," added Rosalind. "It was only a photocopy, but the last two pages were missing. We could see the bits against the staple."

Barbu and Lieutenant Francès exchanged glances. Finally Barbu turned back to the others.

"Okay. I heard this from Dreyfus already last summer. The mysterious crime five hundred years ago that someone is covering up still today. Mr. and Mrs. Tolliver—and Sullivan? You see my position. Sitting in this room, talking with you of Raymond Chandler, of Christie, of Maigret...I agree that persons unknown may be trying to prevent you from completing your research. To me, it is fascinating. But have you any idea—"

Now Lieutenant Francès began to laugh and Barbu turned to look at him and nod agreement.

"Yes...have you any idea how this story will look as a written report in certain offices in Paris? No—let me finish—" as Rosalind started to protest.

"In the present atmosphere, when terrorists are bombing targets all over the civilized world, authorities in Paris will look at a report like this and only wonder how to punish the imbeciles who wasted their time."

"But...but someone attacked a policeman!" exclaimed an aroused Rosalind, who was waving her hands. "They almost killed Inspector Dreyfus—"

But Dreyfus was already shaking his head, resigned, as Barbu went on. "Inspector Dreyfus has a distinguished record. He has sent over one hundred stupid criminals to prison over the last ten years. The powers that be, here in France, see fit to let even violent criminals out after only a few years, perhaps seeking revenge. Who knows who this mime is...or was?" Barbu once again was trying to wave down objections from Spencer and Rosalind.

"I assure you, I am sending my report—a *descriptive* report— simply listing the events that seem to be linked. I am completely sure that the National Police will pursue very seriously the attack on Inspector Dreyfus. We do not permit police to be attacked in this country. But about the events of 1545? I must warn you not to be optimistic."

TO:Juge d'instruction, Avignon

FROM:Ministry of Interior

RE:Recent violence in the department of Vaucluse

With reference to your request for an investigation of the incidents enumerated in yours of 16-10. Despite the suspicious disappearance of a witness after the death of Professor Lebarbe, the case must be listed as accidental death. Reports of a death-dealing nun are due to an overactive imagination and should not be repeated in official correspondence. This is a direct order from the minister himself.

Monsieur Rousset drove off the road after lunch on a hot day. An old man, with an alcohol level almost over the legal percentage. An Englishwoman saw a nun—these nuns again—inspect the car and then leave. The Englishwoman was almost three hundred meters from the scene. There is no evidence of a truck on the scene, after consultation of all the logs of construction companies operating in the Luberon that afternoon. Once again. No nuns.

As to Monsieur Tolliver's adventures in the USA, we decline to comment. We understand that he reported both incidents to the Federal Bureau of Investigation, which has promised to investigate. An informal communication from a colleague in the FBI advises us that unless Muslim terrorism is involved these incidents must remain of the lowest priority. And the attack on Inspector Dreyfus is undoubtedly a reglement de comptes, some misguided criminal arrested by him long ago, seeking revenge. The ministry continues to insist that criminal sentences be longer and enforced, to prevent this kind of retaliation. We ask you to instruct Inspector Dreyfus not to speculate further on extraneous motives for the attack. At the same time, we suggest a commendation be put in the files of both Inspector Dreyfus and Corporal Abdelaziz for their courageous counterattack on the criminal, whom we expect to apprehend shortly.

The official from the Ministry of Interior in Paris looked over his letter. He made a satisfied twist of the lips that could almost have been a smile. *There*, he thought. We silence any talk of nuns. *We make a commendation of a Jew and a damned Arab policewoman. All pressure groups taken care of. Except one.*

And he picked up one of the phones on his desk. The call was answered at once. The person on the other end answered cautiously.

"I see your number on the phone display. Does this mean the matter we spoke of is laid to rest?"

"As much as possible. And your person down there will stay informed. Don't call again. The ministry has no further connection with this *connerie*."

CHAPTER TWENTY-TWO

Dreyfus and *Leyla Abdelaziz* were looking at film from the surveillance cameras down in the underground parking of the Palais des Papes. The times of the film scrolled across the top of the screen. They were looking at vehicles that had entered the parking on level two, east side, from 1100 on the previous morning. Cars came and went on the grainy black and white film.

"There!" exclaimed Abdelaziz, pointing at the screen. A dark green Renault Espace slowly stopped, backed, then reversed into a vacant parking space.

"That's the space!" she said excitedly.

"Quiet...just watch," cautioned Dreyfus. The driver's door opened and a man got out, wearing a black overcoat. He removed it, revealing his black suit, then took out a small suitcase and placed it on the seat. He opened it, revealing a mirror built into the lid. He looked closely into the mirror, took out a sponge and added white powder to his already white face. He then took out a black top hat and what looked like a short nightstick, locked everything else inside the car and walked off camera, tucking the night stick under his coat.

"Back up the film," said Dreyfus. "Let's get the licence number when he comes in."

The screen *flick*ered, steadied, revealing a vacant corridor. Now appeared the Renault van and Abdelaziz stopped the film. "Can you make it out?" she asked.

Dreyfus had a magnifying glass. "Ends in 30. That's from Gard. 320...no, 328...GV 30 That's it. Get on the computer to Nîmes and see—" But Abdelaziz was already phoning.

A shadow fell across the desk. A large man in a dark suit.

"Dreyfus?"

"Yessir. We were just—"

"Is this about the attack yesterday?"

"Yessir. We identified the car—" Behind him he could hear Abdelaziz talking with someone on the phone.

"Inspector. I'm sorry. You are off that case. It is inappropriate for a police officer to investigate a personal attack on his own person. It smacks of retaliation. Understand?"

Dreyfus knew better than to argue. He nodded his head. "Yessir. I understand the policy. But here is the film of the assailant's car. If the department wishes to—"

Abdelaziz interrupted him. "Inspector. Nîmes says the car is of a dentist and was reported stolen two nights ago."

One of Michael's favorite chores was taking out the garbage. It was ironic, he always thought, remembering the agony, the pleading, the excuses, even managing to escape his parents' house in the evening when he knew he would have to take out the garbage. And there, in Palo Alto, the garbage only had to go out the back door and directly into one of the galvanized cans standing in the driveway beside the garage. Maybe a task of twenty seconds.

Here in Barigoule there were village garbage collection bins at each end of town, partly concealed behind attractive stone-walled enclosures. Although they were about equidistant from the Tolliver house, Michael preferred the collection area to the west, which stood next to the village *lavoir*, about sixty yards from his back door. There, emerging from the side of the low wall holding back the cliff two lead pipes set into a decorative carved stone plaque spurted spring water out into a small basin. From the side of the basin a stone trough led over to the *lavoir*, the much larger ancient stone basin where the women of Barigoule had once done their laundry, as recently as the decades after the Great War. Thirty years ago, a thoughtful mayor noted an unusual surplus in the village budget and decided to beautify the *lavoir* and fountain. The drainage was set to rights, the muddy ground was capped with handsome cut stone bricks, and a roofed shelter using antique tiles was built over the *lavoir* in the manner of village architecture from previous centuries. The unlovely garbage bins next to the *lavoir* were enclosed, mostly out of view, and now when tourists entered Barigoule from the west they tended to pause and admire fountain and basin. Everyone in town now had hot running water in their homes and most had washing machines, so the *lavoir* stood only as a monument to former days, to tweak the nostalgia of elderly Belgian, Dutch, and German tourists. In the warmer parts of the year the fountain was much visited by groups of cyclists, who knew from the cyclist grapevine that the spring water of Barigoule was pure and safe.

Michael loved walking at night down a side street—an alley, really—to take a sack of garbage down to the collection point. By nine in the evening everyone was home, the houses dark and shuttered, emitting only slits of blue light from television sets, except for the glow from Jeannot's café at the other end of town, where a few locals lingered over coffee and marc in a cloud of cigarette smoke that could drive out the tender-hearted. There were few streetlights in Barigoule, and these were of an economic wattage, casting only a dull orange light in their immediate vicinity. Michael could imagine himself totally alone in the world, walking down the long alley between stone houses and looking up at the sky, where he could see the constellations of the north—the

Bear, Cassiopeia——with a clarity unknown to any city dweller. His only companions in the blackness were the village cats, either shadows that quickly slipped away before an intruder, or well known friendly cats that would rub against his leg as he passed their houses. As he passed a side alley, a dog would always bark, a German shepherd owned by a nervous widow who believed she had to keep the dog out at night to preserve her from the dangers of the neighborhood.

Michael was walking down to the village garbage bins, relaxed as usual, mind emptied, savoring the utter quiet of the night. He passed the alley of the German shepherd and was surprised. For once no dog barked. *The curious incident of the dog in the night time,* he thought, and grinned. Once at the bins, he lifted the lid of the nearest and slung his black garbage bag into the dark interior. As usual, he turned to the *lavoir* and rinsed off his hands in the clean, cold water, wiping them on his jeans. Then he set off back up the lane toward home. Midway along he had to pass a small yard hedged with bushes. Tonight, as he came abreast a quiet voice came out of the bushes, almost giving him a heart attack.

Monsieur Tolliver!

Oui? He responded, stopping and looking to his left.

The voice continued in English. "Please keep walking. Just remember...there are some here who will help you. You are not alone." There was a rustling in the bushes and he sensed that the speaker had left. Obediently he kept walking. He was almost to his own back door when he heard the shepherd, in the distance, begin to bark.

The next day Michael had just gotten off the phone with Dreyfus and was reporting to the Sullivans, who had joined Michael and Nicole at their house for breakfast. The table was littered with the remains of croissants and scrambled eggs. Nicole was making another pot of coffee.

"Dreyfus says he's been taken off the case and that the ministry has no intention of pursuing the question."

"What a ridiculous—"

"What bullshit—!" Spencer and Rosalind began to respond. Michael put up a hand.

"He was being very formal...recorded, undoubtedly... just letting us get the message. But I have a feeling that he's still interested and I bet he'd like to be kept up to date, anything else we find out. He made a point of asking if we still had his cell number."

"In other words, don't call him at work," Rosalind was swift to point out.

The day outside was sunny, crisp and clear and the countryside was inviting. Nicole was looking out the window, bringing the coffee to the table.

"You know," she said meditatively, "I was just thinking...you know the dream I had? About the grotto?"

"The dream? But you dreamed about our house," Rosalind started to say, but Michael was nodding, yes.

"No, it was part of the same dream. I told you about the house being burned...but it went on, the dream, and I wound up somehow in the grotto—and you remember, I never actually went in with you guys—but there I was in the grotto, looking up at the roof, and I saw, clear as anything, some writing on the ceiling. And in some way, I felt that the writing was protecting me from this other voice telling me just to give up. And then Michael woke me up. You know, it's such a nice day, maybe we could go up there again, take really good flashlights, and see if there's anything written there..."

The Sullivans looked at each other. Michael started to say something, but Rosalind spoke first.

"Yes! By God, let's do something! We can take some good lights and—"

"But, do you suppose it's safe, with what's been happening?" Spencer sounded unsure.

"Come on! Let's do it. And let's call Jeannot...ask him to bring that monster dog."

"But he's working today—" Spencer had lots of excuses, obviously thinking more of his burned house than of discoveries in a dank cave.

A call to Jeannot's bar. Yes, Jeannot could join them and bring Simba, not to worry.

The last time they had visited the grottos it was May and it had been warm. Today it was fall, clear and sunny, but with a bite to the north wind. The Sullivans and Tollivers parked up the old dirt road at the only point where they could park without blocking the road to residents further along. They stood in a stand of pines and waited until Jeannot arrived in his BMW. Simba bounded out of the car and pranced around like a puppy, sensing adventures. Jeannot led the way along the footpath, the cliff face to the right.

"You know, in the summer some kids went in the grotto, the main one, and found a narrow hole leading back into the rock. They had flashlights and were having a great time until they got to a narrow place no one wanted to go through. So they decided to come back...and only then they discovered there were some branching of tunnels they hadn't noticed on the way in. So they took the one they thought was the right one...and it ended. So they went back, but they didn't know which tunnel they had turned off from, you understand? And then the batteries in the flashlights started to go dead. So these children were smart, they thought, we must just stay in one place, our parents know we are here, when we don't come home they will come find us. And you know? The parents came and called into the grotto. And there was no answer. Then they were terrified and called the firemen and they were lucky that two of the firemen were, how do you say, *spéléologues*, cave explorers. They went in leaving a string behind so they could find their way back. And it was not until the next morning, finally, that the children were found. Now the department is thinking, they should put a gate on the grottos."

"Oh no!" said everyone except Nicole, who didn't want to go in the grotto at all. But it was her idea, and now she was committed.

"It reminds me of *Tom Sawyer*." Spencer was stalling a little. Jeannot looked at him curiously.

"It's a famous American *roman*," said Michael. "*Tom Sawyer* and his little girlfriend were children who were trapped in a cave like this with a maniac."

"Thank you for reminding me, Mikey." Nicole was looking anxiously at the slope ahead. They had reached the point where the steep hillside, overgrown with small oaks and brush, climbed up to the limestone cliff face. Michael led the way up a narrow trail, ducking beneath oak branches and trying not to let brush snap back in the faces of his followers. The slope was slippery from the last rains and Spencer, grumbling as usual, was the first to slip and come up with mud on his hands and knees. They finally gathered on the ledge at the top of the slope and looked about.

"The grottos are to the north," said Jeannot, and led the way with Simba. In the fall some of the trees had lost their leaves and they could see where they were going. They passed the first cave, then the grotto where the rock overhead had fallen in, leaving it open to the sky. Jeannot ventured in a few steps.

"No dead animals today," he said. "When I come up here I always look, just in case some idiot hunter or truffle poacher has fallen in." There was a moment of silence as all the implications of such an event were considered.

"It has happened, you know...last time was maybe ten years ago. A hunter, in winter. He was lucky...a broken leg, broken back, but someone heard him yell the next day. They came, they called the firemen, luckily, because they are medically trained and saw the back was broken." Jeannot was looking at the ground in the middle of the clearing.

"And you know what? Right under where this hunter was lying, they saw just the end of a bone, and they dug down and there was a whole skeleton."

"You mean...someone had fallen in and never been found?" Rosalind was excited with the mystery.

"Someone. Yes. But they did some tests and found that this mystery person fell into the open grotto more than 4,000 years ago."

"My God! And did archaeologists come up and continue the—" Now Michael was excited.

"Archaeologists? I am afraid not. The local departmental society of archaeologists asked to conduct a small—how you say, *fouille*— excavation, thank you, Mike...but you know, the grottos lie on the land of the chatelain, and he said, 'I will have my people excavate.' And he is very influential. Up in the castle he has a huge collection of artifacts from the ancient...very ancient times around here. He has many stone axes, flint knives, and skeletons—who knows how many—but he lets no one into the castle to see."

"But that's ridiculous!" said Michael. "In the U.S., all ancient ruins have to be excavated publicly, even on private land—"

Jeannot held up a hand, smiling gently. "Maybe. You could check. But in France we have the same laws. Unfortunately, there are matters of greater interest. The Roman shipwreck at Madragues. The new cave paintings in Ardeche—and even there the local owners are suing the government and I think they won. Here? Our grottos are a...what did you say the other day, Michael?"

"A blip on the screen?"

"Exactly. A blip on the screen."

"Are we going to the main grotto, or what?" asked Nicole, hugging herself against the cool wind.

They passed the sheepherder's grotto, inched around a curve in the cliff and saw before them the same opening that Michael had seen months ago, fleeing frantically from the boar. It was an innocent pool of darkness at the bottom of the cliff, still lying in shadow; the morning sun had not crossed the meridian yet. The prospect was singularly uninviting and everyone immediately felt much colder than the outdoor temperature warranted.

"Give me the flashlight," said Nicole, grabbing one from Spencer's willing hand and stalking toward the cave. Some spirit had electrified her and she felt compelled, beyond all fear and hesitation. She dropped to her knees at the entrance to the cave, crawled to the inner opening quickly, and looked back, trying to compose her features into an impish laugh.

"Last one in...is—"

"We're right behind you, Nicky," said Michael, just behind her, shooting his light in ahead of her. The assembly took a few minutes. Neither Spencer nor Jeannot had an easy time squirming through the hole on their bellies. Simba could not be tempted to enter and prowled around outside, whining.

Once in, they could all stand up and examine the inner cavern. This time, they had a much greater concentration of torches and the space was almost as light as a small apartment living room at night.

"Up there," said Nicole, pointing to the back of the cave. There the wall rose and then curved back into an alcove a few feet deep, providing a flat platform below the ceiling of the main cavern. "In my dream I was lying up there, I swear...I know I've never been in here before but it's so clear—"

"Maybe I should go up there—," Michael started to say.

"No, no! I have to go first. And give me the strongest light!"

Jeannot had a six-volt lantern with a magnesium bulb that was almost too bright, but Nicole took it and with a boost from Michael climbed up into the alcove, lay on her back, and focused the lamp directly overhead. She was silent for a tick or two.

"I can't really make anything out...so dusty...could someone pass me a hanky, anything, rub some of this crud away. Thank you Jeannot...shit! It's all crumbling down on my face, in my eyes...just a minute, if I can squinch over to the side here a bit..."

They waited, Rosalind biting her tongue, desperate to say something, anything at all, to help.

"Oh my God! There *is* something written here!"

It was almost an anticlimax, everyone having assumed that Nicole's dream had some basis, such is our irrational faith in the supernatural.

"It's in French...well, of course, wouldn't it be? Or maybe not. It starts...well, it's almost Latin...'*veramen vous lou dise...*' does that sound like something?"

"It is Provençal," said Jeannot, in a strained voice.

"Oh, great! And we all know Provençal, right?" said Rosalind with a sarcastic laugh.

"But you see, we have the camera," said Spencer. "Just take two or three shots, make sure you cover the whole thing, then we can get a text, have it translated...there's got to be someone around here who knows Provençal—"

"Even me, a little bit," said Jeannot, nervously, making it sound like "a *leetle beet*." "But then we have to have the pictures developed, and printed, and how long—"

"No, no," protested Spencer. "It's a digital camera. We just go home and put it on the screen, blow it up, amplify the contrast, whatever. You'll see."

Nicole now had the camera and quickly took four flash photos of the four quadrants of the ceiling, blinding everyone in the cave. There was a sudden, almost imperceptible twinge in the rock beneath them, a feeling any Californian would immediately diagnose as a tiny earthquake.

"Oh Jesus!" cried Rosalind. "The whole thing's going to cave in!"

But the feeling subsided immediately and they relaxed.

"I thought they didn't have earthquakes here," said Spencer. "It's the one reason we came." Simba was now whining in a higher voice outside the cave.

Rosalind laughed. "That and no gophers. Why else?"

"Help me down," said Nicole quickly. "So we can get out of here." And the five of them crawled rapidly out of the cramped entrance hole, to be greeted with wet kisses by a joyful Simba.

"There have been a few little earthquakes over the centuries, they say," mused Jeannot, on the way back to the cars. "But never anything big. Your own house would have fallen in, Michael, those days, the state it was in."

They all gathered at the Sullivans, in order to view the digital photos on Spencer's fancy computer. No one wanted a real lunch so Rosalind passed around platters of sausage, ham, cheese, and bread. A bottle of a good local Côtes de Ventoux was opened.

There was a bit of cursing when the pictures refused to download at first, but Rosalind reinterpreted the dialogue windows that kept popping up in French and suddenly the screen was filled with a crystal-clear photo of a rough stone surface with smudgy black writing on it. Spencer quickly printed out the four exposures, scissors and tape were found, and with only a little heated discussion the various parts were cut and joined to produce a readable text, which they all stared at in wonder.

Veramenvousloudise ni a daqueliquesouneici

Quenoungoutarandela mort d aquiquevegonlou

Fieude l omevenidinssounreinage

"It looked like charcoal or something," said Nicole. "And when I was brushing the surface I could feel that it was like scratched in first, and then blackened with something."

"Maybe written with the burned end of a stick, bit by bit, lighting the stick again," added Michael. "After all, if that was written, uh, back then, there were plenty of people to help. It's a good thing you didn't rub too hard...we'd have lost it."

"Yes. But what does it say?" Spencer sounded mystified.

"*Veramen*...it sounds like Latin. Could that be Provençal, Jeannot?"

Jeannot leaned forward. "*Veramen vous lou dise*...could be something like *'en verité vous le dis—'*"

"My God," broke in Rosalind. "'Verily I say to you...' It's from the Bible, I bet. And probably from the Gospels, everything we know about the Vaudois—"

"You mean...you think someone from the massacre actually wrote this? An old Vaudois?" Jeannot sounded dubious. "You know, in five hundred years many people went in the grotto. A hundred years ago everyone still spoke Provençal here. It could have been anyone."

"But my dream...it was so real—." Nicole stopped suddenly and laughed. "I know it sounds ridiculous, basing theories on dreams. You're probably right, Jeannot." Now she was hugging herself again, almost shivering. "But, you know, I had the dream, and we just went there and found what I saw in my dream...it's creepy."

"First things first," said Spencer, firmly. "Let's translate the bloody thing and see if it means anything. What did you say, love? 'Verily I say to you...?' Okay, then what?"

"But everything Jesus says in the Gospels starts like that," put in Michael. "It's like any puzzle; we have to narrow it down, find other parts we can solve. Jeannot?"

"I have been reading it over and over, Mike. Sometimes when you say it quickly you can guess the French. The next part I don't get, but then, que soun eici que noun *goustaran de la mort* sounds like '...*qui sont ici qui non gouteront de la mort...*'"

"'those who are here who will not taste of death...'" translated Rosalind. "Don't we have a Bible somewhere, Spence?"

"Of course. It's in the library next to the atlas and the Indian cookbooks. But look, I was talking with the priest up at the cathedral a few days ago...he's a nice old man, he'll know the passage right off, why don't I just call him." And Spencer picked up the phone, dialed, and then nodded his head at the company... yes, he's there.

Spencer made small talk in French with Father Jean-Claude for a few moments and then claimed that he and his guests were trying to remember something from the Bible, probably the Gospels, that went, 'Verily I say to you...some who are here who will not taste of death...' They could all see Spencer waiting for an answer, then nodding his head, raising his eyebrows, and finally thanking the priest and hanging up.

"Well. Father Jean-Claude was fine at first but when I asked him about the quote he sounded nervous and irritable. He hemmed and hawed for a bit and then he said he was sure there was nothing in the Gospels like that. Can that be right?"

"He's an old man. The young ones don't know the Bible any more, but if Jean-Claude says it's not in the Bible, I think he's right." Jeannot seemed convinced. Michael and Nicole were not so sure, but then Rosalind came back into the room triumphantly, holding a Bible.

"You know, I've always been a fast reader so I just started skimming... looking through the Gospels, and there it was, in Matthew, the first one, near the beginning. You want to hear it?"

"Maybe it's not the same in French—," Jeannot started, but Rosalind began reading.

"'Verily I say to you, that there are some here who will not taste of death until they have seen the Son of man come with his kingdom.' And look here!" She looked around in some confusion. "This is Matthew 16.28. But there's a note to Mark 9.1 and Luke 9.27..." She turned pages rapidly. "Here's Mark... yes almost the same, and...Luke...same thing. Now how in the world could Father Jean-Claude say there wasn't anything in the Bible like that? And it's there *three* times!" She turned to Jeannot questioning him, as if he were responsible for the mysterious ignorance of the village priest.

Jeannot shrugged his shoulders, smiling a little. "Me? I don't know. But I have to get my dog home soon. Dani told me, don't be too long." And he rose to go. They clustered at the door, everyone thanking him for his company, for the reassurance of a huge dog.

When he was gone they all sat back down in the living room and looked at each other. Michael was shaking his head.

"Something's wrong here. The priest should have known—"

"And Jeannot wasn't reacting right, either," said Spencer.

"Okay." Rosalind was going to take the lead. "Okay. We know the passage *is* in the Gospels, not once but three times. But what does it have to do with the grotto? If someone shut up in there did actually write this on the ceiling, what was the point? If they were praying it should have been *Let me out of here!* Something like that." Michael and Spencer laughed.

Nicole had been quiet, but spoke up now. "I've been thinking, something I read in college...maybe in the medieval history course, about myths that were created about Jesus and the early

Christians. It's not really the same context, but there's the legend of the wandering Jew."

"You mean, the one who wouldn't let Jesus rest on his doorstep, when he was carrying the cross?" Spencer was immediately alert.

"Yes, and supposedly Jesus said something to him like, 'Well then, I won't rest, but *you* rest here until I come again.'"

"Gives me goosebumps," said Rosalind. "Was that in the Bible too?"

"Not a bit," said Nicole. "It was made up of whole cloth in the Middle Ages and I think it was derived from something like that passage in Matthew. You know, sort of like, 'You will not taste of death until I come again with my kingdom.' And the legend claimed that the wandering Jew could never die, but wandered all over the world asking people, 'Has He come again?'"

"That would be some curse," said Spencer. "But Jesus saying it is one thing, some Vaudois spell worker is different."

"St. Gens made a wolf plow his field," Rosalind reminded him. "And that was right around here. I think we're in the right place to look for magic, curses, spells, whatever. How about another *vide grenier*? Look around for magic books? There's one Sunday at St. Saturnin."

"Okay." Michael agreed. "But in the meantime, I'm going to tell Dreyfus what we found, send him a fax of the inscription."

"He's Jewish. Do you think he'd be interested?"

"That's the point. He'll have a different perspective, at least."

The late afternoon sun had sunk beneath the cloud cover and light now streamed through the western windows of the great chateau of Barigoule, illuminating ancient tapestries on the stone walls in the smaller reception hall. They were the only source of color, hanging in the light above a small group of men, posed like figures in a doll house amidst ancient black and brown tables and chairs. A large man was the only one seated, in a cracked black leather chair in front of a feeble fire in the enormous fireplace.

The big man was cursing furiously. "How can someone write something in the grotto and no one finds it until now? Unbelievable! Intolerable!"

The two old men standing in front of him looked at each other nervously.

"The archaeologists even dug up the floors in there. Two different expeditions, fifty years apart. And they never thought to look over their heads? Explain that!"

"The woman...Jeannot heard her say that she dreamed she saw it. That's why they looked there."

This produced another outburst. When the big one calmed down he fell silent, thinking for a few moments. The two men didn't make a sound, waiting him out.

"Well, Jean-Claude did what he could, told them it wasn't in the Bible. But now what? Will this stupidity pass further? What if the police—"

"Ah...Avignon called just a little while ago. One of the Americans sent Dreyfus a fax of the inscription—" A fresh tirade cut off the old man.

"Dreyfus! The fucking Jew! He was off the case. Now it's time to do something. Is...is Maurice any better?"

"The mime? He's out of danger, they say. But the bullet nicked a lung. He should be out of action for a bit, the *toubib* said."

"He's a good thinker though. Have him make a plan, *hein*? Make this Dreyfus go away, an accident, a crime, anything!"

CHAPTER TWENTY-FOUR

Inspector Dreyfus was not in a good mood. He had been about to leave for duty for the noon shift when his office called and informed him that his hours had been changed to the midnight-to-seven shift. He met *Leyla Abdelaziz* at the station and one glance at her angry eyes let him know that she was as irritated as he was. The station was nearly deserted late at night, but a desk sergeant was on hand to pass on their assignment.

"They are concerned over the car thefts and possible drug sales at the eastern parking garages." He pushed over a simple map with red circles drawn on it. "Some discos in the area have become popular, young people flock to the area, their cars are broken into, they buy drugs, even a rape last week." The sergeant shrugged. "The politicians demand to clean it up. They all say you have the best record with the *voyous, hein*? What can we do?"

Dreyfus and Abdelaziz, simmering silently, signed for a supposedly civilian vehicle, although every criminal in Avignon, even the stupidest, knew that a dark blue Renault sedan was an undercover cop car.

They drove through black and empty streets, now glistening a bit under the streetlights from a minor drizzle. As they approached the vicinity of one of the suspect parking garages they began to hear the annoying bass notes of a rock band, amplified beyond all reason, buffeting the windows of their car, and they could see a halo of light outside the club, and a few groups of revelers clustered outside the door, waiting for a vacancy. It was almost one o'clock in the morning. To their right hulked the four-story parking structure and Dreyfus drove to the entrance, took a ticket from the automatic machine. Once inside, he backed into an empty parking slot.

"The *roulottiers*, the little assholes, are going to be on the top floors going through cars," he said. "If they're there. I'm taking the elevator up to the top, and I'll work down. You—"

Abdelaziz started to protest.

"No!" he insisted. "They can be dangerous! How many years have I done this?"

"But...but so many are North Africans. I can speak Arabic and¬¬—"

"Yes, and when they see a woman, a woman of the police, who is an Arab, they become out of control. You know your own people, the young men, how they despise women. I don't want some young punks suddenly getting macho, trying to prove something." He saw the stubborn anger on her face.

"Listen, Abdelaziz, they gave us a shit assignment, something I never heard before, sending out a Jew and a woman to arrest young Arab punks. I don't know why, but I'll go up now. If I catch some, I'll call you on my phone, we'll call the *panier à salade* to come collect them, they know they'll be booked and released with a court date three, four months from now, which they'll never go to. Why make them mad?" He left her slumped in the front seat, still mad, but the phone in her hand.

The lonely elevator took Dreyfus to the third floor of the parking structure, where he left it. The parking area was brightly lit and he surveyed it silently until convinced that no one was prowling around the cars. Then he silently climbed the stairs to the fourth floor. In the shelter of the top stair enclosure he stopped to look and listen. It was completely dark up here, meaning that someone had either broken the light, or unscrewed it. In a remote corner of the level he could now hear the creak of metal being bent. A *roulottier* was breaking into a car, going after the radio, tape deck, maybe the airbag, a thoroughly modern prize, worth 200 euros at the knackers. Dreyfus loosened his Beretta in the holster, speed dialed Abdelaziz's cell phone.

"There's one here," he whispered. "I'll keep the phone open," and he tucked it into the handkerchief pocket of his jacket. He walked quickly toward the sound of metal, letting the screeching of torn aluminum cover his footsteps. In the reflected light from the street outside he could see a solitary figure bent over the door of a new Peugeot 607, a luxury car. The robber had made enough purchase in the upper corner of the door with a tire iron to get his fingers around it and was now bending it slowly outward, his foot propped against the lower door.

Dreyfus stopped. He was ten feet away and directly behind a large black Mercedes, the kind that always had an expensive and loud car alarm. So he drew his Beretta, then rocked the Mercedes violently. Immediately the car alarm responded with a raucous *doo dah doo dah doo dah!* The car thief spun around and suddenly the lights on the top floor went back on. Dreyfus was confronted by a car thief with a pistol in his hand...almost unheard of...and behind him he heard running footsteps. He knew instantly that he had been set up.

His reaction was instantaneous. Without turning to see who was behind him he fired a quick shot at the car thief, then threw himself to the ground as several shots went screaming and ricocheting around the concrete structure. He rolled quickly under the car that was being robbed and paused in the middle of his roll to take aim at an ankle right in front of him. He fired and there was a scream of pain, then he completed his roll to the other side and vaulted over the next car, rolling over the hood to the ground and crouching, trying to locate the remaining attackers. The car he had just rolled over was offended and joined its alarm to the general cacophony. Dreyfus now heard a powerful car screaming up the ramps to the top floor and knew that it was Abdelaziz responding to the alarms and shots she had heard on the phone. He left the cover of the car he was hiding behind, fearing that the attackers would now be waiting for Abdelaziz and would shoot her the moment her Renault rounded the fourth floor ramp. The last thing he heard was a screaming ricochet as a bullet hit something in front of him and a massive darkness hammered him in the forehead. He fell to his knees, knowing that he should do something, take some action, but half-blind, paralyzed by the blow to the head, he could not make his muscles obey him. Vaguely he heard three shots, as if in the far distance, then he started to crumple.

Leyla Abdelaziz had heard the gunfire above and disregarded all previous instructions. She already had the car idling and in gear; now she squealed out of the parking space and started the long spiral up the ramps to the fourth floor. Along the way she was able to punch on the police radio and shout out the code for "officer down" and the location. Rounding the corner onto the fourth floor she saw a man squared, directly in front of her, both hands on a pistol and ready to fire. She simultaneously ducked her head below the dash and tramped on the accelerator. A shot crashed through the windshield in front of her, sprinkling her with bits of glass, but she also felt a crushing impact at the front of the car. She slammed on the brakes just in time to avoid smashing into the line of parked cars in front of her and then was out of the car, using it as a shield, trying to see any adversaries on the other side. A man in black emerged suddenly from between two cars and took a snap shot at her, but her Glock was in her hand and she put a round into the middle of his chest. She vaulted to the side of the car and took in the scene at a glance. There were three bodies she could see, two still, one moaning and holding his leg, and she could see one more underneath her car, not moving. Where was Dreyfus? Just then a sorry figure came crawling out between two cars, dripping blood onto the concrete. Dreyfus still had a gun in his hand and was groggily looking around for someone to shoot.

"Dreyfus!" she screamed, and dashed to his side. "Are you shot? Please, please tell me!"

"Not...shot..." he croaked. "Head hit, something...look out... they'll kill you..."

"They're dead!" she said with great satisfaction. "Can you get in the car?" And with her help, he was able to get off the ground and stagger to the passenger side of the blue Renault. She hesitated, looking back at the injured man, her pistol still in her hand, and Dreyfus, in a fog, still realized that in her fine rage she might just finish off the wounded.

"No, no!" he said. "We need someone alive, to tell the story, whatever it is...," and he slumped against the seat.

Abdelaziz didn't bother dealing with the payment machine at the exit. She just accelerated and snapped off the barrier. And then racing down the driveway to the parking structure they encountered a *panier à salade*, a police van with a cage for prisoners. Its siren was on and lights flashing. The two vehicles were window to window and Abdelaziz shouted across.

"My partner! Shot! I'm rushing him to the hospital!" There was a flurry of questions from the van.

"Go! Go! Fourth floor! They're all dead but one. Hurry!" And she pulled out into the rainy streets of Avignon.

Groggy as he was, Dreyfus soon realized they were not heading for any hospital of which he was aware. He put his hand on her arm.

"Leyla...where are you going?"

She almost slapped his hand away. "Dreyfus. That was a setup! One thing only they wanted! To kill you! If you go to a hospital now you will die before dawn. Someone is after you. What is it? The drug people? Slot machines? Who is mad at you?"

She had immediately named the most likely assailants in southern France. Both the drug networks and the mafias that controlled slot machines were notorious for settling scores against their enemies or competitors. They did not usually attack law enforcement personnel, but it was not unheard of for a severe judge or a vindictive police officer to be assassinated, just as a warning.

Dreyfus held up a feeble hand, trying to laugh. "No, Leyla, it is the fucking Barigoule thing. I can't believe it! I have no old enemies in drugs or *machines à sous*. None at all. Now where are you going?" Abdelaziz was driving side streets toward southern Avignon, a mostly Muslim enclave. But she was on her cell phone, not trusting the police radio, and all he heard was a rapid stream of Arabic. He put his head back and was soon unconscious again.

He awoke to find Abdelaziz and a large man helping him out of the car. He was able to limp across a driveway and into a building and then endured an agonizing trip up a flight of stairs, hoisted and assisted every step of the way. There was a room and a light and a bed, and Dreyfus was able to collapse once more. Abdelaziz and the man helping her managed to strip off his overcoat and pull a blanket over him.

"Look at his head. Do you think it is really bad?"

"Who can tell? I know a *toubib*, just around the corner. I can call him, if he'll come at this hour." Abdelaziz nodded and the man took out his cell phone and dialed. It rang obviously for a long time, waking the man on the other end. Lulled by a stream of animated Arabic conversation, Dreyfus slipped once more into darkness.

There was a stab of pain in his forehead and Dreyfus awoke and struggled to get up. Strong arms held him back.

"David, David? Listen to me. We are cleaning your forehead. He says it is not bad but we must medicate the wound and bandage... David?"

He had never been called by his first name by his partner before. Somehow the use of his name calmed him.

"You found a doctor?"

"A good one, don't worry..."

Shutting his eyes against the sting of antiseptics, Dreyfus could hear soft conversation in Arabic, a language he had studied, had practiced on the streets, and could almost understand.

"This flic...your partner?'

"A good man...other flics tried to kill him tonight."

"So now the bastards kill each other?"

"It is a strange thing, Amad...not all bad...I am a flic too, you know!"

Dreyfus's eyes opened and he saw an old man in a shapeless suit staring at his face. Seeing him conscious, the old man grinned.

"So. The fuckers tried to kill you too! A strange world, isn't it?" He was holding a large gauze square.

"Leyla. Hold this bandage while I tape it."

Dreyfus felt something cold on his forehead as the bandage was pressed down and the pain started to go away.

"A simple antibiotic with painkiller in it," said the doctor. He handed Leyla some capsules. "Some codeine, a relaxant," he said. "He must sleep and rest."

"David...?" She took his hand, leaned over him, anguished. "David? I killed a man. What shall I—"

But Dreyfus was out again.

At the headquarters of the *police judiciaire* in Avignon there was consternation.

"We have three dead assholes and one cripple," said the sergeant who had arrived with the van. "They are all well known. From the mafias."

"They were robbing cars?" Commissaire Barbu was incredulous. He had been roused from his bed by a frantic phone call in the early morning hours and was sitting in the office wishing for a coffee.

"It looks like they were trying to kill Dreyfus. A setup. The guy with the broken ankle. We'll find out from him maybe. In the old days—"

"Yes. But it's not the old days. Easy going. Make him think Dreyfus was killed and he's up for the chop. He'll rat out the others. And where is Dreyfus?"

"His partner was taking him to the hospital. We found an exterior mirror smashed on the ground, covered with blood. We think a bullet hit it and knocked it into Dreyfus's face. Shouldn't be too bad. David's got a hard head."

Barbu laughed. "Okay, we won't worry about him for a while. These bastards trying to kill a cop! That's what makes me mad! That's the priority for now."

But fifteen minutes later his phone rang, not the office phone but his personal cell.

"Commissaire Barbu?"

He recognized the voice. "Monsieur...the prefecture is working late tonight, *hein*?" He tried to get rid of the irritation he always felt when the top civilian administrative office called on the police.

"We are always working, Barbu. A judge woke me up, very angry. Can it be true that police shot and killed four kids who were only robbing cars?"

Barbu had to choke back his angry retort. He breathed deeply, long enough to provoke a "hello?" on the other line.

"Only two shot, sir. One other was run over, mortally, I'm afraid. The last one only has his ankle fractured by a gunshot—"

"But this is—"

"And these were not adolescents, sir. Grown-ups. All of them well-known Corsican enforcers from the Casimiri family."

The man on the line was quiet for the moment. "Well, my informant was obviously wrong. And the inspector in charge? He was hurt too?"

"Dreyfus? Yes, sir. A side-view mirror was shot and it ricocheted into his face. Not serious. He is in hospital right now."

"Ah. Good. What hospital?"

It was late night, almost morning, when the two nuns entered the Centre Hospitalier Montfavet in the southeastern sector of greater Avignon. They nodded to a somnolent uniformed guard sitting by the *réception* and proceeded to the nurses' station. A bored orderly was reading a girly magazine, barely glancing up, but then he came to attention, seeing the nuns.

"Yes. Good evening, sisters. How may I help you?" He shoved the magazine out of sight.

The little nun gave him a smile he thought almost too radiant for this time of night. "May we go to the room of Monsieur Dreyfus? His family asked that we pray over him, even if he is not awake."

"Dreyfus...Dreyfus." He tapped the name into his computer, stared at the screen a moment. "Sisters, I am sorry. We have no one by that name tonight. What is his doctor's name?"

The other nun now spoke up and for the first time he noticed how large she was. "Well, we weren't sure Monsieur Dreyfus was here. But also on our list..." And she consulted a small black notebook, leatherbound, with a gold cross on its cover. "Also on our list is Charles Gherini...Is it possible that...?"

It was possible. "Monsieur Gherini is on the..." and his face clouded. "I'm sorry, sisters. Gherini is being detained in the police wing...he is under arrest." The orderly shrugged, spread his hands.

The nuns' faces fell. "Oh. His mother was so insistent that we visit...just say a short prayer. She sent a medal...see?" And the big nun's fat hand was thrust into the orderly's face, clutching a shiny religious medal of some kind. He was suddenly aware that her hand smelled strongly of bacon.

"It is up to you, sisters." He shrugged again. "Third floor, south wing. But there are police guards at the entrance to the wing, and a gate." In the back of his mind he was still wondering why nuns would have been visiting a Jew.

They almost jumped with renewed joy. "Oh, thank you, Monsieur! The police will certainly admit us."

Which was true. The sleepy guards opened the gate without hesitation, asked one of the nuns to sign a clipboard, and pointed them down the darkened hallway past the deserted nurses' station. The guard could hear them chattering good naturedly as they swished down the corridor.

The large nun found the room number. "There are six little bastards in here. How do we find Gherini?"

"Thin, black hair, mustache. Will have a cast on his lower leg, probably elevated." The little nun was consulting some notes.

They entered the room quietly, calm, carrying out their errand of mercy. Five of the men were asleep, but a voice came from their left. "Sisters? For the love of God, please help me! It hurts so badly. Just another shot is all..." They could make out a dark face, a body cast. The large nun went to his side and began to chant softly in Latin. The little nun meanwhile had located the Gherini with the leg in the air and she swiftly took a syringe with an ultra-fine needle from under her habit. One of Gherini's hands was out of the covers and she could see a prominent vein amidst the hair on the back of his wrist. Without hesitation she slid the needle into his vein, watching his face the whole time, smiling in case he should wake. But he was obviously under medication and didn't even twitch as she depressed the plunger.

As she turned from the bed she began to worry as the complainer in the other bed raised his voice to the large nun.

"Sister! Enough with the Latin shit, all right? I'm suffering terrible pain here..."

The large nun made a soothing gesture. "Of course, my son. My colleague is the qualified nurse. Sister Euthanie? Do you have the other syringe? The Dreyfus syringe?"

"Of course!" And the little nun came to his bedside, examined his elbow briefly and then expertly inserted her needle. "In less than a minute you should feel no pain, my son," said the large nun." And they crossed themselves, turned and rapidly left the room. The invalid would have been surprised to hear them giggling as they walked back down the hall.

"Might as well. It shut him up."

"'Sister Euthanie'? Where did you find that one?"

"Hee hee! Any way, no witnesses is always best."

"And my dear, two for one..." They stifled a snicker as they approached the guard at the gate.

CHAPTER TWENTY-FIVE

A fine drizzle was falling on the Luberon as Spencer drove through the vineyards on the way to Bonnieux and the *vide grenier*. There, in the French equivalent of a garage sale, but spread over an entire village, they hoped to find the woman Annie Serre—the only person still alive who had seemed to know something about the last days of Barigoule on that terrible day in April four hundred and fifty years before. The countryside was not comforting. The vines on either side were bare skeletons, only a few forlorn leaves blowing in the wind from the northeast.

"Do you think anyone'll be there?" inquired Nicole from the back seat, which she was sharing with Rosalind.

"A little rain like this? No problem," Michael answered his wife, leaning over from the front seat. "Only time I've seen wholesale defections was that street market in Gordes last year. There was a mistral in December that must have lowered the wind chill to zero. The one guy with a stall had onions blowing out of their baskets."

"I remember," said Nicole. "And whoever was there bought everything he had in about twenty minutes. I think they were feeling sorry for him."

They drove up the hill into Bonnieux and found a parking place near the lower *place*. The usual pottery people had their stands protected by awnings. The locals, who had brought all the junk from their attics to sell, were less prepared for bad weather and were either watching their mismatched silverware and cracked dishes drip with rain or were attempted to cover their treasures with plastic sheets that effectively hid what they were trying to sell.

Nicole and Rosalind volunteered to try the upper town while Spencer and Michael started to circle the lower square.

"They're going to make one circle and settle down in the café," said Rosalind.

"Maybe...but I've been thinking of finding this woman again. I know she knows something, even though she didn't want to talk about it. Remember I bought that awful book from her."

"Yes, and now the author's dead. You sure she'll even talk to us? It would scare me. Is it that stand up there?"

Rosalind was right. Annie Serre was cold and distant, barely acknowledging that she had met Nicole before. The two women looked through all the old books on her table while Annie deliberately carried on a long conversation with the stallholder next to her, a thin man trying to sell bronze statuettes of nymphs and stalking ceramic black panthers amidst a hodge podge of similar junk. Rosalind finally lost patience and demanded attention.

"Madame, excuse me. Have you heard of the publication, *Bulletin de la société des études vaudoises*? We are looking for old numbers."

Annie Serre turned white as a sheet, and the man next door turned away rapidly, as if embarrassed at hearing an explicit sexual approach.

"I...Where did you hear of such a thing?"

"This is old Vaudois country, here. We are interested in the research and¬¬—" Nicole tried to interrupt, moderate the tone of the questioning, but Annie Serre put her hands up. She was trying to look angry, but something almost like terror was *flick*ering in her expression. She shook her head violently.

"I have nothing like that. You won't find that here." And then she looked at Rosalind piercingly and lowered her voice until it was barely audible.

"But you know the *Société* itself has an office in Apt," she murmured. And she pointed down the hill. "Right there in the middle of town. You take the little street leading southeast out of the library square. Then first right, second left, and you will find the nameplate...Yes, monsieur?"

An old man was trying to ask her a question about a small escritoire in her collection of theoretically antique furniture. It had a price tag of 150 euros and Rosalind and Nicole realized their allotted time with Mme. Serre was over. Going down the hill, they discussed the new disclosure in tones of wonder.

"I can't believe it," said Rosalind. "Here we've been looking for books and journals, and the whole bloody institute is right here in Apt."

"Maybe," said Nicole. "You know, when I talked to her before she gave me the feeling that she knew more than she was saying about the Vaudois...and she didn't really want to talk about the massacre. You know, why did we want to stir up old trouble, or something like that. And now she suddenly knows about the institute?"

"Well. Still. I tell you what. Let's not tell the boys, alright? They'll just take over and go blasting down to Apt, find the place, terrify some old secretary or whatnot. Tomorrow's Saturday and I have to go to the market in Apt. Come with me? We'll do it better. And can you see their faces when we come back with the—what is it?—1973 number of the journal."

"I'd love to, but I can't tomorrow. Mike and I are going to lunch at the Saule Pleureur, you know, in Monteux, and it takes a while to get there."

"Lucky you. Last time we were there Spencer had the fried lambs' feet. Well, I'll carry on myself."

"Roz! You be careful! you never know—"

"Not to worry. You know Apt. Stodgiest village in Provence. They actually claim there's no crime there."

Dreyfus woke abruptly, completely disoriented, seeing gray light streaming through a window. His first reaction was to move his arms and legs, thinking that he might have been tied up. Policemen had been kidnapped, used to extort the release of some gang member, never successfully. A few had actually been killed but most were soon released... Now he found that he was not bound but that his head hurt. And then it all came back, the set up in the garage, knocked out by...what was it?...a sideview mirror? Taken somewhere by Abdelaziz and—now he sat upright, sending a shaft of pain through his skull, and looked around, remembering that he was in his partner's apartment, his partner, an Arab woman, that an Arab doctor had treated his wound, that no one on the police knew where he was. Putting his hands on his knees he pushed hard and managed to stand upright, only to realize that he was wearing only an undershirt and a pair of boxer shorts, the ancient threadbare olive drab ones he had kept when he got out of the army so many years ago.

"Leyla...," he tried to say, but his throat was full of phlegm. He coughed, cleared his throat, tried again.

"Abdelaziz?" That had the tone of command, and he heard movement in the next room. In a second his partner came rapidly into the room, to his amazement wearing only an oversized T-shirt that barely reached below her waist. His first thought was that this could be scene from an erotic movie. Her legs were long and flawless, the stuff of legends, her breasts were covered by the flimsiest and most imcompetent layer of clinging cotton...he couldn't help staring.

"Dreyfus! My God! Don't try to stand up. The doctor said—" And then she looked down at herself and clasped her arms across her breast, blushing furiously.

"Oh! I'm embarrassed. The doctor said to keep you warm so I had the heat way up, and I was too hot so—"

Dreyfus relaxed, almost smiled. "Don't worry. I woke and I didn't know where I was."

"Okay. Just a moment. I'll be back. And she was, wearing a light gray jogging suit, which did nothing to hide the curves she had just revealed. Dreyfus was flustered, suddenly experiencing a feeling toward his partner that he had never thought possible. He sat down on the bed again.

"Abdelaziz. Have you called in to the department yet?"

Her face had been full of concern. Now it hardened. "You must listen, Dreyfus. There is a bad problem."

"Yes, what—"

"No. First you should eat something. You know it is in the afternoon?"

Dreyfus was startled. But then he became aware that his bladder had not been emptied for...maybe ten hours? He stood again. "I have to go to the—"

"Right through there, first left. Then come into the kitchen, if...you are feeling well?"

Stumbling a bit. "No. Yes. I'm feeling much better. Just..." And he headed toward the bathroom with great relief.

He had eaten a light lunch of bread, cheese, and olives and was finishing his second cup of coffee when Leyla sat down across from him, a frown on her face.

"When I tell you this problem, promise me you will remain calm, OK?"

He was startled. "I'm no longer calm already! What do you mean?"

"It's just that...Well, last night someone slipped into the hospital."

"What hospital—?"

"The hospital in Montfavet...where I told them you were."

"You told them...but I was here, right?"

"Yes, I lied, but I said you were not really hurt, that you went by yourself."

"Oh, that's great. Now I'm in the shit!"

"Not so much as if you were there." She stared at him intensely until he realized there was something he had missed.

"And if I was there?"

"As I said, someone slipped in...believe it or not, the surveillance cameras and the guards show only two visitors."

"They asked for me?"

"Yes, but of course you were not there. Then they wanted to see this Gherini, a Corsican gangster, the one you shot in the leg."

"But he would have been in the jail wing, under guard."

"Just so. And when the two nuns arrived—"

"Nuns again!"

"Listen! Yes. Two nuns. And they walked through, no questions, naturally. 'His mother asked me to say a prayer, blah blah blah...' They find Gherini, and this morning Gherini is dead. Not only Gherini, but a black thief in the same room."

Dreyfus was not fully awake. He shook his head, trying to concentrate. "Gherini. Yes, the man I shot. And why was this thief there?"

"Why was he in hospital? What he did was jump off the roof when the *flics* caught him robbing a bar. Landed on a car. Broke his ribs. So they put him in the hospital jail. But he is unimportant. Can you imagine why Gherini is dead?"

His head cleared suddenly and he saw the whole picture. "He could tell them why they were there, the Corsicans...why they were trying to kill me. Of course. And this black man? In the same room? He was awake and saw...maybe was making a fuss¬¬."

"Yes. Both dead. And no one knows how. No traces of poison. Many punctures in their veins. Of course. They were in hospital, they stick you there over and over."

"Nuns again!" Dreyfus could only shake his head.

"And there is more. I phoned the department this morning...I was going to ask for a day off. Barbu's deputy told me I was on administrative leave anyway until the hearing on Tuesday—there is a big fuss in the press about the shooting—and they want both of us to stay out of the way of reporters—"

"I can understand that...but does the department know what happened last night?"

"Look...you read, it's quicker." And she pushed over the morning's issue of *La Provence*. Dreyfus scanned the headline:

"*OK CORRAL!*" TROIS MORTS! EN VILLE! He glanced at the flashlit photo of the parking garage top floor, now full of police, stains on the cement, and read the story.

For reasons still unknown, the story said, a local mafia had lured two police officers into an ambush on the top floor of a parking garage. The officers, whose names were being withheld, had responded with fatal results for three of the assailants, who were all well known to security forces. A thorough investigation had been opened by the local office of the Interior Ministry and an explanation of events was expected at any time.

Dreyfus expelled his breath. "What a fuckup! And the press doesn't know about the dead one in the hospital yet?"

"I've had the radio on, but nothing yet. Barbu's deputy said it was under wraps. Oh...and the shooters? They were all Corsicans. The Casimiri family."

Dreyfus was shocked. "Casimiri! But they *are* a slot machine mafia. They have nothing to do... Of course!..." and he almost slapped himself on the forehead, catching himself at the last moment before he hit his bandaged wound.

"Of course. They were simply hired. And it must be the Barigoule business. The nuns. Everything fits. He got to his feet too quickly and had to catch the back of the chair to steady himself.

"And we...we have to get out of here. They'll already be looking for us."

"The police?"

"Police, nuns, press...everyone."

"But where can we go?"

He thought quickly. "To...a friend." He looked at his watch. "Too late today. But tomorrow, to Barigoule...we'll see Jeannot, talk to the Americans. Come on, hurry and get ready. They'll find where you live soon enough!"

Abedaziz was driving them out of town in her car, following the NR 7. Dreyfus had intended only to lean back and rest a moment but he was soon asleep. From time to time his partner looked over at him. *Leyla Abdelaziz* had resisted being partnered with a...well, a Jew. But after a few weeks working with Dreyfus she had begun to feel strange urges. She wanted to comb down his hair where it stuck up in back. She wanted to straighten his suit coat the way he put it on too quickly and never adjusted it. She had once brushed croissant crumbs off his tie and provoked a startled glance. It was obvious he had no one taking care of him, and he needed care. He was so serious all the time, almost never ate lunch, and he had this tragic look about him, as if he had lost some great love and would never recover until—. It was at this point that Leyla became angry with herself and made herself stop thinking. But now...she couldn't help it. She had now saved his life, maybe twice, even, had taken his clothes off, mostly anyway, had put him in her bed, heard him groaning in the night and sponged his face. *Leyla Abdelaziz*, she asked herself. *Could you be falling in love with a Jew?* And she thought of her father, retired from the Marseille police after thirty years, back in Morocco living like a king on his pension, and decided, *I could tell him I'm in love with a policeman, and leave it at that...*

CHAPTER TWENTY-SIX

On Saturday morning Spencer was sitting in his big leather chair reading the *Tribune* when Rosalind came downstairs wearing her raincoat and running shoes.

"Going somewhere, sweetheart?" asked Spencer, mildly surprised, as he turned to the sports page.

"It's Saturday. Market day in Apt, silly. We need some veggies and bread. Want to come along?" She knew Spencer never wanted to go to street markets on cold, blustery days.

He tried to give the impression that he was seriously considering the proposition. "Well...I think not, my dear. But why don't you pick up a *pintade* for dinner. And be careful driving if it starts raining. You know the idiots around here never slow down." He turned back to his paper. "I always wonder how sportswriters predict football scores," he said. "This imbecile has the Forty-niners losing 30-14 to the Steelers. He's assuming Pittsburgh is going to kick three field goals. Doesn't he know their kicker sprained an ankle last week. Can you believe..."

Rosalind listened politely, her hand on the door, never having had the slightest interest in American football, until Spencer came to the end of whatever he was saying. Then she quickly said, "Back in a bit, love," and left.

The leaden skies held off rain as she drove down the curving road off the plateau, through vineyards, and onto the fields around Roussillon. On the long straightaway an enormous truck came pelting down the road in the opposite direction and Rosalind felt the first twinge of vulnerability. After all, these people had committed murder by truck and by nun, had attempted murder by librarian and by mime. They were obviously without remorse; it would be so easy to pick her off somewhere in the twelve kilometers of deserted countryside on the way to Apt. *Better look out for yourself,* she thought and started looking cautiously at the few vehicles sharing the road with her.

Once in Apt she relaxed a bit. Apt is not the loveliest of French towns. Colonia Julia Apta was founded by Julius Caesar because it commanded a tight spot between hills along the Calavon river and the east-west route that everyone had to take from Spain to the most convenient Alpine passes. It is now just a prosperous market town for the surrounding farming region, and neither the local business community nor the large Arab community of farm workers have felt it necessary to prettify the industrial approaches to the town or its brutally utilitarian buildings.

Rosalind was an expert at finding a parking space on congested Saturday market day. On the way to the bridge into town she saw someone vacating a space on the other side of the street so she swiftly pulled a U-turn to come up behind the exiting car. She ignored the horns of the cars she had cut off and expertly parallel parked facing back out of town.

She had already decided to do her shopping first, just in case someone was actually trying to catch her at suspicious activity. At her favorite vegetable dealer she bought leeks, carrots, onions, some apples, a cabbage, but turned down the green beans the merchant was pushing. This time of year they were from Morocco, expensive, and none too fresh. In the square of the town library, she circled the tables, finally bought some *boudin noir* to have with fried apples, and a large loaf of country bread, still warm and smelling wonderful. Spencer's *pintade* could be picked up at the butcher on the way back through town. By this time she had positioned herself to be directly opposite the alley leading southeast out of the square, the nameless street supposedly leading to the Vaudois institute.

She had never noticed the alley before, insignificant, too narrow almost for such scooters and bikes as might risk its uneven cobbles. She ducked quickly behind a group of shoppers and sprinted up the alley to its first turning where she warily peeked back behind the corner of a building. The alley was empty. Now she tried to remember the directions: the first right, then the second left. The first right was almost narrower than the alley—a mere cleft between buildings. A spatter of drops fell on her head and at first she thought it had started to rain, but then realized someone had watered plants on a window ledge high above. She did not look up, just hoping that she had guessed right, and walked faster. The first left was wider and obviously led to a wider main street somewhere in town. The second left was the most lifeless, deserted alley she had ever seen in her life. Faceless buildings three stories high soared up on both sides, but none appeared occupied. Doors were chained, entries boarded up, windows were broken. On a bare expanse of dirty gray wall a graffitist had started to write ras de b..."I'm fed up!"...but the line of spray paint veered off and ended, as if the writer had been struck down in the middle of a word. *I certainly hope so!* thought Rosalind. There seemed to be no street numbers or live habitations of any kind until she finally spied a dingy sign down the block. She hurried along to find an Arab tailor shop, but locked and looking ancient and bankrupt. But as she turned to go up the alley she suddenly saw an entryway across the alley, with a real door, and a row of nameplates. She dashed across the alley and peered into the gloom.

Société des études vaudoises. Seulement sur rendezvous. By appointment only. She had been so sceptical of the very existence of the society that she almost started to read the next nameplate.

Then she reacted with a quick indrawn breath and a sudden determination. *By appointment only...bullshit!* she thought, and pressed the bell next to the plate with all her force. Miraculously, the lock in the door beside her buzzed immediately and she burst through it before the aging portal could change its mind. Facing her was a ground floor hallway leading off into such stygian darkness that her knees shook. But there was also a steep stairway, with light coming from above, and now she heard a quavering voice, *"M'sieur-'dame...?"* from what she took to be the first landing.

"Ouais...bonjour, Madame. On cherche la société des études vau—"

"Dites plus...Montez s'il vous plait..."

"I'm coming up," said Rosalind, loudly, wondering why the woman above had said, 'Say no more.'"

At the head of the stairs she saw, under the one tiny naked light bulb that illuminated the stairwell, a figure that exactly matched the voice she'd heard. A spidery, ancient woman, gray hair pulled back in a bun, heavy glasses, and shapeless black clothes. She had a pen tucked behind one ear and was holding a sheaf of papers in her left hand. Her whole attitude was apprehensive and she looked ready to turn and flee. "Good day, Madame," Rosalind said in French, in the most soothing tone she could maintain. "It was a great surprise for me to find your establishment right here in Apt. My husband...my friends are deeply interested in the history of the—"

The woman's first reaction was to peer down the stairwell, evidently expecting a greater threat than a slim Englishwoman. Satisfied that no hostile invaders lurked below, she cut off Rosalind in mid-sentence and beckoned her up the stairs and into an office whose door was ajar, beaming a few shafts of grey light into the hallway. Once inside, the woman almost slammed the door and turned the old bolt to lock it.

She turned to Rosalind intently. "You are the one? Who talked to Annie Serre?" Rosalind nodded, all nerves afire, caught up in the urgency of the woman's voice.

"Finally. Finally I can...I can... Madame, do you know what danger you are in?"

"We are just beginning to realize—"

The woman turned to an ancient, dark oak file cabinet and tugged at its top drawer.

"I think I know what you are looking for. Our little journal, such a harmless thing... It has been more than twenty years since we had to stop printing it. No money...and almost no contributors after the deaths in Paris? You knew about that, certainly?"

Rosalind had to grab the back of a chair, her knees were trembling so. "Deaths? In Paris?"

"Yes, Madame. The authors who edited the testimony of Jean the Miller in 1595 died in accidents in Paris a year after the 1973 issue was printed. You hadn't heard?"

A spray of rain slashed across the window, startling both women. They hadn't realized that the promised rain had started. They turned back to face each other, mute, white faces stark in the grey light coming in through the window. Another flurry of rain tapdanced across the panes.

The old woman had a pile of journals clasped to her breast. Now she put them down on her cluttered desk and started fingering her way through them, taking care to show Rosalind the dates: 1983, 1981, 1976, 1974, 1973. And there she stopped.

"You see? 1973? There should be two numbers. But there is only the spring. The fall number is missing."

"But that's the one we've been looking for!" Rosalind's voice broke. "The end of the testimony! There's nothing else—"

The woman put up a hand. "Are you ready to leave? And quickly? Watch this." She stood shakily on a chair and pushed up a ceiling tile. A cloud of dust descended and both of them coughed.

"Take my hand, Madame, I can get up without pain, but stepping down..."

Rosalind quickly took her hand and the other elbow and the woman eased herself to the floor. In her left hand was a cobwebby yellow pamphlet, corroding at the edges.

"Take it! Take it quickly...and leave. Put it under your vegetables there," pointing at the leeks and carrots.

And she grasped Rosalind by both arms with surprising strength, looked deeply into her eyes.

"Madame, my dear, this truth must come out. We have tried...God knows how we have tried. But here in France these stories of ancient mysteries are like the *cigares volantes*, you know?"

"Flying saucers?"

"Yes. Everyone starts laughing the minute we begin to...But now! Go now! And be careful leaving!"

"But you! Alone here! How can you—?"

For the first time a smile crossed the woman's face.

"*Voilà...*" And she pointed across the room.

"My dog, Chairman Mao."

What Rosalind had taken for an old pile of brown rugs moved slightly, and she could make out the head of an ancient Chow. The dog examined her without interest and went back to sleep.

"He will protect me. He has a terrible temper...But go now, before anyone—" and she almost pushed Rosalind toward the door, then darting down to cover the old journal in the basket with a bunch of leeks.

"I...uh...I, we thank you so much, Madame...?"

"Marron. Madame Marron. But now, goodby...and maybe we shall meet again."

The door closed behind Rosalind and she was alone in the dark stairwell.

Terror seemed to entwine her ankles and freeze her to the top steps, but then she felt a surge of anger coursing through her body. *The bastards! What do they think they can do? I am Rosalind Sullivan and everyone knows I am a bitch! Now let's prove it.*

So she strode off down the stairs, nostrils flaring, almost daring someone to confront her. Still, caution made her hesitate at the entry door and she peeked both ways down the dark alley. No one. She eased herself out, clutching her basket to her breast, and darted back to the nearest intersection, the one that seemed to lead to a livelier part of town. A few steps into the new street and there was life around her, people coming out of shops, a few tourists even, venturing up into the bowels of the town. No suspicious old men in their caps.

On the way back to her car she forced herself to go into a butcher shop and buy a *pintade* for Spencer. *If anyone is watching, I am just a casual housewife doing my Saturday shopping*, she told herself. She overpaid the butcher by twenty euros in her confusion and had to be called back and given the change, to the amusement of the usual crowd in the shop on Saturday mornings. Her confidence returned when the sun suddenly burst from behind clouds as she was crossing the town bridge over the Calavon. Once in her car, she stowed her groceries in the well of the passenger seat, but then, before starting up, she gave the basket a long look. She shrugged, reached into the basket and extracted the long-lost journal and tucked it into the inside breast pocket of her jacket. *Just play it safe. So long we've been looking for it!* But she resisted the temptation to look at it. It was for all four of them, after all the work they'd put in.

Rosalind was past the two roundabouts and had taken the righthand turn for Barigoule when she realized there was a dark red panel truck following her closely. *Nothing too suspicious about that,* she thought. This was the main road to Roussillon, then Joucas or Gordes. But the red truck continued on her tail all the way past those turnoffs, tailgating in the usual French manner.

On the steeper road leading up to Barigoule Rosalind got angry at the tailgater. She downshifted to third, gave the powerful Peugeot some gas, and accelerated expertly around the curves on the winding road, watching the pickup recede into the middle distance. One more corner and she would hit a long straightaway up the hill where the Peugeot could do a hundred or more. Bye bye little red pickup.

But as she rounded the curve she suddenly saw a huge shadow to her left and heard the snarl of a powerful motor. Just in time she swerved off the road to her right, barely avoiding a large construction truck that surged onto the road from the left shoulder. *Jesus!* She thought. *It must have been waiting for me. It was going to smash me like...like Rousset...* And then she was desperately trying to control her speeding car on the rough ground off the right shoulder, dodging boulders and tree stumps, not daring to slow down in the hopes of cutting back to the road. But she misjudged the size of a large rock, hit it square with her left front tire, which promptly blew, sending the car into a 180° degree spin and left it stalled, facing the way it had come, where she could see four men advancing on foot, in no particular hurry. The red panel truck had halted in the middle of the road, the doors open. The massive construction truck was now parked on the right side of the road, shielding the little pocket of land where her car had landed from the view of passersby.

Not that there'll be any, she thought bitterly. It was after twelve o'clock on Saturday and every French person in the nation was eating lunch. So she quickly got out of the car and took stock of the situation.

To her right was sparse pine and oak forest that cloaked all the hills leading up to Barigoule. To her left was the road, and she knew she could run back to it faster than her pursuers—but they had the vehicles and they'd just chase her down. Could she talk them out of killing her, in return for the journal? *No!* she told herself. *We've been waiting long enough to read it. And they'll just kill me anyway, bash me in the head and put me in the car to make it look like an accident.* She made up her mind, held a hand up toward the men approaching her, all looking like the usual middle-aged farmers, in caps and work clothes, windbreakers against the rain.

"Stop!" she said, and almost automatically they stopped.

"You almost killed me with your truck," she raged, her anger natural now. "I'm having the police on you."

"A little too late, lady," smiled the man in the lead, someone she thought she recognized from the village. A farmer with a cherry orchard?

"You shouldn't have poked your nose into things that didn't concern you, American bitch!" said a second man. They were working up some anger themselves.

"I'm not American, I'm English, you idiot."

"English!" And they all looked at each other in amusement. "Such an honor! An Englishwoman. I've heard that the English women are hot in bed, but not the men. Is that true?" They all laughed

"Where is the document?" asked the lead man, grinning, beginning to advance slowly. "Give it to us and we'll let you go, Englishwoman." His false smile oozed treachery.

Rosalind pointed to the ruined car. "It's in the basket. Under the leeks."

"The leeks?" They all laughed again. One of the men started toward the car, but another, perhaps the youngest, gave up all pretense and started toward her.

"Come to me, nice Englishwoman. We have to make sure." And another man started off to the side, cutting her off from the road. He was a fat man and he stared at Rosalind with a leer.

"We'll make sure, all right," he said grimly. "And maybe we'll have some fun too, all of us together." And he cupped his groin with one hand.

Without a word, Rosalind turned and took off uphill. She was thinking rapidly. She had some advantages. First, they didn't know that the Sullivans and Tollivers had been hiking all the forest trails around Barigoule for several years, and only a hundred meters into the forest was one that led up the hill to a little hamlet just east of Barigoule. Second, they did not know that Rosalind had run marathons.

"Roger! Jean-Jacques! After her!" She heard the leader shout. "I'm getting the rifle!"

Sprinting into the woods, Rosalind realized she had only a little time before one of the hunters could get close enough to put a bullet in her back. And she heard pounding feet behind her.

Fuck them! No lazy, woman-hating, chain-smoking, big bellied French peasants are going to catch me. She picked up the pace, figuring the men were running as fast as they could and a few hundred meters on the hill would wear them out Far behind she heard a shot and a bullet whistled by overhead and to the right. Not even close, and she realized that if she could outpace the running men by enough she could take another fork in the trail a few hundred meters ahead and lose herself in a network of trails that lay around an old quarry. Rosalind settled into a fast running pace, just below the frantic sort of speed that would tire her. She realized now that the light drizzle had changed into snowflakes and she hoped she wouldn't be leaving tracks.

CHAPTER TWENTY-SEVEN

eyla Abedaziz woke suddenly. She could see gray light through a dormer window. There was a moment of panic, followed by a far greater anxiety as the enormity of her present situation sank in. Last night's events streamed through her consciousness unbidden. They had left the police car behind and taken her old Twingo. Dreyfus had given directions to Apt, and from there up sinuous mountain roads to a tiny village perched on the hills to the south near the top of the Luberon massif. A friend from the army, he had said. They'd been in the paras together. It had been late in the afternoon when they got there and his friend, a large, drinking sort of man with a beard, had grabbed Dreyfus and kissed him hard—"Why don't you visit, you bastard?"—that sort of thing.

The bearded man was called Manu. The two men had sat up late, eating a rabbit stew with onions, many cheeses, and too much wine, talking, while Leyla, and the woman of the house, a lean and suspicious matron, had remained virtually silent. Dreyfus had seemed reluctant to explain his sudden and unexpected visit, and the men eased their way into the present situation by remembering stories from their past—the paras, rugby matches, who started what fight in a bar somewhere. Leyla wondered at her partner, a man she had always considered serious, studious, an intellectual. But she could see that his friend obviously looked up to him as a tough guy. Then Dreyfus briefly told Manu about the attack in the garage. Manu swore furiously and wanted to start making phone calls—to find out more details, to plan reprisals. Dreyfus calmed him down, arguing the time of night and his injured head. Leyla's offer to help clean up had been repulsed by Manu's wife, but in a friendly way now, and they had gone up into the tiny guest room in the attic. Neither Manu nor his wife had shown any curiousity about their relationship and there were no winks or nudges when they went upstairs.

There were two little beds in the attic and Dreyfus had slipped under his covers quickly and silently in his underwear, giving Leyla a chance at the upstairs bathroom. When she returned he was asleep. But she woke in the middle of the night to hear him screaming softly, his legs thrashing, and when she knelt by his bed and woke him, he was muttering, "They'll get us, kill us... You! You must get out of this before they....!"

Dreyfus had been shaking and she naturally slipped into bed beside him, holding him and comforting him like a child. And so they went to sleep again, holding each other, warm in the little bed. But later in the night she woke to find herself almost on top of her partner, her legs clasped around his thigh. Both of them had awoken from an erotic dream and now continued the slow dance they had been dreaming, moving softly together, brushing lips and finding a little kiss, then a deep kiss, hands daring to feel forbidden curves and crevices, awkward moments to remove clinging clothing, and then finally they were joined and moving in sweet passion toward a burst of jolting energy that surprised them and collapsed them. Both of them shy, they did not speak, just held each other until sleep again claimed them.

And here she was, looking at the peaceful face of her partner, a lean, thoughtful face with a day's growth of beard. As she gazed, his gray eyes suddenly opened, staring right at her, and they were both embarrassed.

"I—," she started to say.

"I—," he responded, but Leyla, unable to meet his eyes, cuddled against him, waiting and hoping for him to say something not about last night—the weather, the stupid Americans, anything. What he said was not what she expected.

"Leyla...I still remember. It came to mind last night as I was dozing."

"David...I—"

"No, no. Listen. I remember when you said, 'David, I killed someone.' And I should have—"

"No, don't worry...I shouldn't have—"

"But yes. Yes! It is an important thing! To kill someone. My first time—maybe the only time, unless that fucking mime is dead—it almost made me resign the police. Even though...even though he was a killer, many times, a gang kid, had shot at my partner, was aiming at me, so I shot him in the body and he fell forward and I had hit a main artery and a pool of blood poured out around him so fast, unbelievable! It was that pool of blood I remembered night after night. And my supervisor made me go talk to the priest all the *flics* talk to, me, a Jew! But he was smart. When I said I was a Jew he said, 'This is not about religion, it's about removing human garbage from the streets. *My* job is to try to make them better. *Your* job is to clean up whatever I have failed to fix.' And my supervisor said I might have to do it again and if I had doubts I should resign. I knew he was thinking I was a sissy of a Jew, so I was angry and told him I was staying on. Anyway, Leyla, I was awake many nights. So tell me when it bothers you."

She was thinking of her police training camp. "You know, we had to shoot at these targets, shaped like a man. And from the first day they said I was a natural...I didn't think, I pointed, like a finger, and the bullet went where I pointed. They joked about it, rough jokes...how did an Arab and a woman learn to shoot like a white man. But someone else, an older man, said, 'she's like her father...if he had to take his pistol out it was all over.' And the officers said I would make a good *flic* and I passed with a top grade. And then, when I saw that man in the garage, it was like the target suddenly popping up, and I did what I was trained to do."

Dreyfus was smiling. He leaned over and kissed her on the neck, making her shiver.

"You were super. A professional. And you know? I thought you were going to kill the last one too. And now we are talking about killing people, I must make a phone call." He reached for his clothes and extracted his *portable*. He was not put through and had to leave a message, but almost immediately his phone rang again.

"Yes. This is Dreyfus, tell Marco. He'll know..." And he waited a moment. Finally an angry voice came on the line.

"Dreyfus! You bastard! Is it true, this bullshit thing in the garage?"

"True, true. They were trying to kill me."

"I made inquiries. Some low-level little asshole I never even heard of took a phone call, agreed to a hit, all on his own, sent out the boys. I suppose he thought I'd be happy. They never told him it was a hit on police. You know we don't operate that way."

"I know. I was surprised, Marco. And now I'm worried that accounts will be settled."

"Accounts settled. Yes, my friend, they will be. We lost some troops, maybe not the smartest, but good obedient boys. But you are out of it. Their families will be told you are not involved. We are finding out who ordered this hit, not telling us that a policeman was involved. Then accounts will be settled, rest assured."

Leyla had been listening, hearing both voices. After Dreyfus hung up she started to ask a question. He cut her off.

"Casimiri. The godfather. One of them, anyway. I've met him several times, here and there. I try to put him in jail; he manages to stay out. It's a professional relationship. I knew he would never try to have police killed...it would be the end of him."

"But you said, *reglement de comptes*...? Settling accounts?"

"Yes, as you know, *reglement de comptes* has a special meaning in the world of our gangsters. There are vendettas over drugs, *poules, machines à sous,* every kind of market share, as the economists say. Everything must be paid back. But they do not settle accounts with police. I had to get things straight with Casimiri." He looked at his watch.

"Now, I want to drive up to Barigoule, see these strange Americans and English who started the whole thing. It's time to find out what is in back of it all, why someone is trying to kill us too."

On the way out he conferred with Manu, who was still eager to mount a campaign on many fronts. Dreyfus was more focused. "You must call Barbu, my boss. He's a good man, not like some of those bastards in the department. Let him know you've seen me, tell him to look into this bureaucrat who asked what hospital I was in. You understand?"

Manu nodded. "We'll get to work. I knew Barbu in the old days...some people in the ministry too. You take the trail in front; we'll follow the trail backward, flush some of these cockroaches out of the drains. Check back again this afternoon, if you have the chance."

As Abdelaziz and Dreyfus drove slowly down the curves of the mountain road gentle flakes of snow started to swirl against the windshield.

CHAPTER TWENTY-EIGHT

"Do you want a coffee?"

Nicole and Michael were just finishing dessert at Le Saule Pleureur in Monteux. It had been a fabulous lunch, but for some reason Michael had felt himself rushing through it, and now he waved down the waitress.

"*Que de l'addition, s'il vous plait*...No, no coffee. I don't know what's wrong, but I think we should get back." He looked out the spacious windows. "And look now...it's beginning to snow. We'd better get moving or we'll never get through the Dégout, have to go round by L'Isle instead."

The so-called *Dégout* was the usual shortcut across the plateau, winding through a deep gorge in the hills, almost impassible when snow was too deep. To the east, the sinuous road over the Col de Murs was even worse. Otherwise, one had to take the long way around through the large village of Isle-sur-la-Sorgue, then Coustellet and Gordes, adding a good half hour to the trip.

They paid up and started over the flat Rhône valley plains toward the plateau of Vaucluse. "This might only be a little snow shower," Nicole said nervously. But as they passed through Pernes the snow suddenly increased in intensity and by the time they started to go uphill past Venasque on its crag Michael was seriously doubting the wisdom of continuing on this route. Only his familiarity with every curve kept him going through the veil of white that his wipers were laboring to displace.

"This is so early for a real snow," Nicole said with alarm in her voice as they passed the guest house at Camp Long, the last habitation for many miles. "November? I can't remember it this early."

And then, once properly into the Dégout, with the cliffs towering on both sides, creeping up the first really steep slope, their usually nimble Peugeot 206D started to slide and fishtail. Michael reluctantly stopped and, looking backward, delicately reversed down the hlll until they found a place to park off the road by a large quarry.

"I'm beginning to wonder if we can even get back to the Pernes road," Michael worried. "There's that downhill stretch with no guardrails and a hundred foot drop. We just made it coming uphill. But going down we could get sliding and—"

"Let's not, darling. You know, we can always walk back to Camp Long and get a room for the night. They'll have plowed the road by tomorrow."

"Maybe. Generally they don't bother to plow until the snow stops. But you're probably right. At any rate we could call Spencer from there—"

"If he can get out of Barigoule by now. It's usually worse there in the snow."

Then they heard the laboring sound of a vehicle and a small red panel truck appeared in the gaps in the windshield. The truck stopped and a vaguely familiar figure got out of the driver's side. *A cherry farmer?* thought Michael. The man was middle-aged, wearing the usual cap and a heavy brown sweater. He trotted to the driver's side window and Michael put it down enough to talk.

"Ah, you're from Barigoule, right, Monsieur? I think you are the famous mystery writer?" A grin crinkled the weather-beaten farmer face, snowflakes catching in his bushy eyebrows.

"Yes, but I don't think we can make it back today."

"You know, we can give you a lift. We have a *quat'quat'*, a four-wheel drive, take you to your door."

Michael looked at Nicole. "You know I wasn't looking forward to walking to Camp Long in these shoes," she said.

"Okay! Thank you! We are very grateful. It's not out of your way?"

"Not a bit. I have to drop my friend at the chateau, but then your house is right down the alley. No problem!"

They locked the car and hurried to the rear door of the panel truck. The passenger greeted them, turning around from the front seat, a slim, neat young man with black hair pulled back into a pony tail, wearing a black turtleneck. The farmer got back in and drove slowly in four-wheel drive up the steep curves of the Dégout, making short work of the snow, which was almost six inches high by now. They made the usual remarks about the early snow. Coming to the intersection with the Gordes road they turned left to Barigoule, the driver staying in second gear and maintaining a slow but steady pace. From the back of the truck Michael and Nicole could see nothing of the road, only whirling white outside, but they were aware when the truck began to labor uphill. Then the shadow of the great chateau fell over them and the truck halted while an electric gate creaked open. Now they could make out the outlines of a great courtyard sheltered from the wind and snow. The little truck turned and then reversed back to a caver*nous* entryway. The young man skipped out of the truck and opened the rear door, smiling and pointing at the arched entrance.

"Monsieur, Madame Tolliver, I beg you to accept the hospitality of the chatelain. He has long wished to meet you both."

Nicole and Michael looked at each other in puzzlement. They had always heard that the lord of the chateau was a recluse and never invited anyone to visit.

"You know, we're right down the hill...it's quite a short walk... why don't we—"

But the driver had now come around to the rear door and was holding a revolver. "I'm afraid the chatelain has insisted." He didn't look nearly as friendly as his younger partner, quite threatening now.

CHAPTER TWENTY-NINE

Rosalind was gasping for breath when the path she had been following finally flattened out at the top of the hill. She'd come out without a hat or cap and now her blond hair was wet and plastered to her cheeks. Her jacket was waterproof but her jeans were damp and her running shoes were soaking. *Thank God, I'd had them on*, she thought, and wondered if any of her attackers were still on her trail. She knew she was east of town, although the snowfall was now thick enough to obscure the usual landmarks. To her left she could see a few dark shapes of houses amid the trees and realized she had come upon the tiny hamlet just outside town where the mayor lived. If she could find the house, she could escape her pursuers, get Madame the mayor to call the local policeman. But suddenly she was blinded by the headlights of a car parked by the side of the road in front of the nearest house. She was about to dart to the side and continue running when the door opened and a tall gaunt figure stepped out, waving to her. She recognized Marius.

"Madame! Madame Sullivan! You are in great danger. Please get in immediately. There are some terrible men who are trying to kill you!"

Rosalind tried to think, make some sense of the crazy events of the day. But she realized the accuracy of what Marius was saying. There *were* terrible men trying to kill her, rape her, whatever, and she dashed to the passenger side of the car and flung herself into the car.

"Help me, please! Those men can't be far behind!"

"Yes. There is craziness in the village. The only safe place now is the castle." Marius spun the car around in the snow and drove deliberatly, sliding a bit, but maneuvering up the gentle slope across the plateau, through the barren fields, and to the great gate of the chateau, now standing open, a sight Rosalind had never seen before. In the great courtyard a door flew open and a portly woman in a maid's uniform came trotting out with a huge umbrella. "Madame...I beg you, please come in quickly. Oh! Your poor hair! May I bring you a towel?"

Rosalind was too bewildered by events to do anything but agree. The maid let her through dark halls and through innumerable doorways, Marius bringing up the rear, until they emerged into an anteroom of some sort, stone floor, stone walls hung with tapestries and faint light coming in through high windows. A huge oaken door obviously opened into some important part of the castle. The maid darted through a narrow door, evidently a bathroom, for she returned promptly with a thick white Turkish towel, with which Rosalind gratefully mopped her head and then wound it into a turban.

"And your shoes! I must fetch you some slippers, Madame."

I should be feeling more relieved than this, thought Rosalind, and indeed there was a chill air of forboding in this stone room in spite of the maid's anxious chatter.

Before the maid could return with the promised slippers the great oaken door opened and a handsome young man, dark-haired with a pony tail, stood in the opening. He was wearing a black turtleneck and black leather pants. Rosalind thought immediately that he would have looked quite normal at a theatre party in London, but here in this medieval castle in Barigoule he was disturbingly out of place.

The young man appeared to catch sight of Rosalind as if by accident and immediately froze in an expression of delighted surprise. "Madame Sullivan! *Quel honneur!* Or would you rather speak in English? No? Very well. I have heard you speak French beautifully. Would you please come in!"

The first thing Rosalind saw was the size of the room. It was the central hall of the castle, built like a small cathedral, sixty feet long and at least forty feet wide, with tall columns leading up to Gothic arches overhead, where many windows let in the afternoon light, such as it was. Sconces on the walls held dozens of lights. Ancient oriental carpets covered the stone floors from wall to wall. At the end of the room in front of a massive fireplace full of glowing logs was an arrangement of dark leather chairs and couches, grouped comfortably around a huge low circular table. And then she suddenly saw Michael and Nicole sitting forlornly together on the couch to her left. She ran over quickly, threw herself into Nicole's arms and started sobbing, giving way finally to the day's horrors at the sight of a friendly face.

"Oh my God, Nikki! You can't believe...they were going to kill me—"

But Michael interrupted. "Roz, listen. I'm afraid there's something wrong here...." Then they all started to talk at once, but Nicole shushed them. "Let's talk in order." And she described how she and Michael had been stuck in the Dégout and had been picked up, luckily, as they had thought, by a little red truck, but then delivered to the chateau and forced to come in. A farmer, she said, but now with a revolver, and now they were locked in this goddamn castle.

Rosalind could not help interrupting. "A farmer in a red truck? Those bastards were trying to kill me. They caught me on the Apt road and I had to run all the way uphill...at least I made those little fucks run a bit!"

"This is what I think is happening," said Michael, and he began to describe what he thought was the nature of the organization that had gradually impeded their research into the massacre at the grotto, had taken the chance of killing Lebarbe and then Rousset, and had evidently had a long enough reach to assault him in Berkeley, and even attempt arson at a harmless religious institute in Arkansas.

"But why!" Rosalind was angry. "A crime four hundred and fifty years old." Then she suddenly considered. "But...Spencer! He must have missed me by now...he'll probably call Jeannot—"

But she paused as the great oaken door opened once more and her husband came in, looking bedraggled, and followed by Dreyfus and *Leyla Abdelaziz*, the woman looking furious, Dreyfus with his normally detached expression. Marius with a shotgun over his arm brought up the rear.

"Spence! Great fucking Christ! Did they hurt you? I'll—"

But Spencer shook his head ruefully. "No, my dear. Dreyfus and his lady came to call and we'd just gotten talking when that asshole Marius knocked on the door. When I opened he came in with that old farmer, both of them armed. I was going to put up a fuss, but Dreyfus said, 'No, let's go with them.' But they took his pistol. I don't know what the hell he's going to do—"

Dreyfus was patting the air with both hands, trying to calm everyone down. "Messieurs-'dames...I think maybe we shall now find something out. They—"

But Rosalind interrupted again. "Find something out! Hell yes we'll find out! I have it! I have the journal, with all its pages! We can finally read the whole thing...what what's-his-name...Jean the Miller told the court—when was it?—1595. I've got it right here!" And she reached into the breast pocket of her windbreaker.

Michael looked around quickly, and noted that Dreyfus and Abdelaziz were doing the same thing. They seemed to be alone, unguarded except for Marius, in this huge chamber, but the circumstances made it obvious that they were probably locked in, and undoubtedly being overheard.

Rosalind was now turning the pages. "Where did he stop, the boy Jean? Here it is, the last page..." And she began reading.

'Do you want me to toast your feet some more?' he asked me, using curse words I cannot repeat.

"That's the fucking captain...then he says...":

'The fire will not burn them. But it will suck all the air out and the heretics will suffocate on their way to Hell.' And he gave the command to light the fire. It was a huge blaze and burned for hours. The soldiers cooked their dinner over the coals for they had killed most of our cattle and goats and sheep and the fire helped to make a good dinner for them.

"That's where our copies end," said Nicole. "So go on, please!"

Rosalind looked around, steely eyed, then back at the page.

And we slept there...I should say, spent the night, for I never slept a second, thinking of the children I knew, little Marie-Claire, Françoise, Solange...and all the women of the village, almost, except some brave ones who had gone with the men. And it was cold, that April, and I was freezing and the soldiers were all sleeping close to the fire, but I could not, knowing that it was killing—[the court ordered a recess in order that Jean might compose himself]

But in the morning the ashes were cold and the Captain Mormoiron ordered the coals scraped aside and the bodies brought out. The soldiers were not pleased by this mission but some doughty pious lads—they were Papal troops, you understand—these lads wiggled in the hole and began to drag out bodies one by one, ah! How pitiful! The matrons, the maidens, and worst, the little children!

But then there was a cry from the hole and an arquebusier emerged, bottom first, dragging an old lady. I saw that it was old Madame Serre, our dear spell-worker, whom everyone in the village loved, the most holy and pious lady, who knew the holy writings better than—[Jean was counseled to continue with the events]

And she was alive! Her face blackened, her hands bloodied, she could not move, but her eyes were shining like terrible fire and she was looking around at us all. And she saw me and knew right away that I had told them...told them about the grotto, and she pierced me with her eyes. And Captain Mormoiron was in a furious rage, we thought he would go insane, and he raised his sabre and cried, 'Damned witch! Do you wish to live forever?'

And she looked around again, and then directly at the captain and she said:

'No. I shall not live forever.' And her eyes gleamed, and she crossed herself, and she said

'But you...you will all live forever!'

And Mormoiron with a hideous curse plunged his sabre into her breast and she died. And a very few soldiers cried 'bravo,' but most thought a poor shabby deed had been done that day and we walked back in silence.

[A question was put to Jean the Miller]

Yes, sire. I am now almost seventy years old, praise God, and still run the mill in Barigoule, and I know many of the soldiers, boys from the area they were, who were there that day, and it is curious...not one of us has gone to his reward, and I begin to wonder if what old Madame Serre said—

[Jean the Miller was cautioned that what he was contemplating was grave error and could be construed as actionable heresy and that he should never again think of such a thing. The court then heard a cobbler from Cabrières d'Avignon.]

"And that's the end," said Rosalind, spellbound. The others in the room could not bring themselves to speak, still imagining the scene in the space outside the grotto, hearing the words almost as spoken, until Spencer cleared his throat and intoned,

"And verily I say to you, that some here shall not taste of death until the coming of the Son of man with his kingdom."

"The words on the ceiling…in the grotto!" breathed Nicole, in disbelief. "It must have been her, lying up there, writing on the ceiling—"

"Preparing the spell," added Michael. "And then, trying to stay just alive until she was dragged out, and the other half—"

"How amusing!" A deep voice sounded behind them and they realized a large man had entered. He was not tall, but massive, a large grizzled head surmounting a portly body, clothed in a floor length black cloak. He had piercing light blue eyes, now darting from one to another of his guests, concentrating for a moment on Dreyfus. He traversed the room and sat in a large leather chair in front of the fire. And now they realized that he had been followed into the room by a slim young man, whom Michael and Nicole recognized as the passenger in the truck. Sidling in behind was the farmer, still carrying his handgun, and they joined Marius, still carrying his shotgun. They stood silently against the wall, waiting for the big man to speak.

"I must say that I never thought, when Monsieur Tolliver started his inquiries, that he and his friends"—and he gestured around the room at the Sullivans, Dreyfus, and Abdelaziz—"that they would actually find the secret of the grottos! How long did that publication, the testimony of Jean the Miller, how long was that testimony in archives, and then published for all to read…in a stupid journal put out by an impoverished society of pathetic theologians. Can you imagine how many people read that journal, that testimony? Not many. And of those who read it, who believed the old lady? '*You will live forever!*'" He broke into a high giggle that startled his hearers.

"It is ridiculous. But you, Monsieur Tolliver, you came here and started investigating from another direction. And that I could not permit."

Dreyfus had been letting the words wash over him, concentrating on where they were, and what they would have to do to get out. Was this lord of the castle four hundred and fifty years old? Or was he just crazy? What he did know was that a group of people had gone to extraordinary lengths to frighten these Tollivers and Sullivans, to kill their informants, and then try to kill him. As a policeman, he always wondered, 'What is at stake?' and although in his experience it was always either money or excess testosterone, he was now keenly focusing on what the big man was saying. Soon he would find out what was in back of this *connerie* and then they would figure out how to stay alive. What none of these posturing fools realized was that Abdelaziz still had a pistol. They had taken his but had never thought to search a woman. He had seen Leyla put her Glock .40 in a shoulder rig this morning and her leather jacket concealed it perfectly. And now she looked over at him, they exchanged glances, and he knew they had agreed...she was ready to go to war, if necessary.

Spencer broke the silence. "It's all bullshit, you know! No one is five hundred years old. You'd have putrid flesh falling off your bones. Teenage kids wouldn't even go to see this movie!" And he took Rosalind's arm and started toward the great door they'd come in.

Before he could get there, the door opened and a mime came in, a mime in a dusty black suit, his face a pasty white. And he was carrying a small machine pistol.

"Ah, Maurice!" said the big man. "I'm so glad you could join us." And he chuckled. They all stared at the menacing apparition, wondering why, until now, they had never realized how terrifying a mime could be, dirty, dusty, and with a rigid grimace of hatred that could indeed be centuries old.

"Now you see one of us...maybe not putrid flesh falling off his bones, but not a very good prognosis either. Now please behave, all. Maurice lives only to kill, as Inspector Dreyfus almost found out." He bowed to the policeman, who gave a slight shrug. And then the chatelain glared at Michael.

"Monsieur Tolliver. You started this entire investigation. You say you wish to find out what happened that day five...four and a half centuries ago? Mmm? Are you really prepared to hear?"

Michael stood up. "That's what I want to hear, of all things. And to start, what did you mean about this...this sick-looking mime, if he is a mime?"

The big man sank back against the couch, stretched his arms out on both sides, and considered his audience, person by person.

"All right. I'll start with Maurice. He is a mime because he lost his voice, more than two hundred years ago, under the guillotine." And he laughed at their shocked faces.

"Yes. Yes! Just imagine a sharp forty-kilo blade slicing through your larynx. *Hein*? He has been living forever, as the witch cursed him, but from time to time he has to change bodies, his spirit slipping to some nearby human of weak or unformed character, or low mental capacity. This Jew policeman here shot him in the lung. It should have killed an ordinary man but Maurice has more lives than an alley cat—"

Spencer burst out. "You're doing it again! This is the stupidest science fiction plot I've ever heard!" But neither Rosalind nor the Tollivers seemed ready to agree with him.

The big man sighed. "Will you all listen? Not interrupt for a bit? I want to tell you a story.

"We stood in the clearing, smelling the leftover smoke, looking at the pile of stained bodies, when the witch cursed us. It was the day after Easter, and yet—soldiers of the Pope as we were—we had not been to church, to celebrate His rising, because we were so intent on punishing this tiny hamlet, stealing its goods, and of course, having our pleasure with its women. It was thus we heard the horrid words, "You...you will all live forever!" and we laughed, maybe a bit nervously, but we laughed and watched as our Captain Mormoiron killed her with his sabre, and thought that was it. As we walked back to the town the only thing the men could think of was the regret that they hadn't caught the women alive and had their pleasure...as so many other soldiers had done.

"The document of Jean the Miller is correct. Fifty years after, none of us had died, or fifty more. When we first understood that the curse was real, and we tired of life, and sought to escape the curse, some ventured into military affairs...and there were many wars in the seventeenth and eighteenth centuries. Some were blasted with cannon balls, some were crisped in fire, some shriveled with the many horrible diseases of campaigning... dysentery, pneumonia, gangrene, tuberculosis. Their bodies died and they found themselves—their essential spirits, um, shall we say *transferred* to nearby bodies, persons of weak intellect or character, as I said, and realized that they had to live, live, live on... After a century we realized our fate: to survive, from one body to another, forever over the centuries. You may envy eternal life, but there are certain unpleasantnesses. Ravaillac shot and killed Henri IV in 1610. He was one of us. He was tortured unimaginably for a week and could not die, no matter how he wished it, until they drew all his guts out, winding them up on a windlass, and then tore his limbs apart with teams of horses. Even then he woke up in the body of a hunchback, died again of plague, and was suddenly the simpleton son of a great noble. And then in 1793 he kneeled under the guillotine..."

They all looked over at Maurice the mime, hesitating to believe the unbelievable, wondering how many bodies *he* had occupied since the guillotine. Then Michael interrupted.

"It was a terrible curse, if you are not just spinning some ridiculous story, but there were certain advantages for those of you who went from life to life and realized what was happening."

"Yes," said Dreyfus, speaking for the first time. "Yes, of course. Money and power. Knowledge, experience, more than anyone can learn in one lifetime, learning the mistakes, avoiding them, seeing the opportunities. And that is what they have now and that is what they are protecting. Not the silly story of the curse—real as that may be, who would ever believe it? No. They are protecting the wealth and power they have acquired during the last three or four hundred years. I wondered how a ministry could call off my investigation behind the scenes, how not once but two times they tried to murder me, how they could just send down the order: *Do not investigate nuns!*"

The big man burst into raucous laughter. "The nuns, the nuns! Who could suspect?" And he reached behind him and pulled out a pair of thick glasses and a nun's wimple, pulling it onto his head. They all suddenly noticed that under his black robe he was also wearing colorful running shoes.

"*In excelsis Deo,*" he said in a high voice, squinting and crossing himself. The slim man beside him giggled and all were now aware who the second, smaller nun had been. And then the big man suddenly became angry.

"This stupid heresy drove us to protect the true church, which I had sworn to serve my whole life, and then our lives were ripped apart by the curse of a witch using the satanic arts!"

"No!!" Nicole startled everyone by speaking strongly, angrily. "What satanic arts? We have been in the grotto. We have seen the old lady's prayer written on the ceiling. And those are the words of Jesus himself: '*Some of you will not taste of death until the Son of man comes with his kingdom.*' The words of the Gospel. However it was that she blasted you with those words I don't know, but it was not Jeanne Serre who used the arts of Satan, it was you, and your filthy crew doing the devil's work, the day after Easter, the day after He had risen, killing twenty-five innocent women and children—"

"Stop this stupid nonsense, you idiot woman!" the big man shouted. "Do you think yourselves believers? What do you know of Holy Church? I was a priest that day...and many times I have served in holy office—"

"And then you and your friend put on nuns' clothes and went out to murder innocent people," Michael chimed in. "Professor Lebarbe and Monsieur Rousset—"

"And two prisoners in the hospital at Montfavet," added Dreyfus. As they all turned to face him, startled, he went on. "A Corsican gangster, who was supposed to kill me, and knew too much. And a poor stupid burglar who just happened to be there. The surveillance cameras at the hospital have them coming and going. It could be no one else. Injections of ricin, the doctors said this morning."

The big man stood up. "This nonsense has gone on long enough. I had hoped we might have an interesting discussion about the metaphysics of eternal life, but now I find all your opinions are just boring. Contrary to the Gospel of Saint Matthew, not all of us here will live forever. Maurice? With whom would you like to start?"

The mime's face was contorted with hatred. He jacked up a round in his machine pistol and brought it to bear on Dreyfus. The room echoed with a shot and all turned automatically toward the detective. But it was Maurice with a shocked expression on his face who toppled backward, slumping to the floor with his weapon. Now the farmer started to level his revolver but a black hole appeared in his forehead and another echo crashed around the room. All eyes turned to see *Leyla Abdelaziz* in marksman position, double-handed grip on her pistol, shifting it back and forth between the big man, his slim companion, and Marius, who still had a shotgun but showed no intention of using it. Instead he leaned over and carefully put the gun on the floor.

Dreyfus quickly stepped over to the prostrate form of Maurice the mime and picked up his machine pistol. He pointed it at the big man.

"Are you armed, you pile of shit? Any move and I'll kill you, and your spirit can fly to the rats in the walls here to be born again."

The big man stared back contemptuously. "This doesn't end here. You'll never get out—." But Dreyfus had caught up a heavy ornate candlestick and smashed it across the chatelain's face. Blood spattered the couch as he fell backward and his hands flew upward.

"Maybe we can't kill you, but you can feel pain, no? We *are* leaving, and you are going first, you and your little nun sister here, in case someone is waiting outside that door! Leyla, let's move!" And he kicked the chatelain brutally in the legs until he heaved himself up, uttering little cries and breathing hard.

Between them they herded the chatelain, the little man, and Marius to form a wedge going out the door, Michael now carrying Marius's weapon, a lethal 10-gauge double-barreled shotgun. Whatever the chatelain expected outside the door must have disappointed him. There was no one there at all. They all stopped for a moment. "Wait," called Spencer. "We don't have to go out the gate. Anyone can fire down on us from the towers. There's another exit through the church." And he ventured toward his right. "If my directions are right, the cloister should be out this door."

They found themselves in a small courtyard full of snow with a covered passageway leading to a great door in what was obviously the back of the church. Michael charged to the front of the group and opened the door, gesturing their prisoners to enter. There was a sound of many voices, and as they passed through a narrow hallway and up several stairs they found themselves in the nave of a church one third full of people all gawking at the intruders. The priest, Jean-Claude was staring sideways from the altar, incomprehensibly, seeing this strange parade passing through his church. Several elderly nearsighted worshipers continued to chant a response in the back of the church.

"Father," said Dreyfus. "We leave these persons in your care. Maybe they will be better for it." And Dreyfus, Abdelaziz, the Sullivans, and Tollivers, walked down the aisle to the door of the church, leaving the chatelain and his company to explain themselves to the congregation.

Once outside, Michael spoke up quickly. "Now...while they're thinking it over, let's all get down to our house. Only a hundred meters. With the shutters closed it's like a fortress. And we can try to figure out how to get word out, get help."

But as they trooped down the narrow alley, tromping through snow to their ankles, people came out of houses smiling at them, some clapping them on the shoulders.

"We heard the shots."

"We thought—"

"Don't worry now, there are lots of us here. And we have guns too."

And indeed there were the familiar faces of villagers, here and there a man with a shotgun, or a .22 rifle, and once a bearded man they recognized as the mailman, smiling grimly and holding an AK 47, an arm completely forbidden in France. "You'll be safe," he said. "We've been afraid of them up there too long."

Another man approached. "We know there's a tree down just outside of town on the Gordes road. The road crew won't come out until tomorrow, so we're stuck here. But don't worry. We're going to try to keep the *zombies* up there in the chateau tonight."

At the Tolliver house they secured shutters and doors and then gathered in the great salon. Dreyfus was trying to use his cell phone but Michael told him that *portables* would not work in Barigoule because the nearest relays were out of range. Spencer soon found that the house phones were completely dead.

"Maybe the snow brought down the lines," he said.

"More probably the bastards cut it somewhere," said his wife. "So we're trapped here for the night."

"I wonder where Jeannot is?" asked Dreyfus, and then immediately turned to his partner. "Leyla...I'm sorry! Are you all right? You saved my life up there!" and he forced her to sit in Spencer's great chair. Tne young woman was pale and drawn but she reacted with anger.

"Me...? I am fine! Those people up there are devils and should have been dead long ago. *Djinni*! That terrible man was going to kill you, and then us. And the man with the shotgun. I felt nothing! I would say a prayer for the Corsicans the other night... real human beings I shot. Gangsters and killers, but still human. But these pigs? Cursed by God. Now what? Are they going to appear again? In other bodies?"

Nicole knelt beside her. "Leyla. We don't know. This is beyond all our understanding. We don't know if they get reborn right away, or if they do at all. All we can do right now is stay alive ourselves. Mikey? What do you think?"

"It's dark now, we're snowed in, the phones don't work. Dreyfus said something about finding Jeannot. I've got this shotgun, maybe I'll go down to the café and find him."

Nicole and Rosalind protested, but Michael poked his head out the door, looked around and was gone. Only a minute later he was back, banging on the door.

"Café is closed. Tighter than a drum. I wonder if he and the family went back to Gordes today."

"All we can do is wait then," said Spencer. "Tomorrow, we can walk to our house and get the Landrover. It'll get us to Gordes and the gendarmerie. We can go cross country in that beast if we have to."

Nicole found some sausage and cheese and bread in the kitchen and Michael opened a bottle of wine. At first no one felt like eating but after a few bites their bodies reminded them that they were actually hungry. Dreyfus was munching on a slice of *saucisson* when he intercepted a reproachful look from Abdelaziz. He smiled and shrugged. "I am French first, then Jewish," he explained. Nicole caught the exchange

"Oh dear, I'm sorry! I forgot that you, that both of you—"

"No, only one of us," said Leyla, but she laughed.

"I should have thought...you know, it's no trouble at all to make an omelette."

"No, no, I'm quite happy with some cheese."

"It's a marvelous idea," said Spencer. "I'll have an omelette too. In fact, I'll cook them. No...sit down. I feel like doing something useful."

With omelettes served, Nicole and Rosalind noticed that the policewoman who had been happy with a little cheese made a large omelette disappear in three bites. The momentary distraction, the food, and another bottle of wine made them all more comfortable and Nicole started worrying about sleeping arrangements. The policeman became professional.

"We should take turns on guard tonight," said Dreyfus. "You think they cannot break into this house?"

"The shutters are double-planked oak, with steel slats between the planks," said Michael. "Jeannot built this house like a castle. Still, it's a good idea. I'll take first watch, but come with me now and I'll show you all over the house."

CHAPTER THIRTY

No one slept very well that night and all were anxious to leave the next morning as soon as a grey light filtered through the shuttered windows. They straggled out of various rooms into the salon.

"It's cold," said Michael, sticking his head out the front door. "But it's stopped snowing. Better bundle up."

"Where is Dreyfus?" Leyla was looking around, startled. "David...David?" And she started called up the stairs.

"He had the last watch," said Spencer. "Did he go out when it got light?"

"He must have," Michael answered, looking out the door again. "Footprints, with street shoes. Was he wearing street shoes?"

"Yes...and he has no coat, only his jacket! I must look for him—." Leyla was halfway out the door when Rosalind caught her by the arm.

"We mustn't get separated...that's what they'd want!"

"But...?"

"And we need a police person with us, Leyla. After all, you have a gun." said Nicole, instinctively saying the right thing to remind Leyla that she was, after all, a responsible member of the security forces. "I bet he's just trying to find someplace where his *portable* will work."

"Or looking for Jeannot," added Rosalind. "They're old friends."

"I...Yes, I'll come with you. But how will David know where we've gone?"

"I said last night we'd try for our house," said Spencer. "I'm sure he'll look for us there. I wouldn't worry about Dreyfus. We know half the village is with us, and he does have a machine gun with him, after all."

Leyla seemed reassured once she'd thought it over. Nicole insisted on handing out sweaters. Leyla had to take off her jacket and shoulder rig to put on the sweater and they were all reminded of the heavy pistol she carried and the work it had done the day before. Michael carried the shotgun Marius had surrendered, and Rosalind, to everyone's surprise, turned out to have the farmer's revolver.

"It seemed such a waste, just leaving it there," she said. "It skidded across the floor and I just automatically picked it up."

Spencer started to protest put she patted him on the shoulder.

"You know I can shoot, old bear. And the bastards gave me such a scare yesterday...that fat man thought he was going to rape me. If I even see him I'll shoot his balls off." And then she shut up, feeling ashamed of bragging in front of another woman whom she'd seen gun down two armed men with two deadly shots. But Leyla grinned at her.

"You have the right attitude," she said.

They gathered on the terrace and looked northeast down the back alley toward the main road leading northward to the Sullivan house, and then over the mountain to Sault. There wasn't a soul in the streets. The snow was over their ankles, but once on the main road they found that vehicles had left tracks that were easy to walk in.

The Sullivan house was only a kilometer from the village on the flat top of the plateau and Nicole vividly remembered her dream in the hospital, how she'd walked along along this road, with the wheat blowing in the wind on either side, how she knew someone was following her. Nothing but snow-covered fields this time. She turned around abruptly but the road was empty and she realized that Michael had turned at the same time.

"We're both thinking the same thing," he said and gave her a little grin. But she couldn't help a terrible premonition...that they would come around the long curve and see a smoking ruin where Spencer and Rosalind had lived. Therefore she went weak with relief as the house came into view looking just as she had last seen it.

"Damn!" Spencer was cursing. "I don't think I have the key to the garage with me."

"I do, love," said Rosalind, "but I think the door is ajar. Did you leave it open?"

They soon discovered the bad news. The lock had been forced, the tires on the big Landrover were all flat, and someone had gone to the trouble of loosening the crankcase nut and had let all the oil out. A black pool had spread onto the concrete slab on either side of the car.

For a moment they just stood there. They had all been counting so much on this vehicle, a car that could go anywhere, visualizing a quick trip to Gordes, a welcome by the gendarmes, and a swift visit by the military to put things right in Barigoule. Spencer had been rehearsing what he would say to the press, and wondering if he should mention four hundred and fifty-year-old criminals right away or save it for later.

"I wonder why they didn't just bash in the windows, pry the hood open and wreck the engine?" asked Nicole in a shaky voice.

"I'm sorry to alarm you," replied Abdelaziz immediately, "but it is obvious someone wants to keep your car for himself, and you will not be here any more."

"That's right," said Spencer. "The bastards! Just pump up the tires, put in some oil, and they got a fifty thousand euro Landrover."

"And someone in government will orchestrate new ownership papers," Leyla added. The Arab woman's eyes were flashing. "We now know their intentions and perhaps we should reexamine our position."

"Well, we can't stay here," Michael was saying. "Back to our house, anyone?"

"It seems like such a step backward," said Rosalind. "You know that the Hauers live just up the road to Sault. It can't be more than another kilometer or so. And the judge has a citizens' band radio, I know. He was bragging about it last time we were there, how it was illegal in France, all that bullshit. We're almost halfway there. Let's find out how illegal it is."

They walked up the road, almost enjoying the hike. Although the temperature was still around freezing, the sun was peaking out from time to time and they were treated to a landscape from another time. Not a soul to be seen, not a vehicle, dead silence now that the wind had dropped to nothing. The only other living things they saw were a few magpies in the distance, swooping from tree to barren tree. The road led northward, through mixed pine forest, and still the tracks of a vehicle through the snow made an easy path.

But as they came around another curve they saw that a tree was down right across the road, and beyond it, no vehicle had gone. No one was pretending that this tree had blown down in the storm; the marks of the chain saw were clear. The snow on the roadway ahead looked deeper than what they'd been through, maybe knee high, and they knew they couldn't walk very far in that direction.

All eyes turned to the track that ran off to the left. The car, or truck, whose track they had been following had obviously turned here to go down the track, leaving them one obvious route to follow. The Sullivans and Tollivers looked at each other, knowing very well what lay down that track.

"Not a very good time to visit the grotto again, I don't think," Nicole shivered.

"But you know that big farm just down this road, what is it...a half kilometer beyond the grottos, just a few minutes more," said Rosalind. "The Claparèdes. I was talking to her in the market just the other day. And they'll have a farm truck or something. In fact whatever made these tracks is probably one of their trucks."

At that moment they heard the dogs in the distance, the unmistakable yelping of dogs on the hunt. The sound came from the south, toward town, from where they had come and from the west, down in the valley to their left.

"Jesus! They're doing a *battu* on a day like this?" Spencer sounded outraged. A *battu* was a carefully planned encirclement of a wild boar, or boars, using hounds to draw them into a valley where they could be cornered and shot down.

"Who could catch a boar in these conditions?" wondered Michael. "Usually the boars can fool the hounds even on dry ground. The dogs can't smell a boar today."

"They are hunting us," Leyla said solemnly, and they all realized she was right.

"We made a wrong move and put ourselves in the country, where they can pin us down."

"But the Claparède farm is just ahead," said Rosalind. "If we just—." But Michael cut her off, raising his head and sniffing the gentle northwest breeze in their faces.

"Cigarette. And just ahead. There's an ambush. Those assholes always smoke when they're hunting. That's why they never catch anything."

Then there was a moment when all eyes turned to the right, to the gentle slope up through the scrub oaks, now leafless, to the path beneath the cliffs and the grotto. It was a moment of comprehension, as they all realized their position and knew where they would have to go.

"We're trapped here," said Spencer.

"And they won't expect us to go to the grottos."

"Or maybe they do?"

"Still, they'll shoot us down out here in the open," said Michael. "We know they can't shoot anyone in the grottos. They know we're armed." And he started climbing the slope. Spencer was just about to object when they heard a shot from far off and a branch fell off a tree to their left. That settled the argument.

"I've got some brush here," said Rosalind. "I'll bring up the rear and sweep our footsteps."

"I think they know where we're going,' said Spencer. "But you're right. Why make it easy for them."

Inside the outer cave they paused, listening for the hunt. The hounds now sounded closer, and down in the valley two men were shouting at each other. Nicole looked terrified, but she was the first to speak.

"I guess I'll take the lead," and she turned to the dark entry hole, which looked smaller and darker than they remembered.

"I'll go next," said Leyla. "And I have a small light." She held up a pencil flashlight. "We always carry them."

Michael was last in, having done the best he could to obscure their footprints in the dust. They huddled away from the entrance in the large inner chamber and were silent, hoping the hunters would pass them by. The yelping grew nearer and nearer and then converged. They now heard footsteps and knew that the hunt had reached the entrances to the grottos. And then suddenly a dog came right through the entrance hole, wagging his tail, and started nuzzling Nicole, a white and red spaniel mix.

"Now what?" blurted Spencer.

"It's that damned Nox, down the street from us. His owner is a jerk, lets him roam, and Nicole feeds him sometimes."

There was a whistle outside and Nox reluctantly crawled back out the hole. Then they heard a familiar voice.

"The Tollivers, I believe. And Monsieur and Madame Sullivan. How convenient. And you have your two little policemen with you, I assume?"

"He doesn't know Dreyfus isn't here," whispered Rosalind to Leyla.

"Perhaps I could persuade you all to come out?...No?...Well I'm sure you know what comes next." And in fact they had already heard the sounds of brush being dragged into the outside cave.

Leyla responded by snapping a quick pistol shot out the hole in the direction of the voice. There was a cry of pain and a curse, then angry shouting. Several shotguns discharged at once into the grotto, almost hitting Leyla before she could scramble back.

"Ah, history repeats itself! I remember how we tried to fire into the grotto. But there is shelter in there, I know. I'm afraid you've done for poor Anselme. But Gérard here says he has brought a hand grenade. An improvement over the technology of the sixteenth century, *hein*? Maybe quicker than the fire. All right, Gérard, give it a toss. And everyone stand back..."

Michael quickly knelt by the entrance hole, a shortstop waiting for a ground ball. "We still have a chance here... " And at his last words they heard a pop outside and then a oval green object came bouncing hard into the grotto. Michael pounced on it unerringly and in the same motion hurled the missile underarm back out the hole. There was a sharp crack of an explosion and bits of shrapnel peppered the back of the grotto. A moment of silence, then screams and curses outside.

Inside the grotto there was cheering. "Great shot, Mikey!"

"Super!!" Leyla was laughing excitedly.

"That's it for you bastards!" The chatelain's voice was high and pained. "It's the fire for you now. Come on, drag them away... bring more brush!"

"At least we got some of the bastards," hissed Rosalind.

"I'm afraid I got tagged a bit myself," said Michael, holding his arm, and even in the dim light they could see the dark stains on the sleeve of his jacket.

"Some of the shrapnel. But I don't think it's serious."

Nicole insisted on taking his jacket off and checking the cuts on his arm. They were bloody but superficial and Michael was grumbling while Rosalind and Leyla were debating a quick dash outside to try to gun down as many as possible. But there was a *whooosh* outside as someone hastened the ignition of the brush pile with a bit of fuel. If anyone had retained an objective curiousity about the fate of the martyrs of 1545, they could now see clearly that smoke did not penetrate the chamber, but they could almost feel the air in the chamber flowing toward the fire.

"How much air do you think we have?" wondered Nicole.

"Maybe someone will spot the smoke," suggested Spencer.

Michael was pessimistic. "We can always hope, but farmers burn their cuttings all winter long. The only hope is that Dreyfus got out somehow and is on the phone."

Rosalind had been inspecting the back of the grotto and sounded suddenly excited. "You know, there's a current of air coming in from the back. Come here! You can feel it!

Michael crouched next to her. "My God! You're right! But how could...why did the others die then? Jean testified that they were all suffocated.

"Some earthquake, maybe? Or a new opening way in back there? Professor Lebarbe said these limestone caves keep dissolving slowly. But can anyone get through?" Spencer was thinking of his own girth.

"We have to try," said Rosalind firmly. "Remember, Jeannot told us about those kids who got lost. They got into the tunnels and so did the *speleos* who rescued them. It seems to me you just keep the current of air on your face and follow it."

Spencer agreed to lead the way, but he got stuck at the first turning of the narrow tunnel and had to be pulled back by his ankles. He was breathing hard and sounded distraught, on the edge of panic. "I'll just have to wait here, guys. Good luck!" His voice broke.

Rosalind was resigned. "Then I'm staying too with you, big bear. After all, I've got a gun, and if they try to come in after the fire I'll shoot them."

Michael had his head and shoulders in the tunnel, investigating with the little torch and now his voice came back. "It gets wider. There seem to be two branches ahead and I'm pretty sure the air is coming from the one that goes right and upward."

In the end they decided that Leyla and Nicole would go with Michael as both showed signs of increasing alarm and wanted to do anything rather than just sit in the cave and wait to die. The shotgun was left with Spencer and Rosalind, as it only got in the way.

Crawling, sliding on their backs and bellies, climbing through vertical cracks they made their way, stopping now and then to check the current of air. Michael led the way, using Leyla's little flashlight. They were passing through cold, smooth grey limestone tubes, so round and sterile that they almost looked manufactured.

Nicole had a tiny keychain light that gave more reassurance than visibility. At one point, on hands and knees, Michael put his hand on nothingness.

"Hold up a second...there's a drop here." The torch showed not just a drop but a large round hole, perfectly large enough to swallow a careless explorer. Michael could see no bottom with the light, so he looked around for a pebble and let it drop. Three seconds went by and then he heard the unmistakable *plop* of a stone hitting water.

"That answers one question," he relayed to the women. "Something dropped out of the floor here into a lower cave, and it's *way, way* down! There's just a ledge here to get by on. I'll go first and then shine the light back."

Gradually they edged their way around the hole and then continued. At times it seemed that they could feel no current of air, but Leyla had a box of matches and the flame always fluttered reliably. Then they came to one small chamber that seemed to have no exit until Leyla, searching by touch and feeling for the air current, found a wide crack in the ceiling of the cave to the right side. She checked with a match.

"There is air coming down," she said. "If you give me a leg up I'll see if I can get through."

Michael objected. "No. You should give me the leg up. If I can't get through, I'm stuck anyway. If I can fit through, and there's more room up there, I'm stronger and I can pull both of you up." The women were convinced, seeing the logic.

Leyla cupped her hands and Michael stepped up into the crack. Clawing at every handhold, blind without the flashlight now, he scraped his way between walls slimy with damp limestone and finally reached a horizontal shelf with enough room to turn around. He stuck his head back the hole and saw Leyla and Nicole looking up, but too far down for him to reach. He also noticed that the flashlight was getting yellow and he realized if they didn't get somewhere pretty soon, they would be operating in complete blackness. He took off his belt and made it into a loop.

"Nikki, grab the belt, and Leyla, give her a boost up." He was correctly assuming that the policewoman was stronger than his wife.

Nicole came through the slot fairly easily with Michael tugging on the belt. Then it was Leyla's turn to grab the belt and be dragged over the rock. Michael was exhausted now and at one point the belt slipped a bit in his sweaty hands, but Leyla managed to keep her position, losing a fingernail as she clawed at the rock, and crying out in pain. Then she was on the platform with them, all of them panting with the exertion. For a moment no one could talk. And then the flashlight went out.

They all fought to control their panic, Michael trying to reassure them and himself. "As long as we can still feel the air current..."

But they couldn't. Leyla lit a match and it made a motionless flame pointing straight up. They'd come around too many corners, up too many slopes. They started to slump in resignation.

"You know," said Nicole suddenly. "After that match went out I thought my eyes were still adjusting to the dark. But actually I think I see some light."

They clustered around her as she pointed ahead and slightly to the right and upward. There was a tiny thread of grey light at the end of a long crevice.

"You're right! But can we get through there?" Leyla's voice quavered. They were so close...too close to be frustrated this way. Feel this rock," said Michael. "It's not smooth and water worn like the rest of the cave. It's really broken rock, as if the roof fell in sometime. I bet we can pull enough rock out to get through." And he began tugging at a slab directly in front of him. It moved easily and as he slid it out of place it was followed by a small avalanche of smaller rocks up the slope. Now there was more light and they could see that there was room to crawl up a medium slope. The light was coming from the right and as Michael reached the corner he saw what they had all been dreaming of.

"We're out!" he exclaimed. "There's the forest. And we seem to be on a cliff. I hope it's just not a hole into midair…it looks like a long drop down to the ground."

Then as he clambered to the edge of the hole he saw a ledge leading off to the left. Narrow, maybe too narrow, but the top of the cliff seemed to be just above and there were tree roots growing out of it. He turned back to the women.

"There's a tricky bit here. But there are handholds. I think we can get on top of the cliff on this ledge. Just grab a root and make sure it's a solid one. And he began to inch along the ledge.

"Yes!" he called behind him. "The top's right here!" And that was when he turned back again and saw a pair of boots planted on the dirt in front of him. For a moment he was panic stricken and then he looked up and recognized the face.

"Jeannot! Thank God! We thought we were stuck in there! Give me a hand up."

But Jeannot's face was grim. "I'm sorry, Michael, I wish you had never gotten this far. Now you have to go back."

For a moment Michael couldn't comprehend what he was hearing. Nicole was behind him asking, "Is it really Jeannot? Where are we anyway?" And then he realized there could only be one explanation.

"You're with them!" he shouted accusingly. "How could you, you bastard—"

"No, not with them," Jeannot interrupted. "I am one of them. I'm sorry Mike, Nicole…I wished this never would happen, never get to this point, but—."

"What do you mean, 'one of them'? You can't be⌐⌐—."

"Ah. Yes I am. I have been for so many centuries."

"You were one of the soldiers?" Michael was incredulous.

Jeannot was silent for a beat or two. "No, not a soldier. But I was there. I was there because I betrayed the women and children."

"You were...you mean you were, are—"

"Yes. Jean the Miller's son. Jean, who built the dam. Jean, who was tortured with fire and was too weak, who gave away the women. And the witch looked me in the eye and it was like a knife going in my brain. And I have been trying either to live or die ever since."

"But you're not going to stop us...kill us? How could you!" Nicole couldn't see Jeannot, but she'd heard the exchange. Like Michael, she couldn't believe it.

"It's been so long. You can't believe the things I've seen in my life...all my lives. And always I sought war and violence, thinking every time I died it might be the last time. But it never was. I died...just the last century, I died in Flanders. Poison gas. I fought in the resistance in the next war. They put me in a camp and I starved to death.

I was just a boy when DeGaulle ended the war in Algeria, or I would have gone there. But there was a bomb, protesting DeGaulle, and I was blown to bits."

"I can't believe I'm hearing this," said Nicole. And then she realized that Leyla, behind her, was prodding her with something hard. She turned around and saw it was Leyla's pistol.

"Pass it to Michael," the policewoman whispered. "I can't get around you."

Would it work? Nicole wondered. *Could Michael shoot his old friend? Are we all crazy?* But she took the gun and, slowly, out of Jeannot's sight started prodding Michael in his left leg, which was under the cliff.

Jeannot was finishing his story. "So when I retired from rugby I met Danielle, and for the first time I had a life I loved, a woman I loved, my little Gaby, a daughter I loved. And I thought, I can live out at least one life peacefully, and maybe God will give me back the gift of death. So I worried when you started digging into this stupid grotto thing...so long ago. I always thought, maybe when everyone has forgotten the grotto, then the curse will be over."

Michael had now figured out what Nicole was poking into his leg. His left hand, concealed from above, slowly reached back and Nicole placed the pistol in it. *But how can I shoot Jeannot?* he thought. And he remembered suddenly that night outside the café, when he had punched Jeannot so hard, and the man had swelled up like a goblin and he'd been afraid for his life. Now, all Jeannot had to do was kick him and he'd be on the rocks below, and now he realized where they were. On the rim of the grotto whose roof had caved in, the grotto into which animals fell to their death.

"Michael, I have to preserve this life. I tried to tell the chatelain and the others not to cover up, that they'd only make things worse."

"But the journal...your own testimony! It was there in black and white for everyone to read! How could you hide that?" Michael was trying to transfer the pistol from his left hand to his right without Jeannot noticing.

"Yes, it was printed. And who read it? Those who did just laughed. It was like your flying saucers. No one believed, no one cared, no one investigated." Jeannot raised his head, sniffed the air.

"And now I think the fire is burning down and they will go in. Mike, you have to go back. I can't have this happen. It pains me so, but if you have seen one tenth of the things I have seen in four hundred and fifty years you would know, to me it is a hard thing, but not that hard. Today I will go back to Danielle and Gaby and open the bar as if nothing happened." His voice hardened. "Now, back down the hole, or down the cliff, I don't care which."

The boar had heard the beginning of the *battu*, the men parking their cars, the hounds running around like crazy, baying. As always, long experience had taught him that the best way was uphill. He had been down in the valley, eating the remnants of pumpkins in the Claparède fields, and he had immediately headed for the hills. He had been hit by a lucky shot three weeks ago, a .22 bullet that was still in his shoulder, and the pain was getting worse. As he reached the top of the cliffs, there in the scrub forest, pines and oak, he knew he was safe. The hounds had stopped yelping far away, and for some time there had been burning. He knew he was no longer in the trap.

But then his keen nose picked up the human. He approached warily, his snout circling the air to pick up any scent. There were no dogs, that was sure. And there were no guns, no reek of the loud noises that could hurt and kill. But he picked up the odor of the ones who so often tried to kill him: garlic, cigarette smoke, sweat, male sexual odors. And there was something dark and evil about this one's smell. So the pain from the bullet in his shoulder told him, *Kill this big one! Get the tusks in him, throw him in the air, stomp him to death!* And he crept without a sound through the underbrush until he could see the big man with his back to him, a man with the smell now of anger and killing. And without another thought he charged.

Michael was about to bring up the pistol, take a last chance, when he heard the insane squeal, saw out of the corner of his eye the great brown beast charging across the clearing at the top of the cliff. And he could not help shouting, "Jeannot! Look out!"

The big man was slow to turn, looking for a trick, but he'd heard the squeal too and swiveled, fast as light to meet the threat. There was a medium-sized oak right next to Jeannot, and he could have swung up into the limbs, but that was not the way Jeannot lived, or had lived for four hundred and fifty years. He faced the boar, gave a great shout and charged it, head down, arms apart, and Michael saw that he was going to try to grab it, lift it off the ground, and use its momentum to throw it into the pit.

Jeannot set his feet, felt the boar's tusks bite into his calf, grabbed the animal around the shoulders and heaved as hard as he could. He had not counted on a beast that weighed quite a bit more than he did. The animal came off the ground, shrieking with hate, and a tusk took Jeannot at mid thigh and cut to the bone. He staggered backward, made one attempt to turn and loose the boar into the void but his leg wouldn't answer, his boot heels scrabbled in the pebbles at the edge of the cliff and the two creatures, man and beast, entwined, fell out into thin air and crashed into the bottom of the pit.

Michael, Nicole, and Leyla watched unbelievingly. The two forms below them were motionless. It was Nicole who first got her wits about her.

"Mikey! Let's get out of here! Who knows who else is coming!" The thought was compulsive and Michael, grasping roots, made his way to the cliff top. From there, lying on his belly, he was able to help first Nicole, then Leyla to safe ground.

"Now what?" Nicole asked.

"That man," said Leyla. "He must have come from a road up here. Where—?"

"Of course," Michael exclaimed. "He must have come up the road to Sault, cut through the forest here. We should head, let's see...about due east." And indeed, it was easy to follow Jeannot's route in the snow and where he had forced his way through the low shrubs. They were in sight of the road when they suddenly heard a familiar sound, a *whick, whick, whick,* from above.

"Oh Jesus! Don't tell me they have helicopters too!" moaned Nicole, but when the chopper came into view it was dark blue and they could see the letters, *Gendarmerie de France.* It landed on the road, sending up a spray of snow in all directions, a door opened and suddenly Leyla was running down the slope toward the figure that had emerged.

"David! David!..." It was Dreyfus, and behind him three gendarmes in full combat gear, assault rifles at the ready.

CHAPTER THIRTY-ONE

Rosalind and Spencer were huddled at the back of the grotto next to the tunnel where the current of air was reassuring. But smoke had been filtering bit by bit into the cavern and Spencer couldn't stop coughing. Then suddenly they heard shouting outside and the reports of shotguns. The shotguns were immediately answered by the rattle of machine-gun fire and now they could hear the *whick, whick, whick* of a helicopter.

"My God!" Spencer said hoarsely. "The cavalry is here!" And there were voices outside, they could see boots kicking the fire apart, and then someone shouted into the entrance hole, "*Gendarmarie de France! 'Y'a personne?*"

"*Oui, oui! 'Y'a nous deux...* Jesus, Spencer, do you think the others can get back here?"

They saw snow being thrown onto the ground outside the hole, hissing at first and then just melting. A head came through the hole, a fine young man in camouflage uniform. He was testing the temperature of the ground.

"I think you can come out now, it's cool," he said in French.

The Sullivans exited clumsily but quickly, coated now with mud and cinders from the remains of the fire, found themselves facing three gendarmes in commando gear. A helicopter hovered overhead, still trailing the ropes the soldiers had come down, but it now put its nose down and took off toward the south.

"We have some friends…" Both of them started talking at once. "There are three more of us," Rosalind went on. "They went back up the tunnels in back of the grotto! Can we—."

One of the gendarmes interrupted. "Your friends were lucky. They came out the back, up there." He pointed. "They told us you were here and these terrorists were trying to kill you." And now the Sullivans noticed for the first time that there were bodies on the slope, including a fat man in a black robe.

"They shot at us first, so we had to fire back. I think we got two, maybe more. The others ran away, back up the track there. Don't worry, we'll get them."

"There are two words that get the attention of French police," said Dreyfus. "Terrorist and cult. I told them you were being hunted by a terrorist cult and they had a helicopter in the air in ten minutes."

It was evening and they were sitting in the Sullivan living room drinking coffee and cognac. After the rescue they had been hauled off to the clinic in Gordes to be examined and Michael's wounds had been treated. Then there had been endless interrogation all afternoon by both gendarmes and by departmental *police judiciare* from Avignon. Dreyfus had managed to slip a word to them first. "Remember! These men who attacked you belonged to a cult and believed they were four hundred and fifty years old. Stick to that story." They did, and the police believed it as if there was nothing unusual. Now Dreyfus was explaining.

"France has a history of crazy cults. Ten years ago there was a group in the Alps that believed they all had to commit suicide because a space ship was coming to pick up their souls. But also, these cults usually force their young and brainwashed recruits to sign over all their property to the cult, and this offends French laws about inheritance and the alienation of family goods. Anyway, the gendarmes came immediately, and now they believe they have the complete story, including the Lebarbe and Rousset murders."

"Now, finally," said Michael, "tell us how you got out, where you went this morning."

"My God! Was it only this morning?" Nicole was shaking her head.

"I left the house thinking that if I could just get down the road closer to Joucas I could use the cell phone. It took me almost an hour and I had reached the Mas des Herbes Blanches and the phone still didn't work. But the Mas was open and their phone lines were still up. All I had to do was tell my friend René there at the gendarmerie that there was a terrorist cult murdering people here and they had a helicopter on its way from Avignon with a commando team. They picked me up at the hotel and we came first to town but then we saw some people outside your house shouting up to us and pointing north. And then, of course, we saw the fire, and then Leyla and you."

"And what happened to the...the old ones?" Rosalind wondered.

Dreyfus told the story. The chatelain had fired at the chopper and been killed immediately, together with another ill-advised hunter. The rest had been pinned down on the road back to town and were now in the Gordes jail, as Barigoule did not have one. They had also found a third body, identified as Anselme, who had caught most of the grenade blast. Townspeople had helpfully given the names of the other "cult" members, who were obviously well known. Dreyfus and some gendarmes had hiked back to the open grotto and saw Jeannot on the ground. He had evidently hit the rocks on his back with the boar on top of him and had been fatally shattered and crushed. And Dreyfus said they were standing there looking down at Jeannot, with the boar lying beside him, when the animal lifted his head, stood up groggily, shook himself and trotted off.

"That was one tough pig," he said. "Too bad about Jeannot. I would never have believed it of him."

"Nobody can!"

"And now they will begin to follow up the others, not only here but in high places. Because they left evidence, phone calls, faxes, showing that they were sheltering the cult, protecting it from investigation."

And in the following days there were mysterious disappearances all over France. Deputy ministers, police officials, a few top managers of great corporations, a banker here and there.

One ministry official in Avignon was a little late in trying to disappear. He was taking a taxi to Marseille airport when the cab suddenly turned into an industrial park in the outskirts of Marignane, a van pulled up and several men asked him to get in. He pretended outrage, but they wouldn't listen, just hustled him in, handed him a *portable* and he found himself talking to Mario Casimiri.

"You ordered a hit on a *flic*, you piece of shit, and you got four good boys killed." The ministry official protested but the Corsican had hung up. In the end they rolled him up tight and helpless in a sheet of linoleum, wound it around with duct tape, and that night carried him somewhere, he knew not where, and covered the linoleum with rocks and gravel. He heard a rough voice.

"They say you don't die, you just flit from body to body." He heard other men guffawing.

"Well, we'll see. Tomorrow they're going to pour three hundred cubic meters of concrete into this bridge foundation. You can flit your way out of that. *Bonne chance, petit con!*" And the others laughed uproariously.

CHAPTER THIRTY-TWO

As far as the French government is concerned, the curious episode of the cult of the immortals at Barigoule is history, all cleared up—some members dead, some in prison, some disappeared, and good riddance. The media have been cautioned not to speculate too much because there are questions of national security involved.

Inspector Dreyfus has been decorated and promoted for his perception, his sound investigative technique, and decisive actions. Agent Abdelaziz has also been promoted and there is a commendation in her *dossier* for her excellent marksmanship. Dreyfus and Abdelaziz are living together for the moment, and the arrangement may or may not lead to something more permanent.

Michael and Nicole and Spencer and Rosalind are still living in Barigoule. A week after the narrow escape from the grotto, Nicole had a dream of such intensity that she woke up sitting upright in bed and panting as if she'd run several miles. Michael was awake instantly.

"My God! Nicole! What's wrong?"

"Michael! We have to back to the grotto!"

"No! no! I'm never—"

"No, listen! I had this dream and it was the voices again in the grotto and I was lying there, but it was the good voices...you know? I told you before? The voices about the writing on the ceiling? And this time the voices... actually it was one voice, an old woman's voice—I think it must have been Jeanne Serre in my dream—and she said, 'Nicole. Nicole, go back to the grotto and erase the writing, the words of Jesus. Erase them all and let them go.' And in my dream I started thinking of being back in the grotto and I freaked and that's when I woke up."

The next day the Tollivers and Sullivans held a conference on the substance of Nicole's dream. No one wanted to go back to the grotto, but Nicole had become insistent.

"We have to go...I have to go anyway. I know it sounds crazy, but just think about it! All those terrible spirits are still alive out there, getting into other bodies. And all it costs me is a few minutes lying there with, what? A wire brush and some 409, something like that. Even if the dream is just a dream, wouldn't you take the chance? Just the vague possibility that we could rid the world of all those horrible people?"

And so they did, one afternoon, when the weather had improved. And Nicole lay on the shelf and scrubbed the ceiling until the words

Veramenvousloudise ni a daqueliquesouneici

Quenoungoutarandela mort d aquiquevegonlou

Fieude l omevenidinssounreinage

were compleely removed from the ceiling. And at that moment they all felt something like a sigh deep in the roots of the cliffs where they were standing, something like the noise a computer makes when you turn it off and it winds down.

"Do you think that does it?" asked Nicole as they were walking back the trail to the car.

"How will we ever know?" said Rosalind.

"If I see one of them coming my way down the street in Barigoule, I think I'll go back and bomb the grottos," said Spencer.

They all laughed.

EPILOGUE

In the alpine foothills, in the sanitarium of St. Etienne for the Insane, a harsh December wind was blowing sleet against the tall shutters in the night, making them creak. One shutter, not fastened well, came open and started banging against the stone wall. The security lights from the fence outside streamed through the window and fell on the sleeping form of Lomu, crazy Lomu. He stirred in his sleep and then the slamming shutter and the lights awakened him. He sat up, his dull eyes open, his jaw slack, a puzzled look on his face as if he was trying to remember a dream. He sat on the edge of his cot for a moment, staring out the window. And then suddenly a gleam of clarity glowed deep in his eyes and his jaws snapped firmly shut. He rubbed his face and head hard, tensed all his muscles. Then he slipped out of bed and began to dress quietly, except for a little tune he was humming under his breath. If anyone had been close enough to hear they might have recognized the old song, *Un jour tu verras, on se rencontrera...*

One day you will see,

we will meet once again...

Santa Barbara

Murs en Provence

1 May 2004 .doc